Copyright © 2019, Mick Morris

Blue Tree Books

ISBN: 9781690967460

Imprint Independently published

Division

Mick Morris

Blue Tree Books

ACKNOWLEDGMENTS

I gratefully acknowledge the contribution of my friends Andy King and John Ward in the production of this novel.

Andy's generous help, not only with proof reading, but also with his numerous helpful suggestions regarding the grammar, structure and presentation of the story emerging from our many discussions, has been invaluable.

My grateful thanks also to John, whose advice regarding the accurate representation of many procedural and technical issues, of which I would otherwise have remained blissfully ignorant, has likewise been indispensable.

Any errors that remain in those areas will be the result of my seemingly incurable predisposition to tinker continually, and will surely not be a reflection on Andy's or John's excellent work.

Thanks also to my wife and many friends, for patiently enduring my obsession over the past few months. Their suffering, I am sure, has, as always, been far greater than my own.

MAM - August 2019

PREFACE

This is a novel. The characters deployed and the scenes and events depicted are entirely imaginary except as stated.

Most of the political actors mentioned in the prologue as having been involved in connection with early attempts to forge a union of European nations are of course real, as are the events with which they are associated. There seems no very good reason to disguise them. The secret meeting between Jean Monnet, Paul Henri Spaak, Altiero Spinelli, Arthur Salter and others however, may never have taken place as described.

The description of some scenes and events in London are based on news reports of such events at the time, but all others are the product of the author's imagination, and I sincerely hope will remain so.

Hans Andersen once said that, `out of reality are our tales of imagination fashioned'. This is undoubtedly true, however, during the writing of this book, I did not anticipate that fantasy would be overtaken quite so frequently by reality.

MAM - August 2019

"There are no moral obligations in the game of empire"
A.H. Septimius, Crowns Of Amara

Chapter 1

"Remember, remember the 5th of November"

1

Docklands, London, Tuesday 5th November 2019

Outside the Orb and Sceptre, the streets, it seemed to Jonathan Shawcross, were unusually quiet, even for a cold, wet Tuesday evening in November. He had been standing in the shelter and shadow of the pub's entrance for three or four minutes now, and in that time he had seen not a single pedestrian or vehicle, apart from one police patrol car that had driven unhurriedly by.

It was the fifth of November, but no-one appeared to have heeded the words of the old rhyme which enjoined all to remember the day. The celebrations that traditionally accompanied such remembrance were intended to remind people of the failure and repercussions of a botched and cowardly attempt to bring about a premature change of government, but Jonathan could not help suspecting that, for many, it instead commemorated an admirably courageous effort.

He remembered how he had used to look forward to Bonfire Night celebrations in the Derbyshire village where he had spent his childhood, and where it had seemed as if every garden competed to put on the most impressive display of pyrotechnics. It was one of many things he missed since moving to London after his divorce eight years earlier.

When he and Sheila had married, he had wanted nothing more than a decent ordinary life. A decent ordinary bungalow with decent ordinary friends and neighbours and a decent ordinary job. But it had soon become obvious that Sheila had other priorities. She delighted in being the centre of attention and was never happier than when out enjoying herself with her friends which, it seemed to him, had increasingly become most of the time. He knew it wasn't working for either of them and it had not surprised him when eventually she had left him and moved in with her boss at the estate agents where she worked. But when he realised that he didn't miss her, he knew that it was probably for the best. Some men in his position would have welcomed the return to bachelordom and would have made the most of their regained freedom. But Jonathan had chosen another option and had instead reverted to being a solitary man. Perhaps that had been the problem all along. Perhaps, even in the marriage, he had been a solitary man.

As he stood now in the cold, damp night air

finishing his cigarette, he also reflected on the introduction of the ban on smoking in `public places' some years earlier and silently cursed those responsible. Jonathan looked at his watch. Eight forty-six. He stubbed out his Marlboro and dropped it into the outdoor ashtray fixed to the wall of the pub and, as he did so, two briefcase-carrying figures in dark overcoats emerged from a side street, twenty or thirty yards to the right and on the opposite side of the road. Right on time, Jonathan noted. The two men walked towards the car which was parked there, their footsteps rippling the reflection of the street lamp on the wet pavement. Under the lamp post they stopped and spoke for a moment, exactly as his friend Martin Armstrong had promised him, and exactly as they had done on several previous occasions. Then, after shaking hands, Armstrong, the younger of the two, began to walk quickly away. The car's interior light came on as the other man opened the driver's door and, with an agility that belied the blue `Disabled' badge prominently displayed in the vehicle's windscreen, slid quickly behind the wheel and started the engine.

Jonathan recognised him immediately as Brendan Roberts, a senior civil servant who had been advising the then British Prime Minister, Kenneth Heywood, during the final stages of the negotiations. Jonathan took a mobile phone from the pocket of his overcoat and entered a number. A few seconds later, he watched as the car pulled away and, returning the phone to his pocket, walked back into the Orb and Sceptre to finish his drink. Picking up his Evening Standard from the table where it lay, Jonathan left the bar and walked down the corridor to the pub's rear entrance and out onto the dockside.

The mobile phone made only the faintest of splashes before sinking silently into the dark water and mud of the Middle Dock. He turned and followed the walkway around Cabot Square before turning again into the North Colonnade, still brightly lit, despite very few people being out and about. He passed the Terazza where three other brave martyrs to the evil weed huddled pointlessly for protection under a small tree which had lost most of its leaves. Then past a tortilla café where a flickering red neon sign intermittently advertised `Real Californian Burritos and Tacos' and seemingly mesmerised a lone diner who sat, silent and staring blankly, as if lost in contemplation of the contents of the bottle of sweet chilli sauce on the table in front of him. Soon Jonathan was in Jubilee Park and approaching Canary Wharf tube station. With luck he would be at South Kensington in half an hour or so and just a ten-minute walk from the flat where once, not long ago, Hannah would have been waiting for him to arrive home. With luck he would be home in time to catch the ten o'clock news.

As he left the station and crossed over into Old Brompton Road, the rain began to fall more heavily and Jonathan cursed the fact that, as Hannah had used to take great delight in informing him, he was one of those unfortunates whose head, for some reason, just couldn't come to terms with a hat. He increased his pace, and within a few minutes, turned left into Roland Gardens and towards the entrance to the apartment block. Once inside the flat, he took off and hung up his wet overcoat, poured himself a large single malt and turned on the television.

BBC `Breaking News' headline.

`Reports are coming in of an explosion in London during the last hour in which a man was killed in what appears to have been a car bomb incident. Scotland Yard's head of counter-terrorism, Assistant Commissioner Nigel Carter, said that whilst no-one had claimed responsibility for the attack, it had clearly been a deliberate act and accordingly he was treating it as a terrorist incident. Assistant Commissioner Carter also said that there had been no other casualties and no intelligence at this time to suggest any further danger to London or to the UK as a whole.'

Solemn-faced, the newsreader informed viewers that the Prime Minister was about to make a statement and the cameras now switched to the scene outside 10 Downing Street where, behind a hastily positioned lectern, Paul Jameson stood, facing a bevy of bedraggled reporters while he himself was protected from the rain by a large umbrella held aloft by a functionary.

"No effort will be spared", said Jameson, "to bring the murderers to justice and to rid the United Kingdom of the scourge of terrorism."

Then, after praising Roberts as `a dedicated and hard-working public servant who had devoted his life to the service of his country', the Prime Minister, reading from his prepared statement, went on.

"Once again, evil and cowardly individuals have struck at the heart of British democracy, and once again a good and innocent man has lost his life. And I say to them now as I have said before, that such tragic, violent and despicable acts will only enhance our resolve to ensure that the God-given freedoms in which we believe, and which are the foundation of British democracy, will in the end, triumph over the acts of such evil men."

Fine words indeed. But there was another way of looking at it. What was it that Lord Summerisle had said to the unfortunate Sergeant Howie? Something along the lines of, `That is good, for believing what you do, we confer upon you a rare gift these days, a martyr's death.' Yes, that was it. That was much better.

Before turning the television off again, Jonathan poured himself another whisky, smaller than the first but easily large enough to evoke a memory of despairing shakes of the head from Hannah who, though having gradually got used to his having suddenly developed an interest in watching television news, had always made clear her disapproval of or, as she had put it, concern for, his drinking. Strange, he thought, that people were said to drink in order to forget, but that for him it never failed but to do the opposite and bring back painful memories.

2

How the hell had it come to this? All they'd ever had to do was listen. It hadn't been much to ask. Just for them to keep their promise. But even as the words came to him he knew that it wasn't as simple as that. Listening alone was never enough. How many times had he heard politicians say, 'We hear you. We get the message'? And then nothing. Nothing would happen. Nobody would do anything. Although, strictly speaking of course, he knew that wasn't true because, whilst nobody would do anything useful, behind the scenes, hidden from the public gaze in the offices of the elite, a very great deal would be going on.

Just as a man treads water in a pool, every last ounce of the energy he expends being directed towards ensuring that he goes nowhere, that he remains exactly where he already is and moves not an inch in any direction, so, beneath the surface, in a formicary of furtive activity, the ants of the establishment would be engaged in identifying ways to protect system, servants and subjects alike against the emerging menace of change. But unlike the man in the pool, they never acted, or even thought, alone or independently. Instead, just as in the world of the real insects, their success resulted from combining the tiny intelligence of each of many individual neurons into a single bureaucratic brain that predisposed them to swing into action, both automatically and collaboratively, in response to a perceived danger.

But none of that explained how *he* had become involved. It just wasn't like him. It wasn't like him at all. Jonathan had no party-political affiliations and his interest in all things political was limited to a concern to see democracy work. Unlike Hannah, he thought, whose tally of good causes he had long since lost count of, he had never been an activist, taking part in protests and demonstrations, going on marches, attending political gatherings and so on. And surely, isn't that the way the vast majority of people are? As for why he had he never got involved until now, perhaps it was partly because he didn't always sympathise with the causes, or because he just didn't feel strongly enough about the issues? Probably also because he didn't believe that protests and the like actually achieved anything much. True enough, there had been times when he did sympathise with a cause or recognise the importance of an issue, but something in him still rendered him passive. He would write to the newspapers, talk to his MP, attend a meeting to make his views known but, for some reason that he couldn't put his finger on, he just felt uncomfortable about taking part in visible collective action. The truth was he didn't really approve of such things at all. For Jonathan, the whole point of the democratic system of government was that it ought to `work' without the need for that sort of thing.

But that had been then. It was irrelevant now. Brexit was different. Now, everything he had ever stood for was under threat, and desperate times had called for desperate remedies.

~~~~~~~

Chapter 2

"The New Elite has no program. Its only real
policy goal is that all policy be made by members
of the New Elite"
David Lebedoff, The Uncivil War

1

Zurich, Switzerland, Wednesday 18th August 1952

Jean Monnet had called the meeting. It had now
been more than twenty-five years since he and his
English friend Arthur Salter, then working closely
together as senior figures in the League of Nations,
had first conceived their grand idea, but neither man
laid claim to having been the originator of the
concept. Both knew that more than eighty years
earlier, Pierre-Joseph Proudhon had advocated the
federalisation of European countries and that he had
pleaded for an end to 'the irreparable abuse of
sovereignty', calling passionately for it to be
'dismembered'. They knew also that since that time,
many others had attempted to follow Proudhon's
lead, but Monnet in particular also knew that the
implementation of the project would be fraught with

difficulties. Countries, he knew, would not easily be persuaded to surrender their sovereignty in the way that the European Project demanded. So he had waited and for the past few years had taken almost no part in the movement. Instead, he had bided his time while others had attempted in vain to take the project forward and only now had he decided to return to the fray. Monnet had watched from the sidelines, a passive observer as, first, the plans for an `Organisation for European Economic Co-operation', and then those for a `Council of Europe' had come to nothing. The first had been fatally weakened, just as he had predicted, by opposition from the British Foreign Secretary, as well as others from Sweden and Switzerland, all of whom had serious reservations about what they saw as the unacceptable political components of the plan. As a result, the OEEC had remained a strictly inter-governmental entity, relying for its success on willing co-operation between nations. The clue to its failure, thought Monnet, lay in the weakness of depending on `willing co-operation'.

The second plan had been given initial impetus by a speech made in Zurich a few years earlier when former British Prime Minister Winston Churchill had proposed the setting up of a `Council of Europe', something of which he had long been an advocate. As far back as the 1930s, Britain's own position had been entirely clear to all who had listened. Whilst Britain saw no place in such a federation for itself, a `United States of Europe' would be welcome and would be supported and sponsored both by Britain and its Commonwealth of Nations and by mighty America. To further the project, Churchill announced the formation of an all-party `United Europe Movement', with a cross-party committee which included two members of the Labour Cabinet and several future Conservative Cabinet ministers, among them Harold Macmillan.

When the governments of France, Britain, Italy, Ireland, Denmark, Norway, Switzerland and the Benelux countries began joint talks to discuss the form that such a Council might take, the discussions were led by the French, encouraged behind the scenes by Monnet's old friend Dean Acheson, now US Secretary of State. But it was clear from the outset that deep divisions existed, for the various European federalist groups were determined to draw up plans for the complete political and economic integration of Europe and many regarded British participation as essential, a view shared at that time by Washington.

The federalists' aim, to 'break down national sovereignty by concrete practical action in the political and economic spheres', met with sustained opposition from both British and Scandinavian delegates. In particular, the British Foreign Secretary, Ernest Bevin, was extremely sceptical of the overall goal. His government took the same view as Churchill, that those who wished to take the road leading to political federation should be encouraged to do so but, Bevin made it clear, the British government had no intention of following. At the first session of the `Council of Europe', with the exception of one Australian-born Labour MP, none of the British delegation advocated British entry into a Federal Europe.

By the autumn of 1951, a new Conservative government had succeeded Labour, and Churchill had replaced Clement Attlee. Among the federalist members of the *European Council*, hopes rose that the new government might be more 'Europe-minded', but in the event, the Conservatives proved no more enthusiastic for political integration than their Labour predecessors. The Churchill government stood ready to give its friendly support to the movement for European integration, but there was no question of the British taking an active part.

And in those intervening years there was something else that Monnet had come to understand. He had become aware that the project could never be realised if its true purpose was made too explicit; that his ultimate goal could only be achieved by deception, worked for by stealth, step by step, over many years, until enough of the machinery of the new form of government was in place for its purpose to be brought fully and safely into the open. Two other men had, in their own ways, each come to the same conclusion.

The first was an Italian Communist, Altiero Spinelli, obscure until now, who harboured the same federalist ambition as Monnet and Salter. Like Monnet, Spinelli also recognised that, to bring his vision about, it would be necessary to conceal from the peoples of Europe just what was being done in their name until the process was so far advanced as to become irreversible.

The other was Belgian Prime Minister Paul-Henri Spaak who, having witnessed the collapse of the *Council of Europe* talks, finally concluded that the Council would never be anything more than a talking shop and came to realise that they would have to do without Britain's support if they were to make any progress. He resigned as president of the Council in December 1951, having by then come to share Monnet's view that Britain would never consider joining until, at the very least, a united Europe had become a reality. For the time being at least, the project must confine itself to comprising France, Germany, Italy and the Benelux countries. And it had also been Spaak who had urged on his friend Monnet the idea that the most effective way to disguise their project's political purpose was to conceal it behind a pretence that it was concerned solely with two worthy aims; to ensure peace by controlling the means of production of weapons of war and to engender economic co-operation by dismantling trade barriers in what Spaak had taken to referring to as a Common Market.

Tonight, in the private lounge of the Roter Garten hotel, Jean Monnet and Arthur Salter were joined by both Spaak and Spinelli as well as a number of other important and influential figures. Monnet was the first to speak, his quiet, measured tone belying the passion that he felt.

2

"Gentlemen. I will come straight to the point. We are gathered together here at this point in time because it has become clear that one issue in particular must be resolved before any progress can be expected. We have witnessed the failure of the previous initiatives, and in both instances, the reason for that failure has been the same. At the heart of the problem is the very nature of the relationship between participating nations and the strategy for implementation. It must surely be clear that willing co-operation between governments cannot be relied upon. It is weak, because national governments are transient entities, and also because mere co-operation permits of the possibility of national interests continuing to obstruct our goals."

Monnet's words betrayed the disdain he felt for the very idea of being dependent on co-operation.

"Nowhere is this more obvious than in the obstinately nationalistic position adopted by British governments. But, now, with your permission, I will ask Henri to outline his proposal for your comment and consideration."

"Thank you Jean", said Spaak rising from his seat. "And so, to that end, I propose to tell you briefly what is in my mind, after which I think we should open up the meeting for questions and discussion."

"Firstly," Spaak went on, "I should say that I do not consider British participation to be essential. Indeed, at this crucial stage, I believe it would be counter-productive, that their misgivings would simply give encouragement to others and make it more likely that others would also hold back. Therefore, I first propose that we should proceed without them. Secondly, and I believe more important still, is the matter of how the plan is to be presented. Our governments have all agreed in principle that the proposal regarding the production of coal and steel is the way ahead and I see no good reason to delay the formation of the necessary body. I believe Jean is right in suggesting that such an innocuous beginning to the project will meet little if any opposition and yet will provide the essential platform on which the project may progress stage by stage. In this way, it will be not be necessary to win the argument for eradicating national sovereignty before proceeding. This way, time will be allowed to play its part, and in due course nations will come to see that there is nothing to fear."

Spaak deferred to Spinelli who had raised a

hand.

"Also, it is essential that the people are not involved in the construction of the new state."

"I think that goes without saying", said Salter.

Spaak nodded.

"You have anticipated my third proposition, Altiero."

"It is to be avoided at all costs", Monnet interjected. "They are simply not intellectually capable. We have surely all seen that they are too emotional and too uneducated to be safely allowed to choose even their own governments. No, Arthur is correct. It goes without saying."

"And you believe the project can succeed without any British involvement?", said Spinelli.

"I would say that is the last thing we should wish for", Monnet replied. "It is sufficient to have their political support for the project. I envisage the direct political involvement of Britain no more than that of America or Russia. But I believe that if we succeed, they will eventually join us."

Spaak moved the discussion towards the critical issue of the financing of the project during its early years. Monnet said nothing, but looked over and nodded to Walter Boschert, representing Basler Handelsbank.

"On behalf of our clients," said Boschert, indicating the two men who sat next to him at the table, "I am instructed to inform the meeting that a very satisfactory inward flow of capital since 1945 has been maintained and will be made available."

The two German industrialists nodded. Since 1944, when it had become obvious that the war could not be won, they and the many others who had been instructed to plan for Germany's post-war recovery and ensure its dominance in a new European Empire, had worked tirelessly behind the scenes to set up a network of secret front companies in other countries which sent money through Switzerland.

The tall, distinguished looking, grey-haired American who now raised a hand to speak, had been listening intently and making notes. John Landau had been asked to attend the meeting on behalf of his boss, Monnet's old friend Dean Acheson, American Secretary of State.

"I can confirm Gentlemen, that the United States is with you guys all the way on this project. I am authorised to tell you that funding will covertly be made available to your Action Committee by our CIA, through the Council for Foreign Relations."

~~~~~~~

Chapter 3

"Take heed of the day of the Ides of March."
Plutarch's `Life of Julius Caesar'

1

Dublin, Tuesday 15th March 2016

The walk from the Carlton hotel where the taxi from the airport had dropped him yesterday afternoon had been shorter and, given the time of year, more pleasant than he had expected. Despite the sun having risen scarcely an hour and a half earlier, the day was already acquiring a surprising but welcome warmth and from the quayside South of the river, over the Samuel Beckett bridge towards Guild Street and onto North Wall Quay where he arrived at his destination, took only a few minutes. It was the first time Jonathan had seen the Convention Centre, a magnificent modern facility, its gleaming, glass-fronted atrium overlooking the Liffey in Dublin's historic docklands.

Inside the building, the first of more than three hundred delegates due to attend the `Brexit Breakfast' were beginning to arrive, and from the

Babel of the many conversations going on around him in the cafe' bar, Jonathan soon began to get the impression that he was probably one of only a small number of ardent `Leave' supporters present. And from looking at the programme, it was clear that the imbalance was not confined to the delegates. Of the panel of six, chaired by an arch-Europhile former British government Minister, only one, the renowned academic, writer and broadcaster Dr Gerald Lines, was known to be in favour of the UK leaving the EU. Lines had been one of Jonathan's tutors while he had been at university in the late 1990s and had been a big influence on him. Lines' presence at the conference had been one of the main reasons why Jonathan had readily agreed to attend the conference, and he looked forward to renewing his acquaintance. Gerald Lines was now an Associate Professor of Political Philosophy and Social Policy at Trinity College Dublin and only recently Jonathan had read a report from a study group of economists and constitutional lawyers that he had chaired. The document had sparked a lot of heated debate, not so much because it set out the arguments for 'Brexit', but because it made a powerful case for why, if and when `Brexit' happened, it should be accompanied by 'Irexit'.

The delegates now packed into the room where Jonathan would be the sole representative of BIBC, he listened to the opening address, given by the former British government minister who predictably made an impassioned, but mercifully brief, plea for greater European integration and unity. Next to speak was a prominent Irish businessman whose words introduced into the proceedings a palpable sense of panic concerning the impending British referendum. But, Jonathan noted, his chief concern seemed to be less about the effects on the UK if it left the EU than about the effect it might have on Ireland. Jonathan thought this was entirely understandable; after all, the Irish and British economies were joined at the hip and, whereas Ireland's relationship with the EU in recent years had hardly been a bed of roses, the relationship with the United Kingdom had probably never been better.

As the tall, lean figure of Lines now rose to speak, Jonathan was struck for the second time by how remarkably little the man seemed to have aged in the nearly two decades since they had last met. The first had been when, just a few weeks ago, Lines had been invited to participate in a BBC Question Time broadcast to discuss the forthcoming referendum. He must surely be well into his sixties by now, and yet the only outward sign of the passage of time was the shock of wiry hair which topped his angular features and which, once prematurely grey, was now almost pure white. Perhaps, Jonathan reflected, it was simply that he had always looked older than his years. After thanking the first two speakers, Lines' opening words were delivered in an unexpectedly conciliatory tone.

"I am sure that most of you will join me in applauding the chairman's desire to see greater co-operation between European nations and will rightly understand and sympathise with the concerns of the business community regarding any possible harmful effects on trade. But, in a modern democracy", he said, "I am also sure you would all agree that it is highly desirable, if not essential, that such rewards be achieved harmoniously, by consensus not only between governments, but with the people themselves, lest we unknowingly embrace an elective dictatorship or, worse, one that is not elected at all."

Many, otherwise antipathetic, heads nodded in agreement.

"You will be aware of course that the EU's tendency to tell member states how to behave frequently grates with the Irish people. In the referendum on the Lisbon Treaty in 2008, some fifty-three per cent of those who voted were in favour of rejecting the Treaty. But the EU ignored their views and insisted that the referendum be held again. In my opinion, the government should have stood firm and supported its people. But it did not. Instead it acceded to the EU's demand for a second vote and, needless to say, when a result was obtained which suited their agenda, it was immediately accepted and there were no further referendums."

Lines went on.

"By contrast however, during the bail-out

negotiations following the 2008 financial crash, the EU insisted that the Irish government raise its highly advantageous corporation tax rates. This time however, the government held firm. It refused and by so doing kept its grip on a huge share of foreign direct investment. The government similarly, you may recall, took a dim view when the EU Commission insisted that the IT and media giant, Apricot, should repay to the Irish exchequer what the Commission deemed to be the inappropriate tax benefits they had received. On that occasion, the government again stood firm, considering the benefits to be highly appropriate, precisely in order to continue attracting big employers like Apricot. So what we see is clear evidence that the Irish government is inclined not to resist the demands of the EU when it is only the people that will be offended, but that it chooses infallibly to put up a fight when big business is involved. This is not democracy. It is government by corporate interest."

Lines' observation did not go down well with the business community but again, a surprising number of other heads nodded.

"But, I hear you say, is it not the responsibility of government to act in the national economic interest? Is not good business that which benefits both sides? And the answer of course is `Yes'. Most people are generally happy for governments to make such decisions in their name. But those same people are far from satisfied when their views are ignored in areas which eat away at the very foundations of nationhood, those which threaten national self-determination. However, let us for the moment leave behind us the battles of the past and focus instead on the future. While such matters as foreign investment and corporation tax are important to the Irish economy, the relationship with the UK is even more important. If the UK left the EU, some two-thirds of Ireland's foreign trade would then be with English-speaking markets outside the EU, America and the UK being Ireland's two largest export markets. I would respectfully suggest that now that Ireland has become a net contributor to the EU budget, it might do better to follow its neighbour and closest trading partner out of the EU. After all, both nations joined the EEC together, so perhaps they should leave together too? And of course, such an arrangement would also be ideal for Northern Ireland. Trading between Northern Ireland and the Republic takes place across a land border that, despite having different VAT rates and different currencies, has no obvious customs posts. An Irish exit would almost certainly lead to a very rapid trade deal between the republic and the UK. Ireland, ever since it achieved independence from Britain, has always benefited from a Common Travel Area that allows so many Irish people to live, work and even vote in Britain and Northern Ireland, and the CTA could be extended and enhanced if Ireland were to leave the

EU. I am also convinced that Irish public opinion will move rapidly in the direction of Irish exit if the EU continues its bully-boy tactics and the people of Ireland realise that, rather than being a provider of never-ending largesse, the EU in reality actually represents an ever increasing burden on Irish taxpayers."

To polite but muted applause, Lines concluded with the suggestion that Ireland needed to realise that a future within the EU would not make nearly as much sense if the UK were to leave.

2

The meeting over, the room quickly began to clear. Jonathan guessed that most would be returning to their various places of business. He, however, would not. His employers had been unable to book him a flight back to London City Airport until the following day and so he would be staying overnight. Before leaving the centre to return to his hotel, Jonathan considered that a lunchtime drink in the bar would be in order. First though, he would go and congratulate Gerald Lines on his speech.

He found the professor near the podium, standing talking with two other men.

As he approached the little group, the professor, to Jonathan's surprise, smiled and nodded.

"Well, well, it's Shawcross isn't it?", said Lines.

"Yes", replied Jonathan, shaking the hand extended to him, "Yes it is. But I'm astonished that you recognised or remembered me after all this time."

Lines gave no explanation for his remarkable feat of memory but instead said,

"Gentlemen, this is Shawcross, Jonathan, if I remember correctly?"

Jonathan nodded.

"Mr. Henry Bloom", said the professor holding his arm out to indicate the small, neatly dressed man on his left. Jonathan's first impression was that there was something of the country squire about him. Perhaps, as Agatha Christie had said of Roger Ackroyd, almost too much.

"Pleased to meet you, Jonathan", said the man. "but only Gerald ever calls me Henry. It's Harry to everyone else."

"And Mr. Cormac O'Bierne", Lines said looking towards the big Irishman who smilingly suggested that, "Any friend of Gerald's is a good man himself".

Jonathan knew of O'Bierne as a journalist who worked mostly for the Irish Times, but whose articles also occasionally appeared in British newspapers. He also knew that O'Bierne was a free trade advocate who had written a book arguing the case for Ireland leaving the Eurozone. O'Bierne had played a key role in re-forming the Irish Independence Party and was also associated with the Principles Before Profit Alliance, a hard-left party, active in both Northern Ireland and the Republic, which had made clear its support for an Irish exit and which had made some big gains in recent elections. He wondered what Bloom did.

Introductions out of the way, Lines said, "We were just on our way to the bar, Jonathan. Perhaps you'd care to join us?"

"Thank you. I'd be pleased to."

A few of the conference delegates already stood around the area of the bar itself but the room was otherwise sparsely occupied. Near a large picture window overlooking the old docks, Lines indicated a small table with several chairs arranged around it. He motioned the others to sit while he would organise the drinks.

Jonathan sat down in a chair facing O'Bierne and Henry Bloom.

"You'll have noticed, no doubt, that we are greatly outnumbered.", said O'Bierne with a smile.

Jonathan laughed. "Don't worry. I'm getting used to it."

Perhaps it was his imagination, thought Jonathan, but had Henry Bloom seemed to relax a little at hearing his reply, confirming as it did that Jonathan was happy to be considered one of O'Bierne's `we'?

Bloom was next to speak.

"So, what brings you here, Jonathan?"

"My employers, Harry. I work for BIBC. They thought someone should attend and I put my hand up first", said Jonathan with a smile. "Though I must admit that the prospect of a few days away from the desk and the opportunity to meet up with Dr Lines again played a large part."

Lines caught the last of Jonathan's words as he returned carrying the tray of drinks.

"I'm flattered", said Lines. "But it's Gerald, please."

"So you're one of the fat cat bankers I get to write about?", said O'Bierne laughing.

"I'm afraid not, Cormac. Just a humble economist, thanks in large measure to Gerald."

Bloom spoke again.

"Gerald's contribution to this morning's meeting will not have surprised or alarmed you then, Jonathan?"

"On the contrary Harry, I'm well aware of Gerald's position on the issue, and I must say I found it refreshing and encouraging to hear a message which satisfied the economic logic of the situation without sacrificing the underlying democratic principles", said Jonathan.

"Praise indeed", said Lines, "but I fear, Jonathan, that the encouragement you derive from my words may prove to be somewhat premature."

Jonathan wasn't sure he understood.

"What do you mean, Gerald?"

"I mean, Jonathan, that I believe this will prove to be only the beginning of a very long struggle to keep democracy alive. Granted that it is something of an achievement for the people even to have been given a chance to have their say but, as you no doubt gathered from what you heard me say earlier, in the final analysis, it is not the opinion of the people that is listened to."

"Well, I know that the EU managed to overturn the referendum result in Ireland, and that they were also successful in doing much the same in France and the Netherlands, if that's what you mean. But I can't see it happening here in the UK. I grant you that it's very unlikely that there will be a majority in favour of leaving but, if by some miracle there is, then I honestly can't believe that any British government would renege on its promise."

"Forgive me, Jonathan", said Lines, but I suspect that you greatly underestimate the extent of the many vested interests and the power that lies entirely outside our `democracy'; the key role played by the producers of wealth, the transnational corporations. Perhaps you do not recall that, twenty years ago, I stressed the need for those involved in International Relations to directly address two core questions, "What is power in the world system of international political economy? And who has it?"

Jonathan did remember. He remembered that Lines had argued compellingly that if those involved in International Relations and in making sense of international politics were serious about finding an answer to these fundamental questions, they must not fail to take account of international business and its growing power. But he also remembered thinking at the time that it all sounded too much like a conspiracy theory. And Lines' continued in a vein that, even now, did little to dispel that notion.

"In this era of globalization", he went on, "the virtually unlimited wealth of such corporations enables them to influence governments in any number of ways. Campaign funding, lobbying, media ownership, membership of advisory and regulatory agencies etc. Via these and many other avenues, they are endowed with the ability to have laws changed, and, when this happens, it will always be in favour of the corporation, not of the public, for no man can serve two masters.

"And it doesn't stop there", he continued. "It is also necessary to consider the influence exerted by what we may euphemistically call `other interested parties'. They come from many areas, in many disguises and are motivated by many different factors, but they are united by a common interest in ensuring the UK's continued membership of the EU. As well as those MEPs, commissioners and others who are paid directly by the EU, there are those who, in return for their support, receive financial benefits, pensions, grants to fund personal projects etc. There are also others, many of whom ostensibly no longer play an active role in politics, but who nevertheless still wish to be seen as international statesmen. And then there are the professionals, the civil servants and other bureaucrats for whom the EU is a dream come true, the judges whose allegiance to their profession and to their colleagues in other countries far outweighs any concern for democracy or for nationhood, the MPs who have come to believe that sovereignty is theirs alone, that nobody else, not the people nor even the government, can lay claim to it. The establishment is a mighty force Jonathan; one which will not willingly surrender its power nor be so readily diverted easily from its aims as the theory of Western democracy suggests."

"OK, I fully understand that such people might want to prevent the result of the referendum being implemented, but how could they possibly hope to do that? It would cause an outrage."

"There are a great many ways they could do that Jonathan. Try to put yourself in their position. Like their forebears, the founders of the EU from whom they take their inspiration, they would realise the importance of keeping their true aim hidden from view until it was too late. They would not want the people to know that the plan was to kill Brexit stone dead. They would pretend that all they wanted was to inform and warn the electorate of the perils. To this end, their first strategy would be to try to alter the nature of the debate, to move it away from the beliefs and principles on which the decision was made, and in which it is properly rooted, and towards a focus on the economy.

"Having succeeded in doing that, they would

then try to frighten people with predictions of bad things to come. Price increases, shortages of vital supplies such as food and medicine, problems for exporters, chaos on the roads and at ports and airports etc. The list is endless. The cleverer among them would be careful not to directly blame the people. They would simply say that, not only did the people not know what they were voting for, because the government withheld vital information from them, but also that the Leave campaign lied. Others would hint that the referendum itself was a bad mistake because the electorate were perhaps not qualified to make decisions of such magnitude and must therefore be protected from themselves. The less clever among them would risk stirring up public anger by saying that the result stemmed not only from ignorance, but from the basest of motives, including xenophobia, racism and jingoism.

"It would suit them for it to appear as though the people had changed their minds, and to this end they would almost certainly press for a second referendum. This is the time-dishonoured tactic favoured by Brussels and which, as you yourself pointed out, has already been used successfully to overturn referendum results in several other European countries. But there are numerous other options open to them. Parliamentary procedure, new legislation, votes of no confidence, perhaps even a general election."

"And you truly believe they would go that far,

just to get their own way?"

"I have absolutely no doubt about it, Jonathan. These people would stop at nothing."

"So, how then could they be stopped? Is there anything at all that could be done?"

Lines told Jonathan of his plan to form a new group to explore ways of fighting back against the establishment, should that become necessary. His name for the `think tank', as he described it, was PRAXIS, but publicly it would be known as The Institute for Democratic Reform. At Jonathan's request, Lines briefly outlined its ethos and its meaning.

"It is taken from the Ancient Greek word πρᾶξις, meaning the process by which a theory, lesson or skill is enacted, embodied, or realized", he said. "In Ancient Greece, the word referred to activity engaged in by free people. The philosopher August Cieszkowski, who was a major influence on the young Karl Marx, was one of the earliest to use the term as meaning `action oriented towards changing society', indeed Marxism was called the `philosophy of praxis' by the nineteenth century socialist Antonio Labriola. The essence of praxis is the belief that Western philosophy has too often focused on the contemplative life and has neglected the active life This has led humanity frequently to miss much of the everyday relevance of philosophical ideas to real life. Praxis is the highest and most important level of the active life because it is essential to the true realization of human freedom. Our capacity to analyze ideas, wrestle with them, and implement them via active praxis is what makes us uniquely human."

Jonathan began to realise that he had perhaps been naive to think that the referendum would lay the issue to rest. At university, he had read Lines' book, `The Rise of The New Elite - A Critical Analysis of the Threat to Democracy'. He could see that, if Lines was right, direct action was the only hope of bringing about meaningful change.

Lines had been silent for a moment, but now said, "But, I feel I owe you an apology, Jonathan. You must think I'm lecturing you as if you were still one of my students."

"I'm not in the least offended", said Jonathan. "But what about PRAXIS, the organisation I mean?"

"It will not be so much an organisation as a loose alliance of like-minded individuals", Lines replied.

Cormac O'Bierne and Henry Bloom had remained silent while Lines had been speaking and Bloom remained silent now. His part in all this was still a mystery to Jonathan. But when Cormac O'Bierne rejoined the conversation, he spoke with passion.

"As you may be aware Jonathan, here in Ireland we have learned a thing or two over the years about fighting for independence. We have learned the hard way." "But", he said looking over at Lines and laughing, "it's good to know that we are gathering support and recognition in the groves of Academe.

"What we say", O'Bierne went on, "is that Britain out of Ireland and Ireland out of the EU makes perfect political, economic and strategical sense. We want our country to leave the EU. We want to prepare for a time when the whole Irish nation will have the opportunity to make a decision as to what kind of government we should have. I believe it should be a socialist government of course, but whatever the outcome, this government will then be in a position to negotiate with others around the world, stand as a united nation and enter into any agreement which they mutually consent to. But that cannot come about all the time part of our country remains an imperialist-imposed state."

3

That evening in the bar at the Carlton, Jonathan settled into a comfortable armchair with an idea of mulling over the day's events and, in deference to his Irish hosts, a large Fitzgerald's Redbreast for which he had forsaken his usual scotch.

Those last words of O'Bierne continued to resonate with him. It seemed to Jonathan perfectly understandable that an individual should feel a strong affiliation to nationhood, founded on factors such as shared history, culture, language, territory and the like. And would it not be a natural corollary to that to aspire to independence as well? Why should any nation not be permitted to plan its own future and determine how best to achieve it? No, if he had been Irish, that's what he would be saying too.

It was something that, he had to admit, he had never had any reason to devote much thought to. Being born in a small town in Derbyshire he was English of course, but he had never felt the need to make a big thing of it. He was content, happy even, to think of himself as British. That wasn't a crime, was it? Feeling a sense of belonging to one place more than another didn't make you a bad person. It wasn't a competition for God's sake. Or, at least, it shouldn't be.

Jonathan had always been a staunch supporter of a Britain which was both united and self-determining. He was not greatly troubled by the devolution of powers within the UK to Scotland, Wales and Northern Ireland; in fact it made perfect sense to him to aim for a system of government which, so far as practically possible, gave every region and every individual the opportunity to take part in the decisions which affected him or her. Surely, he thought, decentralising political power to the smallest social unit practicable, would give us all the best opportunity to wield influence, both individually and collectively, in the interests not only of ourselves but of the nation as a whole. But devolution wasn't enough for everybody. For many, full independence would always be the goal. And Jonathan had no great ideological problem with that either. Obviously no sensible person would want nationhood to create unnecessary difficulties, for it to become an obstacle to good relations with other nations, but surely it was possible to have both? It is a sorry state of affairs indeed if we have come to the conclusion that the only way to avoid conflict between nations is to dispense altogether with self-determination. In fact, he thought that the opposite was probably true; that the political integration of long-established nations, with their many differing circumstances and disparate ambitions, into a single larger conglomeration was very likely to cause far more problems than it solved. Surely to God, it was not beyond the wit of man to devise institutions and mechanisms that would ensure co-operation of the highest order where it was not only mutually desirable but clearly advantageous?

But if the stance of O'Bierne's Irish Independence Party was perfectly clear and understandable to him, the position adopted by the Scottish Nationalists was anything but. In fact it seemed to him to be very peculiar in several ways. It wasn't that Jonathan begrudged the Scots their independence. How could he when he himself wanted the UK to reclaim its own independence from the EU? No, what troubled him about their position were the contradictions and double standards they employed in order to make their case. Firstly, they wanted to leave the UK but to remain in the EU. `What sort of independence is that?', he asked himself? Secondly, and even harder to understand, was their chosen strategy. They wanted to keep the UK in the EU. Why? From their position, that might make sense if they were planning to remain in the UK, but they weren't. If the UK left the EU, Scotland would leave automatically. So, did it mean that they weren't yet confident of winning a referendum on Scottish Independence and therefore it suited them for the time being to keep the whole of the UK in the EU until the odds improved?

The double standards of their arguments were exemplified by a recent speech Jonathan had heard a Scottish MP give. `It is the height of irresponsibility', the MP had said, `for any government to bring forward a proposition that is going to lead to its people becoming poorer.' Surely, it seemed to Jonathan, there were a whole host of things wrong with this statement. Firstly, was it actually true to say that people would be poorer? And if it was, how much poorer? And would it be just a short-term adjustment or one that would take longer to adapt to? He also doubted whether it was fair to say that the government would be responsible; surely the government would simply be implementing the decision of the people?

And what had money to do with anything

anyway? When, he asked himself, did anyone ever change their mind about leaving an unhappy marriage, simply because of the financial impact it was going to have? OK, so it probably did happen sometimes. The young mother who puts the emotional and financial security of her children before her own happiness; the older woman, lacking in self-confidence or esteem, perhaps even fearful of stigmatisation, or still, naively, hopeful of change or reconciliation; the better off, even wealthy, couple, able to reach an accommodation and reconcile themselves to leading separate lives in order to preserve their joint financial stability. Yes, of course sometimes, in such ways and in such circumstances, the unhappy marriage would be forced to continue. But its partners would pay a terrible price, forever unhappy in their hearts, the dead corpse of the former relationship, floating like flotsam in a sea of resentfulness.

So, if it was so wrong for the UK to leave the EU and pay the price for its earlier mistake, how did the Scottish MP justify the existence of his own party, dedicated as it was to leaving the security of the UK regardless of any financial implications for Scotland? In the Scottish referendum of two years ago, the `No' side had won fairly comfortably, but what if it hadn't? What if the SNP had achieved its stated ambition of independence? What then would it be doing now? For once Jonathan didn't need to use his imagination. He knew that figures published by the Scottish government itself showed that they spent one-hundred and twenty-seven pounds for every one-hundred they raised in tax, a ratio that he also knew was one of the highest anywhere in the developed world. No country could possibly hope to sustain a deficit of such magnitude, such a mismatch between state spending and tax collected. To borrow on world markets, you needed to demonstrate at least a semblance of fiscal respectability. Perhaps, thought Jonathan, they were pinning their hopes on being accepted as an EU member state? But for that even to be considered, Scotland's deficit would need to be reduced to around a third of its present level.

And so, the answer to the question he had asked himself was that an independent Scotland would right now be facing a difficult choice - cut state spending by fifteen per cent, put taxes up by almost twenty per cent, or devise some unholy combination of the two. And yet the man apparently saw no contradiction in roundly condemning the British government for even considering the possibility of taking the UK out of the EU, at a cost which, at worst, would have been minuscule by comparison.

The Jonathan Shawcross that would board the plane to return home to London and Hannah tomorrow, showed every sign of being a more troubled man than the one who had arrived in Dublin just two days earlier.

~~~~~~~

Chapter 4

"And fire came down out of heaven
and devoured them"
Revelation 20:9

1

Stoke-on-Trent, Monday 24th June 2019

It was Midsummer's Day and even at three o'clock in the morning it was still quite warm. Barry Furness lifted up his black tool bag and placed it on the top of the high brick wall. Then, pulling himself up and over, he dropped down into the garden. Retrieving the bag, the tall shrubs hid his presence as he made his way around to the rear of the property. Despite a week having passed since the last full moon, there was still a good light and Barry did not need to use the torch he had bought along just in case.

`Laburnums', in Brenton Park Avenue, was a large five-bedroomed, Victorian detached house, with beautifully tended lawns and flower beds between the wall and the front entrance. On one side, a large double garage had been added and, from the driveway, a path led around to the rear where a scaffold tower had been erected to facilitate some much needed re-pointing of the brickwork to the rear chimney stack.

Barry had taken care to wrap the can in an old woollen cardigan before putting it inside the tool bag he now carried - it was essential to deaden any sound, should he accidentally knock it against the scaffold. He had made his decision to act tonight when, that afternoon, from his crows nest by the chimney, he had seen Lendle's wife put a small suitcase into the boot of her car and drive off after kissing her husband goodbye. He meant her no harm and it was clear that she intended to be away overnight.

He retrieved the ladder from the bushes where he had stowed it after finishing work that day. Quickly and carefully repositioning it to give access to the first lift of scaffolding, he climbed up with a practised ease and within a minute was on the second lift. Removing the screw top of the ten-litre jerrycan, he began to pour the petrol down the chimney. The gulping sound of the liquid as it left the can, and the faint trickling noise that followed as it splashed its way down and over the brickwork, sounded disconcertingly loud to him. But he judged that it was simply so because it was amplified by the stillness of the night and that, inside the house, it would not be enough to disturb anyone. The can almost empty, he pulled from his pocket a piece of rag, poured the last of the petrol onto it and lighting it, dropped it quickly into the chimney. The huge size of the flame that shot from the chimney took him by surprise and, as he reeled backwards, he was thankful for the waist-high safety rail fitted to the top of the tower.

Barry lost no time in descending to the garden where, after putting the empty can back into his tool bag and re-stowing the ladder among the shrubs, he made his way quickly back through the bushes to the garden wall. Before hauling himself over and onto the pavement, he stopped briefly to look back at the flames still belching from the chimney and lighting up the night sky. He looked at his watch. It was almost three-fifteen a.m. and it would take him about ten minutes to walk home. How long, he wondered, would it be before someone raised the alarm?

At seven-thirty, Barry collected another two bags of cement mortar mix from Jewsons and drove to Brenton Park Avenue to finish the job. As he parked his van and opened the door to get out, the pungent smell of the smoking, charred remains of `Laburnums' hit him. The fire and ambulance crews had long since left the scene but two police vehicles remained parked outside the still smouldering empty shell of the property. He set the first of the bags of mortar mix down on the pavement.

"Bloody hell, what's happened?"

"Could you just give me your name sir, and tell me what you are doing here."

Barry explained to the police constable who asked him to wait while he spoke to his superior officer.

The sergeant didn't keep him waiting long.

Yes, he had been working at the house since last Wednesday, but not over the weekend. He had last been here on Friday and had left around five in the afternoon. He had reckoned it would take him one more day to complete the re-pointing and had returned this morning to finish off. No, he hadn't seen anyone suspicious. He hadn't seen anyone at all. Yes, he knew who Mr Lendle was, but he had never met or spoken to him. He thought that his boss had taken the job over the phone and he'd have to ring him now to let him know about the fire. He wondered who would pay the bill for the work he had done. No he wouldn't be going anywhere. At least, he said silently to himself, he hoped he wouldn't.

2

Cheapside, London, Monday 24th June 2019

Jonathan had worked late at the bank in Cheapside tonight and it had made him late for his customary stop at the Whitefriars Tavern, en route to St. Paul's tube station and the half-hour journey home. He hadn't minded too much being asked to help finish off some important work before leaving, because he knew that Mondays were Hannah's late night too. She had said it was something to do with catching up with the weekend backlog of sick pets, which for some reason always seemed to arrive in droves on Saturday mornings. And today she would probably be even later than usual, because she'd taken a couple of hours off to join a protest march and had promised to make up for it by going back to work afterwards. The protest that Hannah and her friends were taking part in today was an anti-Austerity march, organised by `The People's Assembly Against Austerity', which was calling for a general election.

It had been more than three years now since Hannah had moved in with him, though what she had seen in him, he had never managed to work out. When they had met, he was living in digs, sharing rooms in Earls Court with two other men, his colleague David who worked for the same bank and a friend of David's, a university lecturer by the name of Frank. Frank, a staunch Remainer, had left and found digs elsewhere after a heated disagreement with David about Brexit. Then when Hannah had moved out of her parents' home in Enfield, she and Jonathan had first set themselves up in a pokey bedsit in Bayswater and then, two years later, had moved to the flat in South Kensington which was keeping them poor.

On his way to the Whitefriars, Jonathan had

picked up an Evening Standard as usual and he had almost finished the crossword. Just one clue stubbornly remained unsolved, *34d. `Caught in the drain, goes off and is sour-smelling' (6)*. Not liking to be beaten, he knew that the thing to do was to take a break and come back to it later, mentally refreshed. Leaving his pen and the open newspaper on the table, he walked over to the bar and ordered another pint of John Smith's. But instead of returning to his seat straight away, he stood for a moment as the `Breaking News' headline looped silently across the bottom of the small flat-screen TV.

`Prime Minister Kenneth Heywood has announced this afternoon that he is to resign. He has said that he will remain in office until a successor is chosen, which is expected to be towards the end of July. There will be a full statement on the main news at ten o'clock.'

It did not come as a surprise to Jonathan. After all, when the previous Prime Minister Helen Fletcher had resigned after losing the referendum vote, Heywood had been elected on a promise to implement the result, but after three years in the job he had nothing to show for his efforts. He had obstinately clung on for months, even after it had become abundantly clear that the withdrawal agreement he had negotiated was unacceptable to parliament. Three times it had failed to pass, on the first occasion in January being voted down by more than two hundred votes. There was only a small improvement when it was presented again two months later and lost again, this time by almost a hundred and fifty. And although, by the the third attempt the margin had narrowed to forty, it should have been clear to him that it was dead in the water. But Heywood had refused to budge an inch and simply continued to regurgitate the tired mantra that it was `the best we could get'. And he might even have got away with it eventually, thought Jonathan, if it hadn't been for one of his Ministers who finally broke ranks and decided he had to speak out.

Just a few days ago, Heywood's former Brexit minister Nicholas Evans had issued a statement claiming that, more than a year earlier, Dexeu had decided to aim for a Free Trade Agreement with the EU. He then revealed that a few weeks later, the UK had been offered a just such a deal, but that the offer had been rejected by Heywood who wanted to press for a `more highly aligned' status.

"I was rejoicing", said Evans, "We all were. We had pretty much got what we wanted, but that wasn't good enough for him. He wanted to keep us much more closely aligned to the EU, but his plan was never going to work. That was something they were never going to offer. That's why we are where we are now and that's why we've been trying to remove him from office for the past few months. His obstinacy is the ultimate source of all our difficulties."

Evans' revelation not only came as a bombshell, but ultimately proved to be the Prime Minister's undoing. Up until then, most people blamed Heywood for the failure to meet the deadline for leaving, although there had been a certain amount of sympathy for his plight, even from ardent Brexiteers. As they saw it, although his plan was far from perfect, the withdrawal agreement he had tried and failed to get passed by parliament would at least have got us out on time and we could have tidied up the details afterwards. The blame for the failure to get parliamentary approval they said, lay not so much with the plan or Heywood personally as with three distinct groups within parliament itself. It had now become parliament versus the people.

First, there were those who would always vote against any proposal, simply because they didn't want to leave and didn't respect the referendum result.

Then there was a second group who also voted against any proposal, no matter how `good' or `bad', but, unlike those in the first group, not because they didn't want to leave but because they wanted to bring down the government and force a general election. For the chance of getting into power, absolutely nothing would be sacrosanct. They would happily dump the promise made to the electorate enshrined in their manifesto pledges, they would somehow manage to overlook their parliamentary approval to the triggering of Article 50, they would even scrap Brexit altogether if necessary - all to be sacrificed on the altar of a general election.

And then, finally, there were those committed Brexiteers who genuinely considered Heywood's plan to be so deeply flawed that it could not be allowed to succeed and thought, perhaps naively, that they could do better. But now, fearing that those pushing for a `No Brexit' option were gaining ground, they had begun to shift their position from one of `No deal is better than a bad deal', to `Any Brexit is better than no Brexit'.

On the television, the banner item announcing the PM's resignation made its way leftwards and disappeared off the screen to be followed by another.

`Five killed at Brexit `People's Vote' protest demonstration in London today. Hundreds arrested.'

Jonathan had been worried for some time that something like this might eventually happen and only this morning he had pleaded with Hannah to take care, but she had just laughed at him and said, `don't be silly, that sort of thing only happens in France. It couldn't happen here'. But Jonathan had known that the ranks of the peaceful protesters were increasingly being joined by others for whom peaceful protest would never be enough and now he knew he had been right to caution her. Thank God there had been no mention of the anti-Austerity group that Hannah had been with.

It must have been around the end of March, he thought, that he had seen a headline which read,

`Yellow vest protests spread to UK: anti-Brexit protesters demanding a second referendum shut down central London.'

In a march for what they called a `People's Vote', thousands of demonstrators holding signs saying `We Demand Another Vote' and `Say No To No Deal' had taken part in the rally, which ended more or less peacefully outside the Houses of Parliament. A few days later however, Westminster Bridge had been blocked for several hours by `yellow vest' activists. TV news footage that night showed that the incident had caused huge disruption. Chanting `Scrap Brexit now', they were eventually moved on by police but then stopped again outside Downing Street, with further angry anti-Brexit chants heard. In the broadcast, one woman could be heard screaming at police officers to let her knock on the door of Number 10 so that she could `speak to poisonous Kenneth Heywood'. `We intend to make our voices heard', he had heard her shout. Returning to his seat, Jonathan picked up his Evening Standard and turned the page where his eye now fell on an article.

`David Lendle, MP for Furcombe and Linsdale was killed in a fire at his home near Stoke-on-Trent in the early hours of this morning. Chief Superintendent John Masters has said they are treating the incident as a targeted arson attack and are examining CCTV footage from the area. He also confirmed that they are now questioning a man in connection with the arson attack, a twenty-five-year-old who had been arrested two weeks earlier on a charge of damaging the same property by throwing a building block through a front window.'

Masters was asking for any members of the public who had any information regarding the devastating event to come forward. Police confirmed that the MP had feared a possible attack of some kind after receiving death threats in connection with his stance on Brexit, whereby he planned to defy the result in his constituency, despite more than seventy-two percent having voted to leave. There had already been several earlier incidents, both at his constituency office and at his home where damage had been done to the property and `offensive materials' put through the letterbox. Only two weeks ago, the fire brigade had fitted a device to the house's letterbox to prevent flammable materials being poured through it.

`It is understood', the article continued, `that

the arsonist used scaffolding at the rear of the property to climb up to the roof and pour fuel down the chimney. It has been reported that fuel was found in at least three locations in the house: the chimney, a ground-floor room and a first floor bedroom. The force has referred itself to the Independent Police Complaints Commission, which is standard practice when someone dies after having already contacted the police regarding threats received. Mr Lendle's wife Christine was unhurt and was away from home at the time of the incident.'

The item went on to say that Lendle had been very unpopular in his constituency. From the beginning he had been a prominent figure in the campaign to remain in the EU and had made his position abundantly clear. He had his own regular column in the Furcombe Echo, the local newspaper, and week after week he had used it to insult the character and intelligence of his constituents. When the result was announced, Lendle was shocked to the core, but not as shocked as he was when, soon afterwards, he found himself facing and losing a vote of confidence in his constituency. But he was a man used to getting his own way and stubbornly continued to preach his weekly sermons to to the unconvertible. He knew perfectly well that he would be forced to stand down at the next election, but he wasn't one to go quietly, although in the end of course, given that his blackened, charred body showed no sign of him having stirred so much as an inch while the inferno had raged through the house, Jonathan thought it very likely that he had actually gone very quietly indeed.

It seemed that a call had been received by the fire brigade at around three-fifty am. It was made by a motorist who had seen flames in both upstairs and downstairs front windows as he had driven down Brenton Park Avenue. But by the time the first of the two fire engines had arrived less than twelve minutes later, there was no chance of saving the house or its single sleeping occupant.

Jonathan turned his attention back to the unfinished Evening Standard crossword. `Rancid', yes, that worked. `Rancid' was the answer.

3

South Kensington, London, Monday 24th June 2019

Almost ten o'clock and Hannah had not come home. She would be OK though. She would be with the others and they would look after her. If the demo had gone well, they had probably arranged to meet up to celebrate after she finished work. Hannah wasn't much of a drinker, but she had been really looking forward to seeing Mandy again. Mandy had returned only yesterday from a six-month spell on a dig in Portugal. She had probably just had one Lambrusco too many and fallen asleep on a sofa somewhere before getting around to phoning him. He thought of ringing her mobile, but it didn't seem fair to wake her. He would ring the vet's surgery first thing tomorrow morning.

Jonathan had met a lot of Hannah's friends. They were a decent enough bunch, he thought. A bit weird maybe, but decent. And he would never have met Hannah if it hadn't been for them. He remembered being in the Whitefriars after work with David, his friend from the bank and one of the two men he shared the Earls Court flat with. A group of noisy young people sat at a table nearby. Hippies, he thought. Second generation. No, on reflection they were too young. It would have to be third generation. All talking excitedly and laughing. One of them, a pretty, petite, brown-haired girl, of about twenty-one or-two he would have guessed, smiled at him. David had left to go and meet his girlfriend and the young woman had looked over and spoken to him.

"Hi, I'm Hannah. You can sit with us if you like."

`Forward', his mother would have called her, but maybe she was just being friendly and didn't like to see him sitting alone. Something stopped him saying, `Thanks, but I'm OK', and instead only the `Thanks' came out. He had picked up his Evening Standard and pint of John Smith's and moved across to a spare seat at the table where he was introduced to the four others, Gerry, tall, thin and bearded and wearing little, round, John Lennon spectacles was probably in his early thirties and the oldest of the four. Gerry, he was told, was a teacher and, as he soon learned, was married to Lucy and had a two year old daughter. Next to him sat Mandy, Hannah's best friend, and the two of them were inseparable. A few years older than Hannah, he guessed and certainly a good few inches taller, Mandy was what Jonathan's mother would probably call `well-built'. Amanda Curtis, he learned, was an archaeologist who had worked on digs in the Middle East, Europe and the UK. In between projects, she found positions in museums and as a researcher. To Hannah's delight, Mandy had just returned from a year away in Israel and, at the moment, she was working at University College London's Institute of Archaeology. Jonathan couldn't remember much now about what either of the other two young men, James and Dean did, except that one of them worked in IT. Their conversation seemed to be almost entirely aimed at putting the world to rights. Animal cruelty, he quickly learned, was Hannah's big thing, but you could take your pick from a long list of good causes. Ending austerity, homelessness and poverty, scrapping student fees, ridding the world of global capitalism, controlling climate change and, of course, sacking bankers like him. `No, not like him', they'd said. He was `OK', they'd said. That was good to know.

It wasn't so much that he didn't understand or

even empathise with some of them, as the fact that they took so much upon themselves. It seemed to him that they had overburdened themselves with a plethora of individual issues of such scale and disparity that it would be impossible to know where to start. Theirs he realised, was a very different world to his. A free and easy world. A non-materialistic world. A world that, although critical and disapproving, was also trustingly, maybe even naively, optimistic. Not like his world at all.

But when they asked him what troubled him most about the world today, Jonathan found that he was reluctant to give an answer. Not because he didn't have an answer, but because he sensed that he would have to tread carefully. He tried to dodge the question. Putting on a serious face and trying not to sound flippant, he said,·

"It sounds as though all of you have quite enough on your plates already without me adding to it."

But they weren't going to let him off that easily.

"No, honestly, I'd really like to know what you think", Hannah had said. Gerry and Amanda nodded. They had put him on the spot.

"OK. If you insist. Well, the way I see it, most of our problems stem from over-population. Don't ask me how to solve it, but that's what I think. We're doing a lot of seriously bad things to the planet, cutting down forests, polluting the atmosphere and the seas, filling the oceans with plastic and so on, and most of it probably wouldn't be happening if the global population was smaller. So that's my starting point. It's not that I don't share your concerns about a lot of other things but for me that's the big one. In my opinion, if we could somehow put that right, a whole bunch of other issues would become much easier to solve. Some of the biggest ones would even start to solve themselves."

Hannah smiled. Gerry reached over and shook his hand.

"Wow, that's good stuff."

Jonathan was relieved that he seemed to have made a good first impression. His father had always told him that you only ever got one chance to do that. But did the silence that followed mean they wanted more from him? It felt like it, so he told them of his concerns for democracy, but he avoided making any connection between it and Brexit. He told them of his fears that not enough preparation was going into planning for the effects of climate change on the human population, but he avoided going into detail about what that might involve. That would be going too far. There were some things he couldn't tell them. Things they weren't ready to hear.

Now, whenever he now thought back to that first meeting, he found himself asking whether it had in some way changed him. He wasn't sure. But pretty soon, he had become sure of one thing. He loved Hannah. He loved her energy, her resilience, even her naivety. He even loved her when she made fun of him; like when she had once told him that he took things too seriously, that he should learn to `lighten up'. And when he had laughed and said that, with all her concerns about everything under the sun, it was like the pot calling the kettle black. And even when she had retorted `Yes, well, at least I try to do something about it' and part of him had wanted to tell her but hadn't been able to. And then, calmer, when she had laughed and called him an old man and said he'd have to be replaced soon, on his fortieth birthday. But most of all, he loved her trust, however misplaced, and her anger, however misdirected, because these things implied to him a certain healthiness in society.

~~~~~~~~

Chapter 5

"The visions are fragmented and a dark cloud spreads
like spilt ink across the pages of possible futures."
Garth Nix, Lirael

1

London, Friday 24ᵗʰ June 2016

Jonathan's mobile phone rang. Well, actually, it
played *Land of Hope and Glory*, which meant it
could only be his father. Seven-thirty and he'd only
been in bed for three hours. Against all the odds, a
miracle had happened. Leave had won, with the final
tally revealing a massive majority of one hundred
and sixty-eight constituencies and more than one
and a quarter million individual votes. Jonathan had
stayed up most of the night before as the results had
come in one by one but, tired and fearful of a
possible last minute reversal of fortune, he had
eventually turned in. Twice Hannah had woken up
to find herself alone in bed and, finding him still
glued to the television, had shaken her head in
despair. Hannah Kingston and Brian Shawcross
couldn't have been more different. What could be so

important, she had asked, that it was worth staying up all night and then taking a day off work for? By contrast, his father had been ecstatic. For the first time in years, Jonathan heard hope in his voice, for he had long since given up on his dream of living long enough to see his country regain its independence, and had resigned himself to watching, a powerless spectator, as Britain was gradually reduced to being a European state or, as he often described it, a German colony.

As a bonus, the Prime Minister Helen Fletcher announced within hours that she was to resign. Could things get any better? Five months earlier, she had fulfilled her electoral promise and had announced that the date of the referendum was to be the twenty-third of June 2016. Her decision had been a political one, coming against a background of polls suggesting that support for the newly-formed `Exit' party already stood at around ten per cent and was growing remarkably rapidly.

The date set, the ardently pro-EU Prime Minister had immediately embarked on a whistle-stop tour of Europe aimed, she said, at re-negotiating a number of issues known to be of concern with the electorate. It did not go well, to put it mildly. Over the next few weeks, in a series of humiliating meetings with EU officials and other European leaders, she was openly mocked for taking seriously the idea that the people of Britain should be listened to, that their concerns addressed, that rules could be modified to accommodate the UK's desire for more flexibility. It was quickly made abundantly clear to her that reform, in any meaningful sense of the word, was the one thing that Brussels had no intention of even discussing, and when in February Fletcher returned, chastened by the treatment she had received during her grand tour, it was with her tail very much between her legs. Her shopping list had been a modest one to say the least; it had not even touched on many of the most important areas of discontent and yet it had been rejected out of hand.

Like his father, Jonathan was utterly opposed to the idea that Britain should become politically integrated with other European countries in pursuit of the creation of a super-state. It was clear to him that, quite apart from where you stood on the issue in terms of principle, those who believed that it was essential, that, without it, nations would be unable, to work together, to co-operate harmoniously towards the goal of achieving more than each could hope for on its own, were plainly wrong. This simple aim is enacted quietly and practically across Europe every day in the lives of the people, whether they be scholars, businessmen, educators, scientists, policemen or simply travellers, In Jonathan's view, governments had a useful part to play in encouraging and facilitating such co-operation, but to conflate the issue with that of political unification was likely to damage rather than assist the process.

He had been just seven years old when the UK had joined in 1973, and so remembered nothing of it, nor of the referendum on Britain's continued membership, held two years later. But, if he had been old enough to understand and to have a vote, he would very likely, he thought, have voted in favour of joining the Common Market as it had then been called. Like most people, he guessed, he would have seen no good reason not to establish and formalise trading alliances with other European nations. But as time passed and the real aims of the architects of what had since become the European Union had been revealed, he had been appalled to discover the deception by which `the project', as the embryonic EU had been often been referred to by its authors, had been planned and brought into being. Everything he had learned about the project had confirmed him in the belief that our joining had been a huge mistake yet, despite that, he had always considered himself to be a `Reformer' rather than a `Leaver'. But now, after Helen Fletcher's abject failure to secure even the minimal changes she had asked for, Jonathan realised that real change was never going to be an option, that there was no longer any point in pushing for reform. Regardless of where you stood on the issue, the choice from now on was a simple binary one.

Fletcher put on a brave face and tried to sell the few tiny concessions she had managed to wring out of Brussels as successes. Jonathan's father had told him about the first Project Fear back in 1975. How the then Prime Minister had, just like Helen Fletcher, similarly lied to the people and declared that the renegotiation objectives had been substantially achieved. How the government itself had recommended a vote in favour of continued membership and how almost the entire mainstream national British press and media had supported the `Yes' campaign. He had also told him how then, just as now, politicians had warned the electorate that a `Yes' vote would mean rocketing food prices, scarcity, a return to malnutrition, even to famine; how just about every big name in industry, finance and the service sector, from Rolls Royce to British Steel, had campaigned vigorously for Britain's continued membership; how companies like these terrified not just their work forces, but their shareholders, customers, employees' families and even those on company pensions; how CBI members even nominated a `Mr Europe' in each company, who received regular posters and leaflets, commissioned letters and articles to be inserted in company magazines or prominently displayed in the workplace; how they were joined on the front line by consumer organisations, trade associations and the National Union of Farmers. It had been a coming together, Brian Shawcross had said, of a breadth and on a scale never before seen at any British election.

And in the end, the formidable financial power of big business had ultimately proved irresistible.

Despite opposition to continued membership from the Trade Unions, the left-wing Morning Star newspaper, prominent left-wing politicians like Michael Foot and Tony Benn and a handful of Conservatives, the `No' campaign failed to convince people and the `Yes' camp won easily. And the reasons were clear. The donations from Sainsbury's and BP alone had amounted to three times that of the entire `No' campaign By frightening people, by throwing vast amounts of money into the campaign and, most important of all, by keeping the electorate totally ignorant of what the EEC was really all about, the combined might of government and big business emerged victorious.

This time around though, the majority of people had not been fooled and now the referendum had backfired on Helen Fletcher. She had overlooked one very important difference. In 1975 when the nation had last voted, they had been totally ignorant of what was going on and had simply elected to continue to remain party to a friendly free-trade agreement with eight other European countries. But in the intervening years, the so-called Common Market had changed out of all recognition. Treaties had been implemented, often against the will of the people, which had seen the EU transform itself in full view from being a harmless trading bloc, to a fully-fledged political union which now gave twenty-seven other nations influence over many important areas of each individual member nation's own policy.

And the biggest difference of all was that most people in Britain were now aware of where it was all designed to lead.

But at least now it was all over. Jonathan still couldn't believe it. It was incredible. Except of course that it wasn't all over at all, because the Remainers weren't having any of it, and instead of accepting the result, their efforts became increasingly manic and unpleasant.

The focus of Project Fear had, as before, been on economic issues but, despite all the propaganda, it obviously hadn't, on its own, been enough this time. It was time to step up a gear and so new forms began to appear. First came Project Conspiracy. They said that foreign powers, particularly the Russians, were behind it. Then came Project Sneer. The Leave side, they said, comprised uneducated, ignorant people who hadn't known what they were voting for. Nasty people. Liars, racists and thugs. Jonathan wondered which of these he was supposed to be. And he wondered when and how people had become that way. Obviously they hadn't been uneducated, ignorant, nasty, racists when they had elected their MPs. What could possibly have caused them to be transformed so suddenly into such abhorrent creatures? It was a great mystery indeed. They had entered into no Faustian pact. They had partaken not of the Circean pottage, nor had a single drop of Dr Jekyll's serum passed their lips. It appeared that the demonic metamorphosis had miraculously occurred only at the very instant they had voted the wrong way.

2

Cheapside, London, Friday 5th May 2017

The Whitefriars had run out of John Smith's and so Jonathan, having decided that it was too too early for whisky but, equally, too early to go home, had been forced to settle for a pint of London Pride, which to his surprise he found himself enjoying. Opening his Evening Standard and, as usual, leafing through the pages en route to the crossword, his eye fell on a headline, `Man killed in pub Brexit hate crime attack'.

The man in question was thought to have been killed as the result of an argument about Brexit, where `tensions had boiled over and erupted into actual violence'. His badly bruised body had apparently been found in a pool of blood in a dark corner of a pub car park, its throat slit open from ear to ear. Customers at the pub near Leeds told police that he had earlier been heard arguing loudly in the bar with two other men, both believed to be East Europeans.

`Home Office figures', the article went on, `reveal a big rise in hate crime offences, with the police recording a rise of seventeen per cent in such offences in the twelve months since the referendum', although admitting that some of this increase could be put down to what they called `improvements' in the way police record `hate crime'.

The article puzzled Jonathan. It wasn't clear from reading it where the `hate' connection lay. Was it because the man had insulted the two foreigners because of their nationality? Had he perhaps told them they should go back home, or that they would have to do so after Brexit? If so, he supposed, that might have amounted to `hate speech', but would it also be `hate *crime*'? Or was it the murder that was the `hate crime'? The article didn't make it clear, but Jonathan thought it unlikely to be the latter. Killing someone because they voted `Leave' probably didn't meet the criteria.

But regardless, there was no doubt that the division was growing dangerously. More than a year had passed since the meeting with Gerald Lines in Dublin. And it had not been a good year. Within days of the referendum result being announced, all the warning signs had been there. On an almost daily basis, the establishment contrived to invent and circulate new scare stories while continuing to ratchet up the fear level on existing ones, all the time empowering and reinforcing the arguments of those who wanted to remain, whilst gradually chipping away at the confidence of those who had voted to leave. Lines' predictions, he could now see, were coming true, day by day and at an alarming rate, and the country was divided in a way never seen before.

Jonathan had even seen signs of it in his own family when his father and his uncle had got into an argument about Brexit. His father's younger brother Bernard had accused all Leavers of being racist because they wanted to control immigration. And they were stupid, because Brexit was going to bankrupt the country. His father had tried to explain his own position. He couldn't answer for others, he had said, but he hadn't got a racist bone in his body; he didn't worry about where people came from or what colour they were; all he wanted was for our elected representatives to be in control of our immigration policy. Surely, that didn't make him racist? And he told Bernard that the issue was nothing to do with whether we would be better or worse off. It was a matter of principle. He didn't want to see his country give up its independence, its right to self-determination, and become a mere state. We are a democracy, he had said. We wanted, and we had the right, to be governed by people who had to listen to us at least some of the time, if only because they wouldn't get re-elected if they didn't. But Bernard was having none of it and in the end had stormed out in a rage saying, he never wanted to see or hear from him again.

Jonathan had seen it at the bank as well. Workmates who had stopped taking lunch together, too embarrassed at having to avoid mentioning the issue and risk acknowledging the division that had opened up like a yawning chasm between them. He knew others too, who had used to go for a social drink together after work as a single group, but which had now split into two and patronised different pubs. David, his best friend at work, had even left the branch's quiz team, partly he had said, because he felt outnumbered and ostracised and partly because he couldn't stand being surrounded by sniggering Remainers, gloating in anticipation of killing his dream.

And now the Remain campaign had received an unexpected but very welcome gift. Until it had surfaced as an issue last month, the Northern Ireland border situation had not even been considered important enough to mention. How the hell, had it ever been allowed to escalate to the point where it now threatened to dominate things? Everywhere else where an EU member country abuts another which is a non-member, there is a border. Why wouldn't there be?, thought Jonathan. The EU itself insists on it and so does the WTO. It makes perfect sense. And there were already more than forty other borders on the outer fringes of the external border of the EU so what difference would one more make? What is so bloody special about the border between the UK and Ireland? Jonathan knew perfectly well what the answer to his question was said to be, of course. He knew that EU negotiators, having made a tenuous connection between the border and its part in sustaining the `Good Friday' peace agreement between the British and Irish governments, had seized on it as a drowning man clutches at a straw; but it didn't make him feel any better.

He also began to recognise the futility of protests and riots like those he had seen in France. He saw that they had no chance of achieving anything, because the authority unintentionally vested in government by the system of representative *fausse démocratie* meant that the establishment held all the cards. It owned the weapons and the manpower and, most importantly, it owned the law of the land. Riots would never achieve anything much because most people simply have too much to lose. The government would in the last resort simply declare a state of national emergency. The system would deprive you of your liberty and in so doing take away your job, your money, your home, your family. Everything.

The evidence of the past year had taught Jonathan a great deal. He understood now what Ralph Waldo Emerson had meant when he had said that in time, `All democracy becomes a government of bullies tempered by mere editors'. He knew now that when Lines had said, `It is not possible to change a culture of tyranny by adhering to the rules set by those who would themselves change nothing', he had been right. And that Lines had been right again when he had asserted that, `only the people can make it happen'.

But on one point, Jonathan still had doubts. Lines had had predicted that it would not be long before, `every man in every street will see this for himself, and forces will be unleashed which have the potential to alter British society beyond all recognition.' Jonathan had known then that Lines had not been talking about mere protests or riots, but of a level of activism within society on an unprecedented scale and ferocity. At that time, he hadn't been able to help questioning whether Lines was right in supposing that the people really would rise up in anger against the establishment and even now he remained unsure. After all, they hadn't done that for a very long time and, more than anything, he desperately hoped that perhaps there was a chance that trouble could be averted.

But, either way, Jonathan had now made his decision. He had waited long enough, and tomorrow he was to meet up with Gerald Lines on one of the professor's regular visits to Cambridge.

3

Cambridge, Saturday 6th May 2017

Jonathan had driven up from London on a sunny Saturday morning and had met his old tutor in the University's Department of Politics and International Studies where C^{3}I, the Cambridge

International Intelligence Institute which Lines chaired, had been allocated offices which they shared with the Institute for Democratic Reform.

"Good to see you again Jonathan. And may I introduce you to two of my colleagues, Jeremy Benson and Martin Armstrong."

Benson, the older of the two, introduced as Lines' deputy in C³I, looked at his watch.

"Delighted to meet you Jonathan and, well, I hate to appear rude, but I'm afraid I must leave you chaps to it if you don't mind.", and then, excusing himself to leave, "I've got rather a busy schedule today. Perhaps we'll meet up again some time Jonathan."

The second man, Martin Armstrong, he was told, was not only one of Lines C³I colleagues but also a member of PRAXIS. His specialism was international law and he worked as a civil servant, currently attached to Dexeu in Whitehall. Over a leisurely lunch in the garden of the Riverside restaurant, the three would talk.

"I was pleased but, I have to admit, a little surprised to hear from you again Jonathan", said Lines. "As I recall, you said only that you had something you'd like to talk over with me."

"I'll come straight to the point, Gerald", said Jonathan. "Some of the things you spoke of when we met last year are still troubling me."

"In what way exactly are they troubling you, Jonathan? Because you disagree perhaps?"

"No. No, quite the reverse. It's because I realise I have been naive", Jonathan told him. "Foolish even. Because I didn't want to believe what you said, I tried to deny it. But I was wrong. I can see now that what you and your friend Cormac advocated is, in the end, the only way. In circumstances such as are now emerging, direct action is the only solution."

Armstrong nodded. It was clear he had come to the same conclusion and that, like Jonathan, he held Lines in high esteem.

"Do not be so hard on yourself, Jonathan. It is true perhaps that you have only come to understand in your own time, but there are many others who will never reach the level of understanding that you now have."

"You spoke of trying to fight back", said Jonathan. "I'd like to contribute in any way I can, but I'm not sure how I could help."

"There is a great deal that you could contribute, I'm sure. But it is imperative that you trust me implicitly, Jonathan", Lines had said. "And, similarly, I must be able to trust you. There is everything at stake and you need to know that, if you once come on board, there can be no question of turning back."

Jonathan thought he understood what Lines meant. But he didn't.

"You, Martin, and I Jonathan, are not men of action. There are others, better suited in every way, to perform the many functions that direct action demands. But actions must be guided, directed. We are, in Gramsci's words, the `organic intellectuals'. We must engage in the cultural, ideological and strategic work necessary to separate the peoples' conservative consciousness, which they have inherited from the past and uncritically absorbed from the dominant classes, from the consciousness implicit in the actuality of their situation. It is this which, in reality, unites them and provides the basis for the revolutionary action necessary to the practical transformation of the real world."

Jonathan was quiet. There was that uncomfortable feeling again. `Cognitive dissonance', his old psychology tutor had called it. On the one hand, he knew Lines was right. Nothing else would have a chance. But it was pure neo-Marxism, and Jonathan didn't do that.

Armstrong had spotted the signs.

"Gerald is absolutely right, Jonathan", said Armstrong. "We are not the men of action, but neither you nor I need fear that we will be idle. There will be plenty to occupy us, both before and after what the government has euphemistically termed the `transition period'. It will be good to have you on board."

Jonathan had taken an immediate liking to Martin Armstrong. They had much in common. But, lunch now over, Armstrong would return to his work, leaving Jonathan and Gerald Lines to drive in Jonathan's car to meet up with Henry Bloom.

4

Thowton Allop, Northamptonshire, Saturday 6th May 2017

The premises occupied by Midlands Plastics (Machinery) Ltd. were located near Thowton Allop, a small town in Northamptonshire. A turning off the A14, just inside the boundary with Cambridgeshire, led to an industrial estate where Jonathan's Honda drove through the open entrance gates into the car park and a space next to the silver Range Rover in the section marked `Staff vehicles only'.

In the reception lobby where they were asked to take a seat, Jonathan idly picked up a colour brochure from a display stand on a shelf next to the receptionist's desk. Flicking through its pages, he learned that the company's main business was the importation of machinery for the plastics industry. `MPM' it seemed, were the appointed UK sole agents for a number of foreign manufacturers of blow-moulding, injection-moulding, and vacuum thermo-forming machines as well as the raw materials of the industry and a wide range of ancillary equipment such as granulators and hopper feeders. The company also bought, reconditioned and sold used machinery and offered their expertise in modifying equipment to customers' own specifications, to which end, the brochure informed the reader, `MPM boasts a well-equipped machine shop'. They had a small UK sales force and employed several specialist engineers and technicians, trained in the maintenance of the equipment that the company sold in the UK. They also held a large stock of spare parts for the ranges they represented.

Bloom's secretary, an attractive, smartly dressed young woman in her mid-twenties, appeared and shepherded the two men down a corridor to an office where, after knocking and holding the door open for them to enter, she retreated. Henry Bloom rose from his desk to greet them.

"Hello Gerald. Good to see you. And you too Jonathan. I trust you're both well."

In a chair facing Bloom's desk sat another man who turned his head around to see them enter.

"This is Joe", said Bloom. "Joe Corović. Joe's going to give you the grand tour a little later."

"Do you need me any more at the moment, Harry?", asked Joe after the introductions had been made.

"No. But thanks, Joe. I'll give you a shout when we're ready."

"Good man, Joe", said Bloom to his visitors after Corović had left the room. "He's our transport manager. Worth his weight in gold. Twelve years in the British Army, much of it spent with the UN in logistics, organising transport, distribution and so forth. His grandfather was Serbian and he's invaluable to me. We do a lot of business in the

Balkans and Joe speaks the language, understands the culture and knows the region like the back of his hand."

Lines and Bloom remained in Bloom's office talking while Joe Corović showed Jonathan around MPM's premises. First the stores, where row upon row of grey metal cabinets housed hundreds of small `bins' holding strange looking machine parts, each bin carefully labelled and numbered. Larger items occupied the `bulk racks' in a room leading off from the main store area. Then, in the machine shop next door, Joe proudly pointed out each of the many different metal-working machines and gave a cursory explanation of each. Some of the more common ones like the lathes, drills and grinders, Jonathan vaguely remembered from his days at Buxton Grammar School for Boys, where he had briefly taken metalwork classes. He was pretty sure his mother still used the aluminium toast rack he had made and had proudly taken home to give to her one Mothers' Day. But here, there were also rotary cutting machines, welding machines, borers, milling machines, shaping machines and hydraulic presses. Jonathan was impressed. There wouldn't be much they couldn't turn out here, he thought.

Leaving the machine shop, Joe guided Jonathan down a corridor, past an office where the sign on the door said `Accounts' and where, through the window in the door, he could see people at desks working at their computers. Then, past an office marked `Sales' and another for `Engineers and Draughtsmen', to the end of the corridor where another, heavier, door led into a large yard at the rear of the building.

In one corner of the yard stood a mobile crane, which Joe informed him was for unloading heavy machines, and several forklift trucks, one of which was busy unloading wooden pallets of boxes from the back of a flat-bed vehicle and stacking them near a large metal roller-shutter door which, Jonathan supposed, must give direct access to the machine shop. Near the gates at the rear entrance to the yard was a small wooden building which Joe explained was the yard foreman's office. Inside at a desk, the man on the telephone waved at Joe and smiled. Up against the perimeter fence stood a large Portakabin which was divided into two rest rooms, one at either end and, between them, a washroom and a small kitchen with a sink, cupboards and microwave cooker. Joe explained that the Portakabin's main use was to give workshop, stores and yard staff somewhere to take their lunch breaks. On the opposite side of the yard some distance from the main building, warning signs on the doors of three other small buildings, indicated that they contained potentially dangerous materials; oxygen cylinders, acetylene and other fuel gas containers, which needed to be kept well away from the main building, as well as from each other. The third outbuilding, slightly larger than the others, had a sign on the door reading `Customer Projects and Orders Only'.

Back in Bloom's office, Jonathan learned that his assessment of the machine shop's capabilities had been correct, but it shocked him somewhat to hear that Lines and Bloom considered it essential to their aims to have the capability to maintain, repair and modify weapons.

"Although of course, it goes without saying that we all very much hope it will not be necessary", said Bloom, noting Jonathan's reaction.

Lines nodded.

"Of course, we will work tirelessly to obviate the need for armed conflict but, at the same time, I'm sure you would agree that we would be foolish not to prepare for the eventuality."

"Yes, I suppose I can see that."

"However, you and I need not concern ourselves with all this, Jonathan. We can safely leave this side of things in the hands of the professionals."

Jonathan momentarily considered asking who the `professionals' were, but then thought better of it. Perhaps the less he knew, the better.

~~~~~~~

Chapter 6

*"Far be it from thee to do such a thing, to slay the
righteous with the wicked, so that the righteous and
the wicked are treated alike. Far be it from thee.
Shall not the Judge of all the earth deal justly?"*
Genesis 18:25

1

Sevenoaks, Kent, Wednesday 26th June 2019

Derek Johnson sat facing the screen on his desk.
The police controller had a difficult job, and one
which was not the most popular role in the service;
most people don't join the service in order to spend
their lives sitting behind a desk with a radio, a
telephone and a computer, but it needed to be done.
In this era of service cuts, with fewer officers than
there were, Derek spent increasing hours of his day
ringing people back to explain why the police
wouldn't be coming out. As the initial contact for all
calls, it was his job to elicit and record essential
information, evaluate the urgency of the incident,
prioritise action using the graded response guidelines
and make decisions regarding the most appropriate
course of action.

All calls received were assessed on the basis of risk and an element of judgement as to whether people could be reasonably be expected to sort out their own problems. The system is colour-coded, red for life or limb in danger, yellow for priorities, such as a house burglary, road accident or disorder in the street, blue for routine matters. On a busy shift Derek thought how his monitor screen resembled nothing so much as the Colombian national flag.

A 101 call had been received from a man who had asked to be put through to Sevenoaks Police Station and had given the name of his 'single point of contact' as instructed. The caller informed police that he was a Neighbourhood Watch `Home Watch Co-ordinator'. He was a volunteer member of *Country Eye*, a partnership between the rural community, the Police and Neighbourhood Watch, which aimed to help reduce crime, or at least the fear of it, by involving the community and protecting those who were most vulnerable. The caller gave his name as Eric Jones and his address as 2, Furze Green Lane, Bridgeley.

Jones wanted to report what he considered to be suspicious activity in connection with a nearby property, a small cottage a few doors from his own, at number 5. It was the end dwelling in the row of five semi-detached cottages that comprised Furze Green Lane and it had been empty for months, ever since the old lady had gone into a home. Jones used to see her son and daughter come to visit at weekends, but of course that had long since stopped. He had subsequently heard that the old lady had since passed away and he had expected to see the property put up for sale, but no `For sale' sign had ever appeared. Another neighbour had told him she had seen the property in an auction catalogue. That made sense. It was in a very poor, run down condition and, like a lot of those lived in for a long time by very old people, completely unmodernised. He doubted whether anyone would get a mortgage on it and expected that if, it was sold, it would most likely be to a property developer who could pay cash for it - one of those who buys cheaply at auction, renovates to a minimum standard and then rents it out.

And then the men had arrived. At various times, Jones had seen several different ones, he thought at least four or five, maybe more, entering and leaving the cottage at all times of day and night.

"It wasn't any one thing in particular", he had said to Derek Johnson, but `a lot of little things' that he thought added up to something very odd.

At first, he said, "I thought maybe they were builders, you know, planning to renovate and modernise the property. But they never seemed to carry any tools or equipment in and there were no signs or sounds of any work being done. And there were never any women", he had said. He thought that alone seemed unusual. "And they were a real nuisance, coming and going at all hours." More than once, he had been woken up by the sound of doors slamming and vehicles coming or going in the middle of the night.

Presumably the property now belonged to the old lady's son and daughter, or perhaps it had been sold at auction and maybe it was being rented out? But Jones didn't think the latter very likely.

"It's in a shocking state", he had told Johnson, and suggested it was much more likely that the men were just squatting.

"Going by the look of them", he'd said, "and I know you shouldn't judge people by their appearance but they .... well, they just seem so `out of place'."

And then there were the vehicles. Jones had seen several different cars and vans parked outside at various times and had jotted down the makes, models, colours and registration numbers of three of them.

Derek Johnson decided that this was definitely a `blue' report. There could be no doubt about it. No crime had been reported and no-one was in danger. It was not until number plate and stolen vehicle checks were made two days later with the National ANPR Data Centre and the Police National Database, that it began to look like anything more than a case of `nosey neighbour' syndrome. The checks revealed that one of the vehicles, a black BMW X5, was sporting number plates belonging to a different vehicle altogether. Another, a white

Mercedes Citan van, had been reported stolen in Cumbria some weeks previously. It was the Mercedes that was parked at the side of the cottage when PC Ben Cranford, the officer sent to investigate, drove down Furze Green Lane at eleven o'clock on Friday morning.

2

Bridgeley, near Sevenoaks, Friday 28 June 2019

Inside the cottage, two men sat at a small table in the living room. One, wearing earphones and smoking a cigarette, listened, eyes closed, to music on his mobile phone while the other studied the racing results in the sports pages of yesterday's newspaper. Neither was aware of the patrol car that had pulled up outside. Nor, until it was too late, did either of them see or hear PC Ben Cranford get out and walk up the path leading to the front door of the cottage. Patrick McNally took off the headphones and laid them on the table. Rising to his feet, he walked towards the old lady's sideboard, where a half-full bottle of his favourite *Green Spot* whisky stood. He had taken only three steps. The curtains were open, but only as much as was necessary, just sufficient to provide the minimum amount of daylight for Doyle to be able to read the newspaper, but through those few inches, McNally saw the face of PC Cranford.

And he knew that the policeman had seen him.

"Shit", he exclaimed, moving hurriedly away from the window. "It's the police. Only one man on his own, but he's seen me. You'd better make yourself scarce, Willy. I'll get rid of him as quickly as possible."

William Doyle said nothing. He rarely did. But McNally was now alone in the room.

When his knock on the front door was answered, Cranford was confronted by a dark-haired man of medium height and slim build, who he judged to be in his mid to late forties. The man smiled and gave a friendly nod.

"No, the van's not mine. It belongs to a friend who's staying here", he said in response to the policeman's question. "His son came to fetch him earlier, but he'll be back this evening, I shouldn't wonder."

"I don't suppose you'd know where he keeps the vehicle documents?", said Cranford.

"As a matter of fact, I do", replied McNally. "He's a tidy man. He keeps all his papers together in a drawer in the kitchen. Would you like me to get them?"

Cranford thought it best if he kept the man in his sight.

"I'll come in while you look for them, if that's alright with you, sir."

"Of course, follow me. Through here", he said, standing back to allow PC Cranford to enter.

Closing the front door, McNally led the way through the living room, past the bottom of the stairs and into the little kitchen at the rear of the cottage. Crossing the room, he pulled open a drawer in the kitchen dresser and, carefully watched by Cranford standing close by him, pulled out a folder and began to flick through the various papers it held.

"It'll be in here somewhere, I reckon", he said to Cranford. "Just give me a moment."

Out of the corner of his eye, McNally saw the door to the adjoining small bathroom open slightly. He kept his head pointing down towards the folder and its contents, so that his eyes could not accidentally alert Cranford to the presence of the other man who had silently entered the kitchen behind him.

"For Christ's sake, Willy", he said as the policeman slumped to the floor. "There was no need for that."

The two .25 hollow-point rounds, fired from the suppressed Walther P99 at a distance of scarcely more than three feet, had left little sign of the damage they had done. Apart from two small, closely-spaced entry wounds in the occipital cleft at the back of Cranford's skull, and a small trickle of blood that had reached and dyed the collar of his white shirt the colour of an expensive claret, there was nothing to indicate that a very large part of the policeman's brain had been liquidised.

3

Sevenoaks, Friday 28 June 2019

Nothing had been heard from PC Cranford since he had radioed in to the station at 11.04am to report his whereabouts and inform them that the vehicle was there. Nor was he responding to attempts to contact him, either by radio or 'phone.

PC Cranford's police car was still parked outside the cottage when the two-man patrol sent to investigate arrived at twelve-nineteen p.m. After knocking on the front door several times and getting no response, they peered through the gap in the curtains into the living room but saw nothing of interest.

"You stay here. I'll take a look around the back", said one of the two officers." Fifteen seconds later, the other heard the yell of, "Quick, I think he's in here", from his partner. Through the window of the kitchen, the officer could see a body on the floor. Pushing the handle he was surprised to find that the old wooden back door swung freely inward on its hinges. Entering the kitchen, the first of the two policemen paused briefly in the doorway to take in a snapshot of the scene.

The metal plate holding the sliding bolt that had once enabled the door to be fastened securely from the inside now hung uselessly down, held in place by a single screw. The hasp into which the bolt had once slid lay on the floor, and the doorframe to which it had been attached was splintered where the screws holding it had been wrenched out. A single hefty kick, planted squarely on the door near the frame, was probably all it would have taken. The sink was home to an assortment of unwashed cups, glasses, saucers and plates. Plastic trays and foil containers that had once held microwave meals and take-away dishes, lay in an untidy heap on the worktop. On the floor, the body lay on its side, its head turned slightly down and its eyes wide open, as if inspecting the skirting board. Both knew it was that of PC Cranford. Shaking him did not wake him up. One of the officers went outside to throw up while the other radioed the station to report what they had found. The Inspector immediately called for an Armed Response Unit to attend. When they arrived, their search of the cottage took barely a few minutes and by twelve-forty-four p.m. the team had declared everything `all clear'. They had noted a small travel bag in a cupboard in the upstairs back bedroom and had reported their findings to the Inspector at the station.

An hour later, the murder squad and forensics team arrived and found that the bag contained some dirty clothes, a shaving bag and a small hand towel. In the side pocket of the bag they would find a Russian-made Makarov 9mm semi-automatic pistol with a threaded barrel. The pocket would also be found to contain a small blue-covered booklet.

4

Millbank, London, Wednesday 3rd July 2019

To Gardaí Commissioner Aoibheann Kennedy, none of this came as any surprise. She had only recently declared that it had, `never been the force's view that the IRA had disbanded and accordingly ceased to exist'. To the contrary, Kennedy was quite certain that there remained serious `legacy issues', of which defections to other still-active dissident groups was but one. She had gone on to suggest that, `They make full use of their `legacy' reputations and in some cases their former terrorist tactics.' It had not taken long for her suspicions to be proved right.

Nor did it surprise Blake Burgess of MI5 who had recently been tasked with preparing for just such an eventuality. Burgess had been assigned as operational leader of a small inter-service counter-terrorism task force, a team of specialists with expertise in such areas as Intelligence, Covert Technical Operations and Financial Investigation & Confiscation and which included officers from both the Security Service and Secret Intelligence Services. And now, following the discovery of the `Blue Book' at the scene of the murder of the policeman in Sevenoaks, it seemed the fears which had led to his appointment might be about to become a reality.

Burgess pressed the `stop' button on the new

digital music player Oliver had bought him for his birthday. Oliver was a thoughtful boy and had chosen the gift carefully, knowing how much his dad would appreciate being able to listen to his jazz away from home. And he must have spent hours, copying the CDs onto memory sticks and carefully labelling each one, knowing that dad would never get around to doing it himself. But for now, Coleman Hawkins would just have to wait. There were more pressing matters to attend to.

He picked up the phone and rang his wife Jenny to tell her he'd be working late yet again. She knew better than to ask what it was that had kept him from coming home to the house in Orpington several times in recent weeks. He listened while she told him that Oliver had been offered a place at the University of Surrey, subject of course to satisfactory exam results.

"It would be wonderful", she said, "to have him living so near home. I was dreading the thought that he might prefer the offer from Stirling and we'd hardly see him at all, but he seems happy with the idea of lodging somewhere near Guildford. We could see him any time we want."

Burgess was happy that his wife was happy. And he remembered how his own mother had been similarly relieved when, after leaving Orpington Grammar School, he had chosen a career in the Police Force and had been enrolled at Hendon, instead of accepting the offer of a university place in

Salford.

"And how's Emily?", he asked, enquiring after his thirteen year old daughter.

"She's fine", replied Jenny. "She's going to stay over at her friend Rebecca's tonight and I'll pick her up first thing in the morning."

"And Lurch?"

"He's fine. Missing you though."

So that was it. They were all fine. Wife, son, daughter and dog. All OK.

"OK. Look, I'm sorry darling, but I have to go now."

"Love you too".

A few silent seconds passed before the knock on the door. The two younger men entered and Burgess indicated for them each to take a seat. The meeting proper was about to commence.

"So, Howard my boy, what do we have?"

The question was addressed to a tall, athletic looking, younger man who lounged, untidily Burgess thought, in one of the armchairs in the office. Howard Everett, who delighted in the job title of Covert Technical Operations Specialist within the IT, Science & Technical department of MI5, was regarded by Burgess' as his first lieutenant. If he would just smarten himself up a bit, Everett could go far.

"Well, we've got nothing on the Makarov. It's clean as a whistle in fact. Never been fired. And in any case, it wasn't the weapon used to kill the policeman. But, we have made some progress already with the `Blue Book'", said Everett. "You're all familiar with `tracking dots' I take it?"

Burgess nodded. "Vaguely", he replied.

But, seeing that no-one else said anything at all, Everett felt that a short explanation was in order.

"Well, they don't exactly go out of their way to publicise it, and it's a complicated area. It's called printer steganography, but basically, most printer manufacturers build in a security feature that was originally intended to prevent people forging banknotes and suchlike. But it's turned out to be very useful in other ways. How it works is that colour printers embed a coded pattern of dots in the documents they put out. The dots contain the printer's serial number, as well as the date and time the documents were printed. The dots are tiny, less than a millimeter in diameter and a shade of yellow that, against a white background, can't be detected by the naked eye. But our guys can read them of course, and by analyzing the dots in the `Blue Book' they have discovered that it was produced on a four-year old Mitsumo digital laser printer, model number L393, with a serial number of 24736229, and that it was printed on June 19, 2018, at seven-fourteen a.m., at least according to the printer's internal clock."

"I'm impressed", said Burgess. "Do we know yet who the printer belongs to?"

"We know who supplied it and who bought it

originally", Howard replied. "But the trail's gone cold. The guy who initially bought it was running a small print shop in Forkhill, County Armagh, but the business went bust soon afterwards and everything was sold off. We've contacted the firm that handled the liquidation and apparently the printers and other equipment were sold at auction. There's a good chance though that we might find out where they went."

Burgess turned towards another, younger, man.

"Talking of auctions, young Jack, perhaps you'd like to tell Howard what you told me about the house itself?"

James Daniels smiled and shook his head in mock despair. Burgess had always called him `Jack'. It was his idea of a joke. But with a name like Burgess, let alone Blake, thought James, he was really pushing his luck to make fun of other peoples' names. Or at least, he would have been if only he hadn't been the boss.

"Well, it looks as if the guy who made the initial report was right about the men, whoever they are, having been squatting, because when the police arrived to investigate, they found the back door had already been kicked in. The police say the house is now owned by an outfit called Blossom Properties Ltd. who purchased it a only few weeks ago at an auction. It was sold on the instructions of a woman, a Mrs Cathleen Burnette, the daughter of Mrs Agnes Merton, the old lady who died."

Daniels referred to his notes.

"The property company say they were planning to renovate it completely and then rent it out, but that they hadn't got around to starting the work."

5

South Kensington, London, Monday 15th July 2019

The phone rang. It was Gerry. He, James and a couple of others were planning to go for a drink on Friday evening and wondered if he'd like to join them. Jonathan noticed that Gerry didn't ask how he was. Gerry was thoughtful like that. And it was very nice of them to ask him. They must have known he wouldn't be a barrel of laughs, that conversation would be difficult, but they had asked him anyway. They were a good bunch.

"Is Mandy going to be there?", he had asked. "I haven't seen her for a couple of weeks. She seems to be avoiding me."

"No, I asked her of course, but she said she's going to be working late", Gerry had replied.

Jonathan hadn't seen any of the others for a couple of weeks either but, Gerry noticed, he asked only about Mandy. Gerry wasn't offended, but he found it interesting.

Chapter 7

*" There are the workers of iniquity fallen: they are
cast down, and shall not be able to rise."*
Psalms 36, v 12

1

*Marlow-on-Thames, Buckinghamshire, Thursday
18th July 2019*

Like a skylark, it hovered; high, still and silent in the
warm, afternoon summer sun. Shining yet unseen, it
did not move. The powerful lens zoomed slowly in
on the colourful scene below. The throng on the
patio near the house. The lawn, sloping gently down
to the Thames. Ladies in their summer dresses,
chatting together in the dappled shade of the
wisteria-covered pergola, while their men, in blazers
and flannels, stand apart from them and talk of
serious matters. Tables spread with food. The white
and blue striped marquee. The waitresses, like
shuffling penguins in their white blouses and black
skirts, carrying trays of canapés and drinks.

In the back of the van, high on the hill, two
men unhurriedly watched the proceedings on the

screen and waited their moment. They watched as the two young waitresses walked back to the marquee with their empty trays. They watched as a small group of men broke away and walked towards the river and down the steps, stopping near the little landing stage where their plotting would go unheard.

"I reckon that's about the best we're going to get, Mac."

"Aye, you're right, Joe. We're not going to do any better than that. If she goes off near the ground, I don't reckon there'll be too much damage nearer the house. Remember, we're not after the girls, so try to aim for the left hand side, nearest the river. There'll be less collateral damage that way."

As Corović manoeuvred the controls until the sights were centred on a spot midway between the water and where the men stood, about four metres away. McKay did the sums.

"Start taking her down, Joe. Slowly. And stop at sixty-five metres."

McKay watched as the numbers on the altimeter display on the screen responded to his instruction. One hundred and twenty, one hundred, eighty, seventy, sixty-five. Corović held it there and waited until McKay nodded before releasing the deadly fruit.

At another time and in another place, McKay had been trained to have the creature circle for a long time, sometimes even for hours, carrying out a meticulous assessment of the effects and, most importantly, a body count. It had not always been easy, particularly if the bodies were in more than one piece. But today they would not wait around. It was sufficient to have seen that no-one in that group remained standing and that elsewhere people were moving. Others, on hearing the explosion, had come down from nearer the house to see what was going on. The three young waitresses who had emerged from inside the marquee, were quickly ushered away towards the house by a man who was probably the catering manager.

"Bring her home, Joe. Let's get of of here and go and get a beer somewhere."

2

Iain McKay and Josif Corović sat in the garden of the Wheatsheaf, enjoying their reward and watching the coxed eights practising their skills in preparation for the forthcoming `Sons of the Thames' race.

"The old team's still got it, eh Mac?", said Corović.

McKay nodded.

"Aye Joe. For auld lang syne." He raised his glass high and Corović did likewise.

"Have this one on us, your Majesty", said McKay solemnly.

The distant sound of an ambulance siren was just audible. In another garden not far away, paramedics had finished ministering to the needs of a few who had been unlucky enough to need their attention. But casualties had been light, and the main focus had been on removing for examination what remained of the four men for whom nothing could be done.

It seemed that the garden party had taken place at Great Marlow Lodge, the home of the Labour peer and former EU Commissioner, Cecil Arbuthnot, who had been elevated to the Lords, courtesy of his inclusion in the resignation honours list of Helen Fletcher, three years earlier. His unfortunate companions by the riverside had been the Labour MPs John Waterson and Alec Starling and the rebel Tory MP Simon Winterson-Greer. The four were members of a cross-party group that was planning a coup, by mounting a challenge to the appointment of the incoming Prime Minister, Paul Jameson. Their strategy was first to press for a vote of no confidence, which they were optimistic about winning, and then subsequently try to form a government of national unity led by Lord Marlow himself, although of course that would mean him having to relinquish his peerage.

From statements made by guests, police now pieced together a good picture of what had taken place. In all, twenty-five people had been present, four of them catering staff and another five neighbours of the Arbuthnots. The remaining guests comprised personal friends, constituency party members and a few from the local business community.

On the patio directly outside the house, ex-Prime Minister Helen Fletcher, who had been guest of honour, had sat with her businessman husband, enjoying the afternoon sun. She was very taken with the dark-haired young man who, at her request, had surprised her by playing a beautiful rendition of the Adagio from Rodrigo's masterful Concierto de Aranjuez. She would ask him to entertain her personally at her next soirée. All her attention focused on the handsome guitar player, she had faced the house and had seen nothing. But Peter Fletcher, who had no interest in music and not a jealous bone in his body, had occupied himself with more important matters, primarily with steadily emptying the bottle of Louis Roederer Cristal Brut 2008. `Yes,' he had seen what had happened, at least, he `had seen Arbuthnot and the others walk down towards the river until their heads disappeared from view'. It had occurred to him that `perhaps Arbuthnot was planning to show them his new pride and joy, his cabin cruiser, `La Bella Europa'. Then he had heard the sound. It hadn't been that loud, he said, but the bottle of Louis Roederer on the table had shattered and he had dropped his glass.

He remembered hearing Helen Fletcher say, `Oh, you poor thing' and had seen her take the young man into the house to clean up the blood from the graze on his temple. The guitarist himself had seemed more concerned about his instrument, which now sported an extra tiny soundhole. Peter Fletcher had then walked down to the river where he had been one of the first to see the bodies but, somebody having already dialled 999 and so there being nothing to do but wait, he had gone to the marquee in search of a replacement bottle of Roederer and a fresh glass. Clutching his prize, he made his way back to the table on the patio. Where was Helen? She seemed to be taking rather a long time.

Several other people told much the same story. Apart from Helen Fletcher, it seemed that most of the other ladies had occupied the area under the pergola and had seen nothing. One of the young waitresses had suffered a small wound to her arm when one of the pieces of shrapnel that had pierced the marquee had struck her. The enterprising young police officer, who had sketched out the layout of the garden and the positions of most of its occupants at the time the explosion occurred, would surely have been pleased to know that his drawing would be put to good use by MI5.

3

Bearsley, North Yorkshire, Thursday 18th July 2019

The member for Bearsley, Shirley Davidson, was one of many Labour MPs who, in all fairness it must be said, had made their intentions perfectly clear. Despite seventy-one per cent of her constituents having voted to leave, Davidson, who was never one to go against the party line and had consistently voted for greater European integration, intended to defy the voters in her constituency yet again, by voting against any and all Leave options that were presented to parliament.

In her younger days, Ms Davidson had been a `model', interspersed with spells as an exotic dancer, and had even appeared in a few low-budget films. In her first, Confessions of a Caretaker, produced in Soho and set in an all-girls school, she had a non-speaking part as schoolgirl vamp, Vanessa Strumpet, but, having ascended rapidly through the ranks in the time-honoured manner, she had eventually come to play roles in several late-era Hammer films. Her most successful outing had been when she was miscast as the lovely and innocent Mina in, The Virgin Brides of Dracula. Davidson had been thrilled at the the prospect of working alongside Peter Cushing in his usual role of Dr Abraham Van Helsing, only to be disappointed to find that, this time, the part was to be played by someone called

Ralph Bates, who she had never heard of. But now, although still an attractive woman, her glory days were well and truly over, and she had sought to maintain a public profile by moving into politics.

Unaware that, behind her back, many in Westminster referred to her as Norma Desmond, the member for Sunset Boulevard North, she had launched herself tirelessly into campaigning for the Remain camp. The referendum result had come as both a shock and a great disappointment to her, and had also come at a considerable cost to her personally. She had been verbally abused in the street and vilified in the social media. Her car had been vandalised and threats had been received at the constituency office. Davidson was also the chairperson of the *North Yorkshire for Europe* group whose meeting was arranged to start at seven-thirty p.m. in the lounge of the small Bridge Hotel in Bearsley.

"Thank you all for coming along this evening. It's good to see that so many of you are keeping your eyes on our website and Facebook page." Ms Davidson looked around the room at the twenty or so, mostly familiar, faces of the members who had responded to the invitation.

"Before commencing our business this evening, I would first like you to join me in paying tribute to my friend and colleague David Lendle who, as I'm sure you will know, was so tragically killed in a fire at his home just three weeks ago. David was a kind, hard working and public spirited man who will be sorely missed by many, and our sympathies go out to his widow and his family."

Most nodded in agreement and the few grunted `hear, hear's were followed by some closing of eyes and a few seconds respectful silence.

"But now, I would like you to give a warm welcome to our guest speaker this evening." Davidson extended an expensively manicured hand towards the rotund, red-faced MP who had sat on her right at the top table since the meeting had begun and had spent much of his time with his little piggy eyes fixed on her ample bosom.

"Many of you will know Dermot Taylor as the founder and leader of the *Keep Britain In* campaign and I am delighted to tell you that he has graciously accepted the invitation to talk to us tonight. Dermot will explain what he and others are doing, both publicly and behind the scenes, to ensure that the United Kingdom retains its rightful place at the table in Brussels." As Taylor's muttered "Thank you" went unheard in the polite applause, Davidson nodded to the secretary on her left who, under orders from her to arrive at the main agenda as quickly as possible, hurried through the reading of the minutes of the last meeting which, to his relief were swiftly accepted with no matters arising. Now moving on to new business, Davidson herself gave an update on the latest estimate of the likely turnout and results of a second referendum which was received with great excitement. Glancing at the clock on the wall, which told her that it was not yet a quarter to eight, she handed the floor over to a man named Corrigan. Things were moving along very nicely.

Alex Corrigan was keen to reveal to the meeting the draft of a leaflet he had produced and was anxious to have approved before being distributed. The tract extolled (a sceptic might even say greatly inflated) the virtues of remaining in the EU whilst pointing out (another sceptic might say greatly exaggerating) the disadvantages of leaving. Corrigan had been speaking for just two or three minutes when the blast occurred.

In a deafening maelstrom, the lights went out and the room was instantly plunged into darkness as the speaker's table and several others, as well as chairs and those seated on them, were thrown across the room. Some of those who had been seated towards the centre of the room were still more or less in one piece, having been partially protected by the bodies of Davidson, Taylor and others who were not so lucky and were killed outright by the full primary wave of the blast. Several more were killed by fragments, mostly glass from the hotel windows or shrapnel from the paint tins, tools and metal buckets which had contained the explosive. A few, seated nearer the back of the room, and so further away from the source of the explosion, were relatively unscathed and managed to grope their way out of the darkness and the choking dust to the door leading into the lobby of the hotel.

Seated at his desk in the small office down the corridor, the hotel manager heard the roar of the explosion and felt the building tremble. Rushing from the office, he and an assistant from the adjoining bar found a small group of shocked, speechless attendees. A fortunate few, cut by flying debris, were dishevelled and bloody but otherwise unhurt. One man had lost a hand, another a foot and one lay moaning and bleeding profusely, from the stump of what had once been a whole arm, on the carpeted floor of the lobby. All were in a state of great distress. One woman had passed out and another sat traumatised, shaking and sobbing quietly in an armchair.

BBC News at Ten reported.

`Eight people have been killed, and more than a dozen injured, six seriously, this evening in an explosion at a hotel in Bearsley, Yorkshire. The hotel which has suffered serious structural damage has been evacuated. An organisation calling itself the British Citizens' Army has claimed responsibility.'

When the forensics team arrived, the front of the building had already been boarded up and the pavement and part of the road cordoned off. Inside the hotel the full extent of the damage was clear. A ground floor internal supporting wall had largely disappeared and both the meeting room and the room behind it were almost knee deep in brick and plaster rubble. The danger of the first floor room above it collapsing had been temporarily averted by installing several `Acrow' props, supporting scaffold boards, beneath the ceiling joists.

After the police photographers had done their work, the larger pieces of brick, stone and timber had been removed, but not until officers had taken numerous samples using what are known as TERKs, `Trace Explosives Recovery Kits', supplied to them by the UK's government-run Forensic Explosive Laboratories. Each TERK comprises a swabbing kit with enough cotton wool and solvent to take up to six samples which are then sent for analysis. When dozens of such samples had been sent off, much of what remained, mostly debris and numerous body parts, was collected in buckets and also despatched for searching, sorting and analysis. It seemed the police believed that the bomb had been planted earlier in the day, probably by one of two men who had been working at the hotel as painters and decorators. The explosive had obviously been hidden in the lounge of the hotel, probably in a metal paint bucket, itself stowed inside a large built-in cupboard in which the workmen had been allowed to store tools and materials. The device had been set to detonate at eight o'clock, using a timer made from DVD recorder components and powered by a small dry-cell battery, which would send a signal to an electrical detonator.

Police checks on the manager of the hotel, a man in his late forties by the name of Roger Downer, had revealed nothing of interest. He had worked in hotels and bars in the north of England for most of his working life, but apart from a couple of motoring offences he had a clean sheet. According to Downer, the two men had been working at the hotel since the previous Monday morning, three days prior to the incident. How had they come to be given the job? They had come into the hotel bar for a drink the week before, still wearing their paint-splashed overalls, and had asked to see him. They told him they were near to finishing a job just down the road and were looking for more work. They had a lot of paint left over which had already been paid for, they said, and if he had any work for them he would only need to pay their wages. One of them had commented that he couldn't help noticing that the hotel lounge was `looking a bit tired and in need of a lick of paint' and Downer had immediately thought of the meeting booked in for the following week. He knew the room could do with a makeover and when he took them through to the lounge and asked for an estimate, and they had said the job would take about three days and would cost him `no more than five hundred pounds at most', he knew it was too good an offer to turn down. He had stressed to them the need for the room to be in a state of readiness for occupation on Thursday evening and by the afternoon of that day, most of the work had been done. The men had agreed to tidy up and put away their equipment, tools, and paint before leaving, saying they would return the following morning to complete the couple of hours' work that remained. Did they have a vehicle and if so did it have a name on it? Downer said he saw them drive out of the hotel's small car park at around four o'clock in the afternoon in a white Mercedes Citan van. He was fairly certain it didn't have any name on the side and he couldn't remember the registration letters, but he was `pretty sure it had a `66' plate'. The next day, Crimewatch Roadshow broadcast a radio appeal for information.

`Police officers are appealing for information about two men following an explosion in a hotel in Bearsley at around 8.00pm on Thursday, 18th July. The men were working as painters and decorators. One is described as being between forty-five and fifty years of age, of slim build, dark hair and approximately 5' 7" in height. The other man, who is described as stockily built, approximately 5'11" and fifty to fifty-five years of age, may go by the name of William or Willy.

Both men are said to speak with an Irish

accent. Anyone with information about the incident or either of the men should call Yorkshire Police on 101 or alternatively call Crimestoppers anonymously on 0800 999111. Incident Number: 18000692171.'

4

10 Downing Street, London, Friday 19th July 2019

Three o'clock in the morning and, in the Cabinet Office Briefing Room A, the COBRA meeting which had just finished, would be Kenneth Heywood's last important act as Prime Minister. Heywood was a broken man. If he hadn't already resigned, his sense of duty would have forced him to do so now. He had tried to warn them. Couched in the careful language of a bureaucrat, he had said, 'There has not yet been enough recognition of the way that failing to implement the referendum result could damage social cohesion by undermining faith in our democracy'. What he had really meant, but had been unable to say, was more along the lines of 'Any parliamentarian who advocates overturning a referendum result they promised to respect, should not be surprised at unleashing the ugly forces of civil unrest, even violence'. They hadn't listened, but regardless, he still blamed himself for failing to get his agreement through parliament. But he knew that others would now blame him for much more. Why had he ever listened to Roberts? And why couldn't they have waited? Just for one more week. Then Jameson would have had to deal with it.

Heywood had chaired the meeting himself, partly as a public indication of just how seriously he himself took the recent events and partly because he knew this would be the last act anyone would remember him for and he wanted to show that he had personally led the Government's response. It had not been a long meeting. The spymasters had confidently assured him that MI5, MI6, the police and all other relevant security departments were co-operating fully on this investigation. An inter-service team was in operation under the leadership of an experienced officer and some progress had already been made. The Foreign Secretary confirmed that the Irish government was committed to giving their full co-operation, and the Home Secretary that border controls were on high alert. MPs would be warned to take extra precautions when they appeared in public. Police would ensure that members of the public would be warned of the dangers of taking part in demonstrations and would be exhorted to report any concerns or information about suspicious persons, behaviour or occurrences.

Despite the recent spate of atrocities, however, the overall mood could be summed up as one of optimism. In this war of the people versus parliament, there could as usual be only one winner.

5

South Kensington, London, Saturday
20th July 2019

Jonathan sat, smoking his fourth Marlboro and nursing a second pint of warm John Smith's, in the small, sunny rear garden of the Hereford Arms in South Kensington. For the past two years, the Hereford had been the nearest thing he and Hannah had come to think of as their local. But now he sat alone.

The article in The Times which Jonathan had just been reading had made mention of reports concerning the existence of an organisation calling itself the British Citizens' Army which had apparently claimed responsibility for both the drone attack in Marlow-on-Thames and the bombing of the hotel in Yorkshire. According to The Times article, very little was yet known about it, but the BCA, as the newspaper referred to it, was suspected of having close links with other para-military organisations, of which the influence of the Irish Republican Army, for so long a thorn in the side of British governments, was the most obvious. As evidence for its conclusion that the BCA derived its inspiration from the IRA, the article cited the discovery by police of a copy of a manual, presumably issued to BCA `volunteers'. The `Blue Book' as it was referred to, had come to light following the murder of a policeman in Kent three weeks earlier and, although no details were given, it was said to reveal close similarities to the `Green Book' of the IRA. Jonathan put down the newspaper. He had never seen either a `Green' or a `Blue' book of course but, if he had, he would have seen that much of the advice they both contained echoed that given to him by O'Bierne. He vividly remembered Cormac saying,

"You yourself will probably never be intimately involved in direct action, Jonathan, but you are nevertheless one of us, so let me give some some hard-learned advice. Don't talk in public places. Don't tell your family, friends, girlfriends or workmates that you are a member. Don't express views about military matters. In other words, say nothing to any person. Don't put anything in writing. Don't take part in public marches, demonstrations or protests. Don't be seen in the company of known sympathisers. You must remain unknown to the authorities, to the agents of government and to the public at large."

He would also have seen that it echoed O'Bierne's caution regarding the need to understand the danger of drinking alcohol, especially the very real danger of over-drinking. It would tell him that a lot of information had been gathered in the past by enemy forces and their touts from the lips of volunteers who drank too much. It would warn that, whilst drink-induced loose talk was potentially one of the most dangerous things facing *any* organisation, in a military organisation, it amounted to suicide.

Of particular value, both to the individual and to the organisation, O'Bierne had said, was the advice to be followed in the event of arrest. The description of what was likely to happen to you made unedifying reading, predicting as it did the likelihood of a `prolonged period of interrogation, involving humiliation and many other forms of psychological pressure which must be silently endured'. O'Bierne had told him that the prisoner who speaks a little, in order to avoid abuse, is in effect inviting yet more from his interrogators, who will always assume that once someone starts to talk, there is something further they can extract from him. Therefore the best defence, Cormac had said, was to remain cool, collected, calm and say nothing. Jonathan knew that it was very sound advice.

In a significant departure from the text of the `Green Book' however, the BCA's manual opened with a statement which had clearly been concocted from the first words of the American Declaration of Independence.

`When, in the course of human events, it becomes necessary for one people to dissolve the political bands which have connected them with another, and to assume the separate and equal station to which the laws of nature entitle them, a decent respect to the opinions of the people requires that they should declare the causes which impel them to the separation.

We hold these truths to be self-evident, that all men are created equal, that they are endowed with certain unalienable rights, that among these are life, liberty, and the pursuit of happiness. That, to secure these rights, governments are instituted among men, deriving their just powers solely from, and with the consent of, the governed.

Prudence dictates that governments should not be changed for light and transient causes and indeed, all experience has shown, that citizens are more disposed to suffer, while evils are sufferable, than to right themselves by rising up against injustices. But whenever any form of government becomes destructive of these ends and evinces a design to reduce them under absolute despotism, it is the right of the people, it is their duty, to alter or to abolish it, to throw off such government, and to institute a new government to provide new guards for their future security, laying its foundation on such principles, and organizing its powers in such form, as to them shall seem most likely to effect their safety and happiness.

We further hold that the recent history of the government of the United Kingdom and that of the Republic of Ireland constitute a history of repeated injury to the independence and sovereignty of both nations.'

6

Millbank, London, Monday 22nd July 2019

It was mid-afternoon and Blake Burgess was in pensive mood. Last Thursday had been a bad day, although as always, worse for some than others. It had been particularly bad for the four men killed at the Thameside garden party and the five women and three men who lost their lives in Yorkshire later that same day.

Things were going far too slowly for his liking. Not through lack of effort on the part of him and his team, but still far too slowly. The only good news was that Burgess' workload having just risen sharply, Greg Thompson had acceded to his request to enlarge the small team by the addition of Susie Weston and an MI6 man, Peregrine Hanbury-Davies. Susie had jumped at the chance and Burgess was delighted to have her on board. She was good. Hanbury-Davies, on the other hand, he had always had reservations about. Although their paths had crossed only a few times, there was something about the man that he found hard to take to. Still, he was good at his job and his Irish connections would be very useful. Leaning back in his chair, eyes closed and feet on desk, what did he know so far?

The police had made no progress in identifying the perpetrator of the arson attack in Stoke. It had tuned out that the man they took in for questioning had a perfect alibi. He had been arrested for getting into a fight the evening before and had spent the night in police custody. But that didn't concern Burgess overly. Although, like the other two, the target had been an MP and the motive clearly political, there was nothing to suggest that it had been the work of an organised terrorist group.

It had been two weeks now since the purchaser of the secondhand printer had been identified. According to auction room records he had been one Patrick McNally and, at the time, McNally had given an address in Rathmines, an inner suburb on the south side of Dublin, about two miles south of the city centre. But when the Gardaí had checked, they had found that the property was not, and had never been, owned or rented by McNally, but instead belonged to a Mr Cormac O'Bierne, a journalist and political activist well known to them. And when they had visited the property, a three-storey redbrick house in Grosvenor Square, the said O'Bierne had told them that he had not seen nor heard anything of Patrick McNally for more than three years. Yes, McNally had stayed with O'Bierne for a short time in the summer of 2016 after he and his wife had divorced, but he had soon accepted a job offer which took him away from Dublin and he had left. No, he didn't know where the job had been, it might have been in Galway, but he couldn't be certain. And no, he didn't have any contact phone number for him nor did he have an address for McNally's ex-wife. When asked about the nature of his relationship with McNally, O'Bierne had replied that Patrick McNally had been `like family', `a close friend of his younger brother Sean.' The two had been at school together. How would he describe McNally? O'Bierne had said he was a `skinny little fellow, about five feet six inches at most, with a full head of dark brown hair.' Did he know what line of work McNally was in? He'd done a few different things, but O'Bierne thought that mostly he had worked as a draughtsman and later in graphic design. While he had been staying at the house in Grosvenor Square, had McNally possessed any equipment in connection with his work? Yes, he was sure he'd had an Apple Mac and some other bits and pieces in his room, but O'Bierne had never actually seen him use any of them.

But Burgess now knew that O'Bierne had lied. The SDU, the Irish `Special Detective Unit', an elite branch of the Gardaí Síochána, was liaising with its British counterparts and offering its intelligence capabilities to assist MI6 with their work in the Republic. The SDU had suspicions concerning foreign involvement in both of the political parties that O'Bierne was known to be connected with, and this had led to his phone being tapped. As a result, Burgess knew of the phone call O'Bierne had made to a UK phone number just minutes after the Gardaí officers had left his house, for MI6 had played him the recording and Burgess had heard O'Bierne ask the switchboard operator who answered his call to, `put him through' to `Henry'. And when `Henry' had answered, O'Bierne had uttered just five words. And those words had been, "Tell McNally to lie low." The telephone number turned out to belong to a company in Northamptonshire and Everett, having checked out the firm, informed Burgess that the owner was a Mr Henry Bloom. For the past nine days, Everett's section had logged, listened to and recorded every incoming call to the company's switchboard.

Perfect timing. The last strains of Miles Davis', `All Blues' faded as Everett led the others in.

"OK, Howard. Let's hear all about `Henry'."

"So ..", began Everett. Burgess winced. God, that was bloody annoying. "I'm not sure you're going to like this, Blake, but let me give you the facts and figures. The switchboard handles around fifty or so incoming calls each day on average, so we've listened to well over four hundred all told and there doesn't seem to be anything untoward in any of them. Mostly, they're calls for engineering assistance, firms chasing up orders and querying invoices. That sort of thing. Leaving aside those where the caller didn't ask for anyone by name, that number reduces to two hundred and eight. Of those, a hundred and seventy-three were put through to an assortment of Kevins, Anns, John, Sues and Julies in what, if I'm not mistaken, sounded like engineering, accounts and sales offices. The remaining thirty-five were answered by Henry Bloom himself and they were mostly of a more personal nature. Arranging games of golf, fixing meetings, social invitations, that sort of thing. But, and this is the interesting bit, not one of them asked to speak to `Henry'. Twenty-one of them asked for `Mr Bloom' and the other fourteen asked to be put through to `Harry'. Ergo, Bloom is not your `Henry'."

Burgess said nothing.

"But we know for a fact that there was a `Henry' there on at least one occasion."

"True, but we also know now that he isn't there very often."

"Which means, Howard", said Susie Weston "that O'Bierne knew that for some reason he *would* be there that day."

"Susie's right. We need to dig a bit deeper. But we also need to be careful. We can't risk alerting anyone. Leave it with me for the time being", said Burgess.

"Right, moving on. Young Jack. Do we have any interesting names from SOI files yet?"

"Not much yet, sir", replied Daniels who had

been tasked with sifting through the `Subject of Interest' records.

"We haven't got much to go on, but starting with the possible Irish connection, we've been running through SOIs to find any `Williams' or `Willys' that might fit the bill. So far only three names have come to light. There was a William McNally, who we thought was involved in the Manchester bombing back in 1996, but he's long dead now."

"Any connection with the McNally who bought the printer?"

"We're looking into that now, sir"

Daniels went on.

"There was also a William Crawford in the files. He's getting on a bit now, pushing seventy, but still working part-time for a private security firm in Galway. Doesn't appear to have left Ireland in years though."

"And the third man?", said Burgess, apparently seeing no irony in his use of the phrase.

"Here somewhere", said Daniels shuffling hurriedly through his papers until being rescued by his MI5 colleague, who, Burgess sometimes thought, might be rather more than that.

"Thanks, Susie".

Daniels smiled at the tall, pretty girl with the blondish `pixie' hair cut who sat next to him and who, reaching across, had put a finger on a name. `You'd think butter wouldn't melt in her mouth',

Burgess had once said to Greg Thompson, his task force Commander. `But you'd be making a mistake. She's clever, and as hard as nails.'

"Ah yes", said Daniels returning to the question. "This one was in the frame in connection with the Bishopsgate bombing way back in 1993, but nothing could be pinned on him. He's a William Doyle."

That was a name Burgess had not expected to hear and something in his face must have revealed his surprise and discomfort at hearing it mentioned now.

"Jesus Christ."

"You've heard of him, sir?"

"You could say that, Jack."

Something in Burgess' tone told Daniels that this was neither the time nor the place to pursue the matter. Later, when he had researched the incident, he would learn that the police had always believed that they knew the identities of the two men behind the bombing, but lacked the evidence to arrest and charge them. He would read that, when asked in an interview if the police were any closer to catching the two men believed responsible, who had been spotted on a security camera running away before escaping in a car driven by a third man, the Commissioner of the City of London Police had replied, "Sometimes police have a good idea of who might be responsible but are not able to bring them to court. Knowing or believing who committed a crime is very different from possessing the evidential requirements to bring someone to justice."

Daniels would also learn from an older colleague that DC Blake Burgess had himself been injured by the blast which had killed a News of The World photographer standing only yards from him and had injured more than forty others. The explosion, which destroyed nearby St Ethelburga's church and wrecked Liverpool Street station and the NatWest Tower on that Saturday morning of 24 April 1993, had occurred when the Provisional IRA detonated a powerful truck bomb. Burgess had been one of the two officers already on the scene making enquiries about the truck before the first of several telephone warnings were received. The calls were eventually traced to a public phone box in Forkhill, County Armagh, and the anonymous caller had used the correct words, `The code is Triple X. This is not a hoax.' Daniels' colleague would also divulge the names of the two suspects, one of whom had been an enthusiastic young IRA member by the name of William Doyle.

Daniels noted that the boss appeared to be lost in thought and, whilst he had no intention of saying it, reckoned that, for Burgess, this had now become personal. The silence was broken by Howard Everett.

"We need to get on top of this, Jack. And quickly."

"We've already got people looking for him as we speak, but it's not going to be easy. He may well be going under a different name, and the only images we've got of him are poor quality and over twenty-five years old."

"And presumably we don't know what this McNally character looks like either?"

"Not unless he still looks like he did in his school photo", said Daniels, grinning like a schoolboy himself and holding up the image from 1985, taken at St. Patrick's Redemptorist College in Limerick and showing a fifteen-year-old Patrick McNally.

Burgess chose to ignore the comment.

"So we haven't got a bloody clue what either of them looks like", said Burgess, followed by another, more quietly muttered, `Jesus Christ'."

"The best chance we've got", said Susie Weston, "is CCTV."

"Tell me more."

"A Mercedes van like the one the bombers were using has turned up, apparently dumped, in the car park at Bearsley railway station. It matches the description of the vehicle given by the hotel manager in Bearsley and also that of one of the vehicles reported as having been seen by the man Jones outside the house in Sevenoaks where the policeman was killed last month. I don't know why it took three days before it was found, but anyway, the good news is we've got plenty of DNA samples from it and several sets of prints, one of which is a perfect match with some taken from the kitchen in the cottage. Getting back to the van though, surely the important question is, `why'? Why would they dump it at the station unless they were going to catch a train? So I've asked Network Rail for the footage from last Thursday afternoon. We should have it very soon."

Burgess visibly brightened up.

"Good girl."

And then, for a moment, Burgess indulged himself in one of the periodic, and very irritating, silences, for which he never deigned to give an explanation. There was never a, `Just let me think about that', not even a `Hmm...'. He sometimes just stopped talking.

Then suddenly, "Right, everybody, that's it for now", he said, but only when *he* was ready to say it.

"But I want these two characters found."

Alone in his office now, Burgess inserted a different `memory stick' into his new toy and pressed the `play' button. Stan Getz' `Cool Velvet'. Just what was needed. Daniels was right. It had become personal.

7

Fort Halstead, Kent, Tuesday 23rd July 2019

This morning, Blake Burgess was not going straight to his Thameside office as usual. Instead, he had left his home in Orpington at seven forty-five a.m. and had taken the A232, driving South East to Hewitts roundabout, onto the A224 and, after a few minutes, had turned off into the cul de sac which was Crow Drive and which led to only one destination.

The headquarters of FEL, the government's Forensic Explosive Laboratories, a sprawling collection of red-brick buildings and pristine laboratories with curious ventilation chimneys, were situated at Fort Halstead, high on the crest of a steep chalk escarpment of the North Downs in Kent, overlooking the Darenth Valley. At the end of a long leafy lane that ends with a chain-link fence, a gate guarded by police and a visitors' reception, FEL was clearly not a place that liked to advertise its presence.

In the course of his work Burgess frequently spoke with John Walton, the Director of FEL, and over the many years the two had known each other they had become good friends. But it was not often that Burgess had reason to visit Fort Halstead in person and as his car now, for the first time in almost two years he guessed, passed through the gates into the huge complex, he remembered a previous occasion when, flushed with pride following his promotion to Director, Walton had deemed it necessary to regale him with a potted history of the establishment he was proud to think of as his empire.

"This place started life", he had said, "way back

in the 1890s when the War Office bought three acres of land here. The plan at that time was to construct a ring of fortresses around London in order to defend the city against any attempts at invasion. The following year, they bought a further six and three-quarter acres and over the next few years, Fort Halstead gradually came into being."

In the event however, Walton had told him, the fort was never needed for its original purpose and in 1936 they found a new use for it when British interest in rocketry was revived. The Committee for Imperial Defence having decided that the Armament Research Department should develop rockets for a variety of different uses including anti-aircraft defence, long-range attack, air combat and assisted take-off units, Fort Halstead became the *Projectile Development Establishment* centre. Further construction work had begun almost immediately, and by the end of WWII Fort Halstead had expanded massively to comprise around eighty buildings, including specialist explosives-filling sheds, laboratories, workshops, administration buildings, and welfare facilities, such as a canteen. In addition the establishment was equipped with air raid shelters and, near its northern boundary, a housing estate for War Department police. At the end of hostilities in 1945, armaments research continued but on a reduced level and now Fort Halstead also took on the works of evaluating captured German technical equipment and in translating captured documents.

Then in 1947, a further change of direction had occurred when the British government took the decision to proceed with the development of an atomic bomb. Yet more buildings were constructed and the project carried out here at Fort Halstead, its real purpose disguised by its being code-named *High Explosives Research (HER)*. Atomic weapons research and development continued at Fort Halstead for several years until, in the mid-1950s it was transferred to the new Atomic Weapons Research Establishment at Aldermaston, Berkshire, since when Fort Halstead had focused on forensic research and analysis in the field of explosives.

Inside the administrative block, Walton's secretary showed Burgess to the Director's office and asked him to take a seat. Walton would be with him in a moment. He didn't recognise the secretary. She must be new, Burgess thought. But in the office nothing much had changed. It had possibly been redecorated and Walton's pet cheese plant had put a spurt on and was now threatening to take over one entire corner of the room, but otherwise things were much as he remembered. The photographs on the wall behind Walton's desk were still there and still fascinated him. Sir Bernard Spilsbury and Professor Keith Simpson, he knew had been perhaps the greatest names in the history of British forensic science. And Baron William George Penney had been not only a world-renowned scientist and leader of the British Atomic Weapons Research Establishment, but also one of Walton's predecessors at Fort Halstead. But the other name and face, that of Dr. Robert Hutchings Goddard, Burgess did not recognise. He would have to ask Walton about him.

"Good to see you, Guy", said a smiling Walton as he entered the room.

"And you too, John Boy. Still playing with your test tubes I see", he said as Walton removed his white lab coat.

Neither man could resist indulging in their usual time-honored verbal sparring and neither could remember which of them had first started it, but it had been `Guy the Spy' Burgess and `John Boy' Walton almost since day one.

"I like to keep my hand in, Guy but sadly I'm mostly too busy pen-pushing and fending off policemen and politicians these days. What about you? Still taking those afternoon naps while you pretend to be solving something?"

He motioned Burgess to take a seat.

"Talking of solving things, John Boy, what have your boffins got for me this time?"

"The first thing to say, Guy is probably stating the obvious. These two things may have happened on the same day, and they may both have targeted MPs, but that's about all they have in common. Taking the grenade incident first; from the distribution of the shrapnel, I'd say it went off very close to the ground. Barely a few inches above it in my opinion. And a good thing too because, looking at where people were at the time, we'd have had a couple of dozen more fatalities if it had gone off six feet up instead of six inches. And they were lucky in where the grenade exploded as well. As it was, the bulk of the shrapnel that didn't hit the men standing close by, either buried itself in the bank that slopes down to the river or punched holes in Arbuthnot's cabin cruiser. What didn't land on either of those, sprayed out at a more or less harmless angle. From what I can see of the distribution, not much of it made its way to the top of the lawn. There's probably more in the river than anywhere else."

Burgess wondered if there really had been as much luck involved as Walton suggested. To his way of thinking, it had been a highly targeted incident and whoever was behind it had known exactly what they were doing. They could have dropped the grenade anytime and anywhere they wanted. But, by the look of things, they had made sure only to target the politicians.

"What about the grenade itself?"

"Can't be a hundred percent certain, but most likely an M75 or similar. Loads of them still around and a firm favourite with bad boys the world over. They mostly come from the Balkans. It's still awash with them. As for the delivery, it would have been easy enough to hang a grenade from the drone and release it electronically."

"Now, as for the second one, Guy, that's a different kettle of fish altogether. On the face of it, the hotel bombing looks pretty straightforward, like an old-school, almost textbook, IRA operation. But then, I'd be disappointed in you if you hadn't already come to that conclusion yourself."

Burgess nodded but said nothing.

"You'll have the full report tomorrow but to sum things up, it was a crude device. A few kilos of Frangex, probably no more than four or five, and almost certainly hidden in a metal bucket. There are fragments of galvanised steel and also some of a hardened steel, the type used in decorating tools. My boys and girls also sifted out a lot of nails and screws which would have done some serious damage to anyone who got in the way. And glass. Lots of it. Victorian we think. Thick and ornately etched. Probably from the hotel window."

"You mentioned the IRA."

"Yes, apart from the modus operandi, the Frangex is virtually identical to the stuff that Irish Industrial Explosives Limited used to turn out back in the 70s and 80s. Their factory in Enfield, County Meath used to produce over six thousand tons of it every year. It's a form of gelignite, mainly used in mines and quarries but we know that some of it used to find its way into the hands of the IRA. They saw a lot of it here back in those days but, personally, I haven't come across any since my first year at FEL in 1984. Back then, we had all the stuff from the

Brighton bombing arriving here and, as the new boy on the team, I was given the plum job of emptying the buckets and sifting through the contents. Separating the dirt from the digits they used to call it."

"And what about DNA? Fingerprints?"

"Well, you're in luck with the DNA at least. One set of samples from several of the larger metal fragments match those your team took from the Mercedes. Can't tie it to anyone on the database but one of your two suspects at least was definitely in both places. All you have to do is catch him and put a name to him. Plenty of fingerprints too, all still firmly attached to their phalangeal hosts of course, but they won't belong to the villains. This wasn't a suicide squad."

Burgess felt himself shudder involuntarily at the thought. There were some things you never became totally immune to, however long you'd been in the game.

~~~~~~~~

Chapter 8

`Come, my people, enter into your rooms And close your doors behind you; Hide for a little while until indignation runs its course.'
Isaiah 26:20

1

Downing Street, London, Thursday 25ᵗʰ July 2019

"Stephen. I'd like you to hang on for a bit, if you don't mind. There are one or two things I'd like to get moving on."

The first meeting of the new cabinet over, Brent had picked up his papers in readiness to leave Number 10. Most of the other newly-appointed ministers had already departed to take up their duties.

"Of course, Prime Minister."

"Let's dispense with the formalities, Stephen. I'm happy to continue to be Paul."

Paul Jameson returned to his seat at the table and motioned for Brent to do the same.

"Where to start, Stephen. There's so much to do. We've got a good team now. I can feel morale rising already, but we're still going to need all the help we can get."

"Well, you know you can rely on me to do my bit, Paul."

"I do know that, Stephen, but it's not going to be easy. It may even be so bad that I have no choice but to risk going for a snap early election. It's all about the numbers and I don't think it can be solved within government. We shall need help from outside. I'm doing what I can with the press and other media and also with the constituency offices, but that may not be enough. Which brings me to what I wanted to ask. This chap you mentioned. Armstrong I think you said. Is he reliable?"

"Trust me Paul. I've done my homework on him and, in my opinion, he is totally reliable. He's one of us."

"So there's no risk then?"

"There's always a risk, Paul, as I'm sure you know. As you yourself said just now, there's a risk in going for an election. There's also a risk in waiting too long. In politics, there's an element of risk in everything we do."

"Yes, Stephen, but that's not what I meant. You said your man Armstrong knows people who could help. Influential people. In some kind of think tank I believe you said. I don't know who they are or how they might help, and I don't think I care to know, but I'll be blunt. Is there any risk to me personally? Or to you, come to that?"

"I believe I can put your mind at rest as regards that, Paul. The thing about risk is that it needs to be assessed and then managed. Firstly, even in a worst case scenario, Armstrong is not Jack the Ripper. There's not much risk of him being caught out but, even if he were, he could never be accused of anything more serious than leaking information to the Institute for Democratic Reform and plenty of others have done far worse than that in the past. And probably still are. I'm damned sure that Brendan Roberts, for one, is leaking to Brussels and I wouldn't be surprised to find that my man Atkins was helping him. I've been told they still meet up. And someone is passing information on No Deal planning to the CBI. They're all at it one way or another Paul, but a slap on the wrist is all they'd get at most. But the important thing is that you would be able to say, and truthfully, that you'd never met the man. Scarcely knew who he was. As for me, even if they tortured my name out of him, I would deny everything and there would be nothing in writing."

Jameson thought for a moment, then nodded slowly.

"OK, Stephen. You've reassured me and, let's face it, we're not exactly spoiled for choice are we? Let's run with it."

2

Whitehall, London, Tuesday 30ᵗʰ July 2019

The number 12 bus deposited Martin Armstrong right on time, and right outside the ministry building where he had worked for the past three years.

"Ah, Mr Armstrong"

"Good morning, Anne. What's afoot?"

"The minister has asked to see you. As soon as you came in, he said."

"Did he say what it's about?"

"No, but he called a couple of others in yesterday while you were off."

"Anyone I know?"

"Davis yesterday morning. And Simon Atkins after lunch. You'll be the third."

"Is he keeping them long? Only I'm supposed to be at a meeting at ten-thirty."

"No, they were in and out. He probably just wants to introduce himself."

"OK, I'll just get rid of my briefcase and then go straight up."

"Thank you, I'll let him know."

What on earth was Brent doing here so early? Evans had never been known to arrive before nine o'clock. What was going on? Probably dishing out marching orders.

There was something in that theory. Stephen Brent had been Brexit minister, or to give him his full title, the Secretary of State for Exiting the European Union, for just seven days, exactly the same length of time that Paul Jameson, who had appointed him, had been Prime Minister. When Jameson took over as PM, he had been careful not to make the same mistake as his predecessor and had selected only ardent, committed Brexiteers to form his new cabinet. As a result, more than a dozen ministers who did not fit that description, including the Chancellor, the Home Secretary and also the previous holder of Brent's own position, Nicholas Evans, had lost their jobs. Could Brent, Armstrong wondered, be taking a leaf out of Jameson's book? Was he following in his master's footsteps and having a clear out?

Not quite, or at least not yet, was the answer. But Brent was a very thorough man. Much of his first few days in office had been spent learning about his staff. First, the mechanics of his new department. The `who did what and for whom'. Then he had read their personal files, familiarised himself with their CVs, noted who took lunch with whom, and had stored away in his enviably capacious memory every tiny detail that might give an insight into what made them tick.

This was Brent's first cabinet post and he was acutely aware that, by its very nature, it was a transient appointment at best. Screw things up and, for `transient', substitute `very short indeed', but do a good job, and a bright future would await the young politician who had succeeded where other older, but not wiser, heads had failed. Nothing could be more important than knowing who was with him and who against.

Brent's secretary opened the door.

"Mr Armstrong to see you, Minister."

"Thank you, Denise. Come in, Armstrong. Take a seat."

The minister sat in one of the two armchairs by the window overlooking Whitehall. On a low table spread with the papers he had obviously been reading lay an appointment diary, a fountain pen and an open, black, soft-backed notebook in which he had been making copious notes. He motioned to the other armchair. Armstrong's first thought was that perhaps the informality of the scene was intended to put his guests dangerously at ease.

"Now, it's Martin, isn't it?"

"Yes, that's right, Minister."

"No need to stand on ceremony, Martin, it's Steve." Brent smiled and extended a hand. "Good to meet you at last. I'm trying to get round to meeting everybody and I'm sorry it's taken so long."

What a refreshing contrast with Evans. In three years the man had only spoken to him twice and even then, on the second occasion, had managed to get his name wrong.

"I won't beat around the bush, Martin, and I won't insult your intelligence by pretending that this meeting is aimed at anything other than fulfilling a deep-seated need that I have to know who I'm working with here. You won't need me to remind you that things have not gone well for my predecessors."

Martin said nothing, but he nodded and smiled what he hoped was a wry smile, amused, but at the same time, knowing, understanding, showing concern. It was, he thought, an awful lot to put into one little smile and he hoped he'd got the balance of ingredients right.

"One other thing, Martin. Our talk will be off the record. Whatever comes up will be for our ears only. Sorry if it all sounds a bit James Bond but that's the way it has to be, I'm afraid. You have every right to decline the invitation of course, and you have my word that there will be no repercussions if you do. But, before you say anything, let me tell you how I see my position. I believe in openness and honesty, but I am aware that such values make us vulnerable and that, in politics, they are therefore regarded as being dangerously naive. This is why, regardless of what passes between us, the talk we are about to have, assuming of course that you are happy to proceed on that basis, will never have taken place. It is my only protection."

"I understand perfectly, Steve. That's fine by me."

"Good man. And a Cambridge man too. Law at King's, I believe?"

"That's right."

"Two years after me. PPE, Magdalene. But, unlike me, you went back for more and got your Masters?"

Armstrong nodded. That's not a question. You know perfectly well I did.

"And also unlike me, you kept in touch with your Alma Mater. King's College Law Society, Cambridge International Intelligence Institute. I'm rather ashamed to admit that I didn't. Work got in the way I suppose."

"Yes, you're right, Steve. I still manage to pop up to Cambridge from time to time."

"And I commend you for it, Martin. Always good to see the broader picture. Our work can tend to make us somewhat introspective. I suppose you must bump into old Lines occasionally?"

Christ, he's got me summed up inside out. Armstrong felt a little uncomfortable.

"Well, our paths do cross occasionally, although not that often. He's at Trinity now you know."

"Yes, I heard. You'd think he might have retired by now."

"What, Lines?", Armstrong laughed. "I can't see him ever retiring."

"No, you're probably right, Martin. I heard him on Radio Four recently. Still sharp as a button. Talking a lot of sense. And please allow me to say how delighted I am to know that we're both singing from the same hymn sheet. It means a lot to me to have someone here I can trust and confide in."

"Thank you, Steve. Good of you to say so." More at ease now, Martin felt that they were beginning to understand one another.

"It's going to be an uphill struggle. We have made too many mistakes", said Brent. "and they are going to be very difficult to put right. The PM's a good man and he agrees with me on that, but even he can't work miracles."

Martin wondered what Brent thought the mistakes had been. Brent knew what Martin was wondering and happily obliged him

"First off, we played into their hands when we allowed economic factors to take centre stage in the great debate. We should have kept to the nitty gritty, the principal issue of sovereignty, to focusing on what it is to be a country that is able to conduct its own affairs and decide its own future, as distinct from becoming a federal state with the limitation of autonomy that entails. If we had done that, both sides would have been forced to stick to the facts instead of indulging in guesswork that enables each of them to accuse the other of lies. Where there are only facts, there can be no lies."

"That's very true, Steve."

"Quite possibly", Brent continued, "the most serious mistake of all was to risk undoing all the good that the promises made to the people might have brought about. We have known for a long time that people don't feel they're being listened to, not just in connection with the EU and not just in the

UK either, but across a wide range of issues and throughout virtually the whole of Europe. We, and when I say *we* I mean both main parties, promised them repeatedly that we would implement their decision, that on this key issue which arouses so much passion, we would suspend our normal form of quasi-democracy for the real thing. And what did we do? By some twisted logic, we effectively decided that it is more democratic to respect the view of the representative than that of the man he supposedly represents. We reneged on our promise and, as a consequence, I fear we are now in danger of severing the last remaining delicate threads of credibility when we make claims on the people's trust. So you see, Martin, that's a big part of the problem. We have opened the door to too many people, many of them in high places, whose hearts are not really in it. And worse, some who, I'm damned sure, are working for the `enemy' if, purely for the sake of discussion you understand, I may call our friends in Brussels that."

"Pardon me for asking, Steve, but can't you just sack them? Or have them moved on somewhere where they can't do any damage?"

"Good question, Martin. There is as you suggest some scope for change, but it's limited. Paul Jameson, as you will know, has removed several cabinet ministers who were obstacles to progress, but they are still MPs of course, and will still vote against almost anything he comes up with. Two of our rebel MPs have been deselected by their constituencies which will help a little eventually, and although I shouldn't say it, Lendle did us all a favour by getting himself incinerated. And of course, Winterson-Greer won't be giving us any more trouble either. The other side have lost some as well, in the recent hotel bombing and the happenings at Marlow, but overall the numbers are still stacked against us. As for my department, I have a few ideas but I have to tread carefully, courtesy of those idiots who believe it's more important to maintain a politically correct `balance' between Leavers and Remainers than it is to actually achieve anything. God help us, Martin. It's like being a patient in hospital who's being trundled into the theatre for an emergency operation, and then, at the last moment, finds out that, in the interests of `balance', some of the guys who are going to knock him out and cut him up are not actually on his side."

Martin nodded, a grim-faced sympathetic nod this time.

"Strictly between you and me, Martin, Jameson is already toying with the idea of calling an early general election. He knows it's impossible to get the withdrawal agreement through with the current parliamentary numbers and hopes an election would improve things. The problem, he says, is entirely caused by an unbridgeable gap between the views of some MPs and their own constituents, which an election might well put right. OK, we would probably lose two or three seats to the Exit party, but the opposition would lose a lot more and the overall balance would shift in our favour. The trouble is, we'd still be a minority government and we'd have to rely on the support of the IUP and Exit parties in parliament, whereas Jameson would obviously prefer an outright majority. If he could get Brexit done first he'd have a good chance of getting that but, as things stand, he knows he probably wouldn't. On the other hand, he doesn't want to wait too long for fear that the opposition will choose another, more popular, leader and do better in the polls. On balance, he's inclined to think the best thing to do is hope that the recent improvement in the parliamentary arithmetic continues until he can get the bill passed, and then go for the election afterwards."

"Yes, I see. Going for an election without being able to show any progress first could even lead to another disaster like Heywood's. If it were me, Steve, I'd be thinking the same way as the PM. I'd hold fire for a while and see if the numbers continue to improve."

"Quite. And in the meantime, some of the biggest problems come from people I can't dislodge, the PM's advisor for one. You'll remember him of course because, as the permanent secretary here, he was your boss until he clashed with Evans and someone then decided the proper place for him was the cabinet office at Number 10. It was the worst move they could have made because it effectively put him in charge of the negotiations."

Armstrong did indeed remember Roberts. He had been jubilant the day the man had left Dexeu for Downing Street. He also remembered the clash with Evans that Brent had spoken of.

"As I recall", said Armstrong, "it was Roberts who advised Heywood not to accept the free-trade deal that was on offer, by convincing him we could do a lot better."

"It was indeed. Evans may not have been the brightest banana in the bunch, but even he knew that what Roberts promised was impossible to deliver, and he told Heywood so. But by that time, Heywood was only listening to Roberts. He effectively put paid to Evans as well as Ken Heywood. We can only hope that Jameson gets shot of him soon. And in the meantime, I've got one of the worst offenders of all coming to see me this time next week. The appointment was made with Evans of course, I'd never have agreed to it in a month of Sundays, but he'll want to test me out to see how the land lies." Brent reached for the diary and flicked through its pages.

"Yes, here, next Wednesday afternoon."

Armstrong looked at the entry in the diary Brent held out towards him. `Charles Gray, 3.00 pm'.

"Says he's retired from politics now but don't you believe it. Once a megalomaniac, always a megalomaniac. Some Captain he turned out to be.

Now spends his time, and his ill gotten gains, trying to sink the bloody ship. We all know politics can be a dirty business Martin, but Gray is a special case if ever there was one. He's pushing for another referendum, because he believes that the people made a mistake and that he knows why. He is cast from the same mould that gave shape to the forefathers of the EU, and so knows that the people were too unintelligent to have been given a say in a matter of such importance. But now he has educated them. Lesson one, demoralisation. Lesson two, fear. Lesson three, defamation. Three years of schooling in the Gray academy of black arts will have worked its evil magic and this time they will get it right. If they do, that will be the end of the matter. If not, of course, it's back to school for more lessons, so it's important to him that there should not be a general election which could just conceivably upset his plan. So, how about this for a perfect example of doublethink. Just yesterday, Gray complained that Jameson had become PM by default, that he had not been elected by the people. Leaving aside for the moment the fact that the people he is talking about are the very same people he says are too stupid to vote in a referendum, and not to mention the fact that we don't elect our PMs by a Presidential process anyway, this morning, less than twenty-four hours later, he was arguing that it would be unacceptable for Jameson to call a snap election because it would be unfair. And yet I don't believe the man even begins to see any contradiction in what he says. Need I say more?"

Brent looked at his watch.

"Anyway, I'd better let you go now, Martin", he said. "I know you have a meeting to attend in half an hour. I hope we'll talk again soon."

Armstrong was beginning to wonder if there was anything Brent didn't know about him.

~~~~~~~

Chapter 9

*"And the Lord said unto the servant, Go out into
the highways and hedges, and compel them to
come in, that my house may be filled."*
Luke 12, v 23

1

Buckinghamshire, Tuesday 6ᵗʰ August 2019

The truck had already started to edge from the centre lane into the inside lane when, hearing the urgent warning blast from the horn of the other HGV he had just overtaken, the driver suddenly appeared to realise that he had either misjudged the length of his vehicle or the speed of traffic already in the lane to his left. In a desperate attempt to avoid a collision, he yanked the steering wheel sharply to the right to pull back into the overtaking lane, but instead his vehicle spun almost one-hundred and eighty degrees before coming to a halt astride both lanes, blocking the road and facing oncoming traffic. Both drivers instinctively activated their hazard warning lights and the traffic behind them ground to a halt.

Just three cars back from the vehicle causing the blockage, two men sat in a dark-blue Jaguar XJ saloon. Behind the wheel, Alan Greening silently breathed a sigh of relief as the traffic stopped safely. In the back, the other man had taken some papers from a briefcase and sat reading. Then, as if only just realising what had happened, he spoke.

"You'd better let the Police know, Alan. Just in case nobody else has."

"Of course", and he was quickly put through to the relevant desk.

"And you'd better let Marjorie know as well, otherwise she might get worried."

"Will do, sir", said Greening, and within seconds he had relayed the news of the hold up to Gray's secretary at the office in London.

When the traffic stopped moving, there were six cars in between the one Phillips was driving and the HGV now blocking the carriageway. At times, there had been one or two more, at others, one or two fewer but, as instructed, he had taken care to ensure that there were never less than four. His passenger had been mostly silent during the journey; a sullen Scot, was how Phillips had always thought of Mac. A very useful one admittedly, but even so he wouldn't miss not having his company for the rest of the journey.

As Phillips pulled the Peugeot over onto the hard shoulder, the driver of the car immediately behind his saw an untidy, long-haired man clad in denim jacket, T-shirt and jeans get out of the front passenger door of the car, open the door behind it and retrieve a black, padded guitar case from the back seat. With a thumbs up, as though thanking the driver for having given him a lift, the man scrambled agilely up the embankment and, with the case slung over his shoulder, quickly disappeared from view. Hidden by the row of scrubby trees and bushes, he made his way unobserved along the line of the road until he judged he was near the target.

McKay unzipped the case and took out the Ruger Mini 14 with its fitted suppressor. He lay down in the rough grass of his hide and took careful aim at the man sitting alone on the back seat of the Jaguar. As an angry car horn let out a loud impatient blast, the ballistic crack from the Ruger's armour piercing round went unheard by any of the inhabitants of the hundreds of vehicles by now tailing back almost a mile down the dual carriageway.

McKay had anticipated that a double tap would be necessary but, through the scope, he now saw that the glass of the window had taken on a crazed, translucent, pink appearance and knew that another shot would not be needed. `Endex', he muttered to himself.

Within the hour, the first reports were coming in on the lunchtime news. The BBC report said:

`A report has been received that, in the last hour, former British Prime Minister, Charles

Gray, has been killed in an incident on the A41 in Buckinghamshire. It is believed he was travelling from his home to his office in London. According to reports, a shot was fired at his vehicle which had stopped because of a traffic accident. Mr Gray's driver has been taken to Stoke Mandeville hospital but is not thought to have been seriously injured.

We will bring you further reports as we learn more about the situation. Police say they are treating the incident as a terrorist attack and it is believed that the organisation calling itself the British Citizens' Army has admitted responsibility. Police would like to hear from anyone who witnessed anything they thought suspicious and are also anxious to ascertain the whereabouts of the driver of the HGV involved in the incident.'

2

McKay had been trained to tidy up, to `collect the brass' before leaving a scene, and it took him less than a minute to locate the empty cartridge from where it had landed. Housework completed, he put the Ruger back into its case and zipped it up. It was good to be back in action, he thought, but he had never imagined that, when the time came, it would be so close to home. Nor, he thought, as he was joined on the bank by Josif Ćorović and another man, had he expected to be working with Joe again quite so soon.

"About bloody time, Joe. What kept you?", said McKay with a grin. "And you must be Ned?"

The young dark-haired man nodded. There would be plenty of time for introductions later. The three men scrambled unseen through the roadside bushes and emerged into the adjoining farmland. Making their way along the edge of the field, they dropped down onto the towpath of the Wendover arm of the Grand Union Canal and, after following it for just over a mile, were picked up fifteen minutes later by a silver Range Rover Vogue in the Hollowday, at Drayton Beauchamp.

"Have you heard the one about the Englishman, the Scotsman, the Serbian and the Bosnian?", asked Henry Bloom in a rare display of humour.

From there, on to the Icknield Way and into Tring on the B488, it took only ten minutes to reach McKay's lodgings in Old Street. McKay, guitar case once again slung over his shoulder, jumped out as the vehicle stopped.

In the back seat of the Range Rover, Nedim was studying the contents of the brown envelope Josif had handed to him The papers and documents it contained told Nedim that he had just become Branko Kovač.

"Thanks for the lift", McKay called out as the

Range Rover started to pull away.

It was heading back the way it had come, taking the long way home via the A505, then A5 and M1, due to there being a long traffic delay on the A41 for some reason.

3

Only two people had bothered to get out of their vehicles when the traffic had been forced to a halt. None of the others thought there was any good reason to. As far as they were aware, there had been no accident and annoying, as it was, there was nothing to be done except suffer the summer heat while they waited to be rescued.

One of the two who did get out of his vehicle was the British driver of the other HGV, which had somehow managed to pull up safely in the inside lane. Having walked back to the truck which was blocking the carriageway, he was surprised to find the cab empty and, looking around but seeing no sign of its driver, went back to sit in his own truck to wait for the police to arrive.

The other person who had left his car had been sixty or seventy yards further back in the line of stationary vehicles. Dr John Clements, not knowing what he might find, had grabbed a bag from the back seat, got out, and walked towards the two trucks. Clements was ready to assist if needed, but he was not ready for what he came across before he reached the scene.

Greening was sitting on the road surface by the driver's door of the Jaguar, just as he had been advised by the police when he had reported the incident to them. The driver shook, stared with blank eyes, as if in a daydream. He had only briefly taken in the effect of the shot on Gray before instinct had kicked in and he had thrown open the drivers door and half-fallen out of the vehicle. Part of him now denied what he had seen; told him it couldn't have been that bad, told him that he should do something. But another part of him, the part that now saw the grey-pink mush that covered his hands, the same part of him that felt the warm wetness on his face and in his hair and on his clothes, knew that there was nothing to be done. And neither of the two parts wanted to look into the vehicle and face seeing the body again.

In the control room, officers had received an emergency phone call at nine-thirty-three a.m. from Alan Greening, Gray's driver, clearly in a state of great distress. The first police officers attending the scene arrived at nine-fifty a.m. They made their initial assessment and sent a situation report to the control room. They had found Dr John Clements with Greening, still mute and seemingly unaware of his surroundings. The ambulance had arrived just a few minutes after the police and its crew were now dealing with the removal of Gray's body. The vehicle which had caused the incident bore registration plates issued in Bosnia and Herzegovina and its sides carried the name *Transportni Global.* There was no damage to any vehicles and it appeared that there had been no other casualties. But one person, the driver of the Bosnian HGV, could not be accounted for.

In the meantime, control room staff made immediate arrangements for all southbound traffic to be diverted onto a slip road further back, in order to prevent more vehicles joining those already trapped. A recovery vehicle arrived at ten minutes past ten and succeeded in moving the Bosnian HGV sufficiently to permit the traffic to start moving again. Slowly, the backlog of vehicles began to clear as cars and lorries made their way past the six-foot high partitions which, attached to road barriers, completely screened both Gray's Jaguar and the ambulance from the morbid curiosity of rubbernecking motorists who would otherwise slow down to gawk and take photographs with their mobile phones. Now the traffic had began to flow again, but, even when the backlog had disappeared completely, the southbound carriageway of the A41 would remain closed to new traffic until both the HGV and Gray's Jaguar had been removed and police forensic teams had completed their work.

According to the paperwork, the Bosnian vehicle had been carrying `groupage', a mixed load consisting of consignments of insulated electrical cable, machine parts, knitwear, ladies' shoes and other manufactured items, destined for delivery to various UK locations. Now on its way back to Bosnia, it carried two large UK-manufactured electrical generators and some plastic pipes, which had been rejected by the British customer and were being returned. The driver had been one Nedim Tanović, an experienced and trusted employee of the company who, because of his fluency in English and familiarity with procedure, made regular journeys to the UK.

Police questioned the driver of the British-registered HGV. He told them that he had feared that if the Bosnian vehicle collided with his, a serious `pile up' would occur, so he had been forced to brake heavily and had been very lucky to bring it under control. He hadn't seen anyone leave the other HGV, but he was fairly sure there must have been two people in the cab.

"What makes you think that?", the officer had asked.

The driver explained that the Bosnian vehicle had been left-hand drive, and yet the figure he had glimpsed sitting in the cab was in the seat closest to him and that, because the HGV had spun right around, that meant he would have had to be in the passenger seat.

One other driver told police that he had seen a man get out of the car directly in front of his, a green Peugeot 308 estate he thought. The man had been carrying some sort of long black case, it looked like maybe a guitar case he thought, and had scurried up the embankment and into the bushes. This information tallied with what the man Phillips had told them. He had given a lift to a hitchhiker carrying a guitar case at Applebury services near Aylesbury. When the traffic ground to a halt, the man had said something about visiting a friend in a nearby village and he'd get out and walk across the fields. It wasn't far and it would do him good. Phillips remembered the conversation well, he said, because the man had been a `surly Scottish bastard who had hardly spoken before that', and he was glad to see the back of him.

4

Millbank, London, Tuesday 6th August 2019

Blake Burgess sat with his eyes closed, engaged in contemplation that, though both silent and unseeing on his part, benefited greatly from the contribution made by the mellow tones of the Barney Kessel trio playing `Embraceable You'.

Daniels had confirmed that Sean O'Bierne and Patrick McNally had been in the same class throughout their schooling and that Patrick McNally was indeed the son of the late, but not lamented, William McNally, whose name had come up in the

SOI search. Sean O'Bierne it seemed had been killed in a car accident in 1998. Daniels told Burgess that there was still no sign of the other William, that if Doyle was still alive, he had `disappeared off the radar'.

The Data Protection Officer from Network Rail had responded quickly to Susie Weston's request for the CCTV footage from Bearsley railway station. And he had apologised for not being able to provide footage from the station's car park where the cameras were temporarily out of action, due to the upgrade from analogue video tape to digital storage that was in progress. Burgess and his team had studied the images, watching intently the figures that appeared and disappeared on the station's two platforms. They had paid particular attention to three groups of people; those who were men, those who arrived in pairs and those who made an entrance between four and five pm. But at that time of day, both platforms were busy, so crowded with commuters that even filtering them in that way still left a lot of people.

"You can probably rule out the ones in suits and ties", Susie had suggested. "In fact, anyone smartly dressed or carrying a briefcase, and anyone under forty."

For more than half-an-hour, Burgess and his team had watched the footage, occasionally stopping to go back and re-examine a passenger movement or to zoom in on the image. Three times during that period, they watched as trains pulled up at one or other of the platforms and disgorged dozens of passengers while replacements milled around waiting to board. At sixteen thirty-four, they watched again as a fourth train pulled up at platform two and the process was repeated. Then, just as the train was due to leave, two figures ran out from the station building, across the platform and hurriedly jumped aboard a carriage. They moved quickly and were in the camera's view for just a few seconds, their faces seen only briefly and in profile, but they fitted the bill. Both men wore overalls and the smaller of the two carried a black travel bag.

"Run that last bit again, Susie. From where they run out from inside the station. And then let me have the controller please"

Burgess had pressed the button to stop playback at the point where the screen showed a still image of the two men, the first of who had boarded the train.

"That's him", he had said. "Doyle. The one still on the platform."

"You sound pretty certain, sir"

"Age has its advantages, young Jack. By which I mean that I have studied the footage from the cameras at Bishopsgate many times and I'm guessing that you probably haven't."

Daniels decided to risk it.

"We know you were there, sir, but we didn't think you wanted to talk about it."

"I didn't. But I do now. Unless I'm very much

mistaken, that's the bastard who nearly got my wife a police widow's pension after the poor girl had only had the immense pleasure of being married to me for six weeks. Watch the old stuff from Bishopsgate, Jack and compare it with what you've just seen. Then tell me what you notice. Now all we need are some decent mug shots."

Susie Weston had, as usual, been ahead of the game and had already come to her own conclusion. The sixteen thirty-eight from Bearsley was the fast train to Northampton and she had contacted Network Rail staff again, this time to request footage of the train's arrival there. The team now watched again as the cameras at Northampton showed the train arriving at nineteen fifty-four and the same two men leaving their carriage. The images were of a much higher quality this time and some useful `stills' were captured for circulation.

After congratulating Susie on her good work, Burgess had closed the meeting. Alone now in his office, he would look at the information Daniels had come up with regarding Cormac O'Bierne himself and which Daniels had described as making `interesting reading'.

The articles O'Bierne produced, mostly written for the Irish Times where he had a regular column, but sometimes also reproduced in British newspapers, were fiercely anti-establishment. He was a passionate campaigner for free trade and his journalistic output regularly argued the case for

Ireland leaving the Eurozone. The tone of almost every article was vehemently both anti-British and anti-European Union. In fact, as Daniels had said to him, O'Bierne seemed to be anti-almost everything, except a united Ireland.

Burgess knew he didn't yet have enough to go on and yet he was convinced that O'Bierne was somehow involved. It wasn't enough that, along with hundreds of others, his name had showed up in the `Subjects of Interest' records which revealed that, as far back as the early 1990s, he had been regarded as an IRA sympathiser. The record was an old one, a `closed SOI' in MI5 parlance, transferred from an earlier legacy system and no longer active. When, as with all closed SOIs, the degree of residual risk that the subject was considered likely to pose in the future had been assessed, O'Bierne had been put into a low risk category and no notes had since been added to his record.

Turning his thoughts to the incident that morning on the A41, Burgess leaned back further in his chair. Before his team gathered again this afternoon to pool their thoughts, he needed to re-run in his own mind, the logic of the conclusion he had come to.

Point One. One thing was for sure. There had been not one ounce of luck involved in it. Gray's car had stopped - no, correction - it had *been* stopped, at exactly the right place and at exactly the right time. The right time for the killer to be ready and in position and the right place for him to be able to escape unnoticed.

Point Two. There was only one person that could have made sure of these things, and that was the driver of the Bosnian vehicle who had skilfully and deliberately turned his vehicle to block the road at precisely the right time and place.

That was the `opportunity' satisfied, but what about the `means' and the `motive'? The answers to these questions, Burgess decided, would have to wait. Sherlock Holmes, fictional or otherwise, had been right. It didn't matter tuppence that you didn't immediately recognise the picture that the jigsaw puzzle eventually revealed. All that mattered was that it was the right picture, which it *had* to be when the pieces didn't fit any other way.

And so to his conclusion. If you rule out luck, as Burgess did, there were only two possibilities. Either Gray had been killed by the Bosnian driver, possibly aided by an accomplice who had been with him in the truck, or he had been killed by the man who had been seen leaving the green Peugeot estate car driven by the man Phillips. It had to be one or the other because, apart from Doctor John Clements, nobody else had got out of any of the vehicles.

Burgess strongly favoured the first of the two possibilities. If there were two men in the Bosnian truck, as the British driver had suggested, could not one of them have been a marksman? If so, that was the `means' answered too, and only the motive would remain a mystery for the time being.

Or was the assassin the man who had left Phillips' car, meaning that he might be working in conjunction with the Bosnian? But that would mean Phillips himself would have to have been in on it, because the gunman had to know exactly where he'd be in relation to Gray's vehicle when the traffic stopped, True enough, Phillips would have had no choice but to stop his car when the truck blocked the road, regardless of where that happened to be, but only he was in a position to make sure it was sufficiently close to Gray's car. And yet he seemed genuine enough, an ex-soldier, now a salesman for a reputable company and with no criminal record to his name. Admittedly, it wasn't impossible, but it raised other questions and would have been more difficult to plan. For instance, it would mean that the hippie and the Bosnian driver had to be in it together. And unless Phillips had also been involved, how could the hippie gunman, if indeed that's what he'd been, have been sure of getting a lift that would deliver him to the appointed place at the right time? Come to that, how could any of the suspects, the Bosnian, the hippie or Phillips, have known where Gray would be at that time on that day?

Surely, that was the big question, regardless of who had done it? Gray had been due to chair a meeting at his London office at eleven o'clock and had an appointment with the Brexit secretary at

Dexeu headquarters in the afternoon, but how was it possible for any of them have known? Marjorie Ainsley, Gray's distraught secretary, had said that apart from her and two personal assistants, only Gray's driver and personal bodyguard Alan Greening would have known his movements for the day, although, of course, there would be some at Dexeu who would have known about the afternoon meeting.

Burgess didn't like the second theory. It was too complicated, it involved too many people and it raised too many other questions. Like, how was the long-haired hippie going to shoot Gray anyway? With his guitar? No, Burgess preferred the simpler explanation. For some reason that he did not yet understand, the Bosnian had killed Gray and had escaped, at least for now. One way or another, he thought, we now have a Balkan connection.

A knock on the door announced Howard Everett's arrival, followed a few seconds later by Susie Weston and James Daniels who, as usual, Burgess noted, arrived in tandem. Burgess lost no time in giving them his take on things, after which Everett was the first to speak.

"What do we know about any of these people?"

"Not much", Daniels replied. "The Bosnian is a frequent visitor to our shores. Been with his company for fifteen years. Nothing on record about him. Always volunteers for the English runs. Seems to like us for some unfathomable reason, but a reliable guy by all accounts."

"And he left Bosnia alone. I mean, no other driver with him?"

"Seems so."

"So if there was another man in the cab, he must have joined him here, after he arrived in the UK?"

"Yes, but maybe the British driver got it wrong about there being two of them? You know, with all that had just happened."

"Could be."

"What about the driver of the car, Phillips or whatever his name was?", Susie asked.

"We've checked out his story and it seems plausible. In fact he seems a decent enough chap, a rep for a firm selling white goods to the trade. The car's registered to them and they confirm that he was on his way to visit a customer in Watford. The customer confirms that they had been expecting Phillips that morning and also that he had phoned them to tell them he'd been held up and would be late."

"What's the name of the company he works for?", asked Susie Weston.

Howard Everett looked at his iPad.

"White Domestic and Industrial (UK) Ltd. Based in Milton Keynes."

"Could there be a connection between Phillips and the Bosnian driver, Tanović?", asked Daniels.

"Not any very obvious one, Jack", Everett

replied. "Phillips' customers are all UK based."

"Yes, but the company he works for. They don't actually manufacture anything do they? Don't they simply act as UK distributors for foreign manufacturers?"

"Could there be some kind of Bosnian connection there?", asked Susie.

Burgess smiled. He was impressed by Susie's intelligent response, as he always was when someone else agreed with his own line of thought.

"Look into it, Jack. Let me know if the outfit Phillips works for buys anything from Bosnia. And if they do, let me know if Tanović delivers it. But, before you go, Jack, what have you got to tell me about the video footage?"

"We all watched it, sir. And we all see what you meant."

It hadn't been difficult to spot. The grainy old black and white video from twenty-six years earlier had showed two men running away from the truck parked in front of the Hong Kong and Shanghai Bank and getting into a parked car. The first man had run quickly, `like a bloody greyhound', Daniels had said. But the other lagged some distance behind, hampered by a pronounced limp which caused him to drag his right leg. Daniels had showed the video to Elias El-Barouny, a locum doctor working for the Met, who had said it was, `Most likely caused by a malunited fracture of the leg, usually the result of delaying too long before getting proper treatment.'

Then they had watched again the recent footage from Bearsley station. There was the limping limb again, although now it supported the weight of an older, heavier torso, topped by a balder head.

5

Enfield, London, Tuesday 6ᵗʰ August 2019

Jonathan had thought that Monday the twenty-fourth of June had been the worst day in his life; that nothing could ever be worse. For on that day, he had arrived home at around nine-thirty in the evening after working late at the bank in Cheapside and stopping for a drink at at the Whitefriars before catching the tube to South Kensington. At their apartment, he found that Hannah had not returned, then, at just before a quarter to ten, the phone had rung. It was Mandy, who had been trying to contact him since earlier that evening. From Mandy, he had learned that Hannah had been one of the two demonstrators who had been caught in the crossfire between police and protesters. A large group of anti-Brexit campaigners had also taken to the streets of the capital on the same day and at the same time as the anti-Austerity protest that Hannah had been part of. The anti-Brexit and anti-Austerity groups had eventually both arrived in Parliament Square where, both wearing the yellow vests inspired by the French

Gilets Jaunes movement and fast becoming the universal trademark of angry protesters everywhere, they had become indistinguishable from each other.

The police officer who came early the next morning to talk to Jonathan had seemed genuinely very kind and, finding that Mandy had already given Jonathan the awful news, he sensed that she was grateful to have been spared the task. The policewoman had asked if there was anyone who he would like them to contact. He asked her about Hannah's parents and was told that they had been the first to be informed.

Mandy hadn't wanted to talk about what had happened, but Jonathan needed to know and had pressed her to tell him. She told him how one minute they had been laughing and joking and then suddenly Hannah had fallen and had said, 'Mandy, I've been shot.' But "she didn't cry", Mandy said. "She just seemed shocked. I put my coat under her head and ran to one of the police officers while Gerry stayed with her. When I returned, she looked as though she was asleep. So peaceful. An ambulance was with us within minutes and took her to St. Thomas' hospital. Gerry and I waited while they tried everything to save her, But in the end, they couldn't. She didn't deserve to leave this world like that."

But today he knew he had been wrong. Today had been even worse than that first day. For today he had attended Hannah's funeral. Over six weeks had passed since the dreadful day when Hannah had not come home. Mandy had come over that first night he was alone and had found him inconsolable. She had stayed with him on and off for several days but eventually, she had had to return to work and to her own accommodation in St. Pancras. For a while she had kept a close eye on him, phoning almost every day to see how he was and often coming round to see him in the evenings. But the phone calls and visits had become less frequent and he had not seen or heard from her for a couple of weeks now, which he found puzzling and strangely unsettling. He himself had tried to return to his work at the bank after first taking a week's leave, but it had been no use. His employers had been very understanding and had allowed him a further week's compassionate leave, and gradually he began learning to live with the pain of his loss.

Hannah's mother, Gloria Kingston, had identified the body. The Coroner had ordered that a post-mortem be carried out and a pathologist had confirmed that she had been killed, as had the other protester, by a bullet fired from a Glock pistol. The gun was identified as one of the handguns that had been taken from the bodies of the dead police officers by men who had been among the ranks of the anti-Brexit protesters.

A month later, the inquest decided that Hannah and the other victim had been `unlawfully killed by person or persons unknown'. With Hannah's parents, brother and other members of her family, he, Mandy and Gerry and several other of Hannah's friends from work and schooldays had sat on the hard, pitch-pine pews of Trinity church. They had watched as the coffin had been carried in by the pall-bearers, followed by the the minister who had met the coffin at the door of the church. Jonathan had listened as the organist played Vaughan Williams' *The Lark Ascending* and, afterwards, the small gathering had sung *Amazing Grace*. He had heard Mandy deliver her personal and very moving tribute to her best friend, in a voice which, faltering and once or twice almost disappearing, contrasted with the practised tone and content of the short sermon from the vicar which followed.

The organist had played again as the coffin was carried from the church to the adjoining cemetery, and lowered into the place where, one day, Hannah would be reunited with her parents who now stood, with family and friends, gathered solemnly around the open grave. He had listened as the vicar read the final prayers and blessed the casket, but his head had been turned away and his eyes and ears closed when the first handful of soil was scattered into the grave.

Was it his imagination, or was Mandy avoiding him? In the Kingstons' garden, she stood in the shade of an old plum tree, chatting with some of Hannah's old friends from schooldays and veterinary college. Once or twice, Gerry had seen Jonathan look over, as if hoping to catch her eye, but to no avail. Unlike Jonathan, Gerry had worked it out and, when an opportunity arose, he walked over to Mandy.

"You OK?"

"Yes thanks, Gerry. I'm alright"

"Look, I know this is none of my business, Mandy, but I really think you should talk to Jonathan. He says he hasn't seen or heard from you in weeks."

At first, Mandy was silent.

"It's just that I've been busy, Gerry. At work. And I've also got a lot on my mind at the moment."

"That's as maybe. But, whatever it is, it doesn't seem to be making you any happier than it's making him."

Seeing them talking together Jonathan strolled over.

"Hi, Mandy. That was a lovely speech you gave."

"Thank you. It was difficult."

Gerry wandered off to talk to Dean.

"Anyway, how are you doing?

"I'm coping. Getting there slowly I guess. But I've been worried about you. I haven't seen you in ages. Have you been away somewhere?"

"No, just inundated with work at the college. But I might be going away later in the year. My contract's coming to an end soon and I've been offered work on a dig in Egypt."

Now it was Jonathan's turn to become silent.

"Are you going to take it?"

"I don't know. I'm thinking about it."

Silent again.

"Well, at least promise me you won't just disappear. Please."

Mandy smiled an awkward smile.

"OK, I promise."

6

Millbank, London, Thursday 8th August 2019

Young Jack had done a good job, Burgess had to admit. Inside forty-eight hours he'd become something of an authority on trade between the UK and Bosnia. The bad news was that the company Phillips worked for had no connection whatsoever with the Balkans nor with Transportni Global. White Domestic and Industrial (UK) Ltd. imported washing machines, refrigerators, freezers and other equipment from Italy, Germany, Japan and elsewhere to a large warehouse in Milton Keynes, from where they distributed to their UK customers.

But Jack had used his loaf. Jack had looked further. He had asked for, and had obtained, information about Transportni Global's visits to and from the UK. There were a lot of them. Burgess saw from Daniels' notes that, in the last two years alone, the same transport company had made more than thirty return journeys to our shores and almost all of them had been undertaken by the missing driver, Nedim Tanović. Even better, Daniels had proudly presented him with a list of the companies where deliveries had been made and had excitedly pointed out that one of the most regular destinations was Midland Plastics (Machinery) of Northampton.

Burgess turned to Howard Everett.

"Maybe you are right, Howard, that Bloom is not our elusive `Henry', but he's up to something. There *is* a Balkan connection. I can bloody well smell it. Bloom is our man in Sarajevo or I'm a Dutchman."

And now Howard Everett was arranging for surveillance cameras to be installed to keep watch on the premises.

~~~~~~~

Chapter 10

" One who has unreliable friends soon
comes to ruin, but there is a friend who
sticks closer than a brother."
Proverbs 18:24

1

Vitez, Bosnia, Thursday 29 October 1992

It had been a long time since the links that
connected the three men had been forged. The first
had come about when, as a young soldier in October
1992, Josif Corović found himself posted to Bosnia
on United Nations peace-keeping duties. His
regiment, under Operation Grapple 1, part of 7th
Armoured Brigade, was tasked with providing armed
escort to United Nations humanitarian aid convoys
as part of UNPROFOR, the United Nations
Protection Force. A column of Warrior armoured
fighting vehicles belonging to 1st Battalion, the
Cheshire Regiment, had moved up from Split,
Croatia through a white, winter landscape to the UN
operating base at Vitez, where the UN central
depots were located. Vitez was a dangerous area

where the outbreak of the war had seen extensive local violence between Croats and Muslims, with villages and mosques being damaged.

In the town's market place, Josif stood by the Warrior looking into the sea of anxious faces and wondering what it must feel like to wake up to find that a foreign army had occupied your town. How much did they understand? What did they expect of us? Did they know that we weren't there to take sides, that the work of bringing the conflict to an end would not be achieved here in the market place by soldiers like him, but by suited men far from here who decided on every step in the process? Perhaps they did, but he supposed that for the children, their presence was simply a novelty.

The boy was there again. Josif had seen him several times now, each time standing a little nearer the front of the throng of assembled locals. And today he was right at the front, a serious looking boy, of eight or nine, Josif guessed, and today holding tightly the hand of a small fair-haired girl who Josif thought was probably his little sister. From her coat pocket, the little girl produced a small bag of sweets and held it open to her brother for him to take one. Then, to Josif's surprise, she stepped forward and shyly offered the bag out to him. Josif bent his knees and reached down to take a sweet from the bag.

"*Hvala vam puno mlada damo*", said a smiling Corović, thanking the child.

The little girl, as yet innocently incapable of being surprised by anything, lowered her head shyly but said nothing. But the boy stared, eyes and mouth open in amazement, at the realisation that the young British soldier was able to speak in words that he himself understood.

2

Vitez, Bosnia, Tuesday 24th November 1992

It was also in Vitez that Josif had first met Ian McKay. As part of a larger United Nations operation in the troubled Balkan region, D squadron SAS were deployed to Bosnia on 'stand-by' duties. McKay was in Vitez masquerading as a member of the SAS signals Squadron whose members were deployed as United Kingdom Liaison Officers working for the UN. In reality of course, the UKLO remit was simply a cover, under which to carry out intelligence-gathering operations and to be on alert and ready to respond to any significant event.

It was not long before such a significant event occurred, when a soldier from Corović' regiment was killed by Bosnian Serb sniper fire on the north-western outskirts of the town on a Sunday night in early November. Lance Corporal Clive Thompson and Private John Emerick had left the observation post to intercept an incoming vehicle. As they stood together checking the driver's papers, Thompson was hit by a single bullet from the sniper's rifle and killed instantly.

Emerick ran back to the safety of the post, a small isolated cottage at the side of the road. As an observation point the cottage was ideal. It provided unobstructed views of the only two roads leading into the town from the north and west, the road joining Vitez to the motorway and the other that led to the nearby village of Mosenj, and it also offered adequate cover and concealment. As Emerick ran, a second shot from the sniper hit the ground near his feet. From the sounds he heard, he was sure that both shots had come from his left, traveling in an easterly direction and, from the angle of impact, had almost certainly been fired from high ground. The most likely position, and the only one which also fitted well with the range estimated, had to be somewhere on the hill known as *Kalvarija* or Holy Mountain, about eight hundred metres to the north-west of the observation post.

When Corović had joined the regiment, he had asked for the opportunity to be trained as a marksman and his request had been granted. He had been selected by his Officer commanding for sniper training and qualified for his Marksmans badge. Now, permission having been sought and granted from SAS D squadron, Corović found himself, on the orders of his Battalion Commander, teamed up with McKay to conduct a counter-sniper mission, to hunt down and neutralise whoever was responsible.

From a height of just over three hundred metres, the slopes of the 'mountain', densely covered by mostly coniferous trees, looked down on one side towards Vitez to the south-east and, from the other, towards the small village of Mosunj. Further outside the town, the peaks and ridges of white-capped taller hills reached heights of over a thousand metres, but the snow that covered Holy Mountain was light. A wide, winding path, which zigzagged upward through the white-green trees that populated the slopes, led to the top where, in a grassy clearing, stood a small, white church, built long ago by the Jesuits and known locally as the Church of Our Lady-at-the-hill.

From the base of the hill, McKay and Corović, clad in snow-camouflage ghillie suits, silently and separately ascended, some fifty metres or so, and half a minute, apart. McKay went first. They had agreed that, if they found the sniper, McKay needed to be in position before Corović fired a distracting shot. Now McKay saw the man who sat, unsuspecting, with his back up against the front wall of the church and to the right of the arched entrance, clad in black and holding a rifle which looked to McKay like a Russian-made *Dragunov*. The weapon was old now and the observation post where Thompson had been killed would, he judged, have been right at the limit of its range. Whoever he was, this sniper was clearly a first-rate marksman.

But despite any limitations the weapon itself might have, he knew that in the hands of a good marksman, the *Dragunov*, fitted with its superb optic, was still a potent piece of kit. McKay thought that the man looked as if he was probably preparing to leave. On the other side of the opening, a 4x4 vehicle had been parked, which, McKay knew, would obstruct Corović's view. He lay motionless and waited.

From his position among the trees on the opposite side of the path, Corović moved slowly and carefully forward and sideways until he too had a clear line of sight. Unnecessary as it now seemed, he would stick to what had been agreed. If they were successful in finding anybody, they would be too close to risk trying to communicate with each other. Through the scope, he took careful aim at the ground a few inches to the man's left and sent a round into the grass. The man started as the soil and other debris flew up at him, but McKay's single round, its sound superimposed so closely on that from Corović's weapon as to resemble a single shot, had already brought the matter to a close. McKay collected his brass and then made his way through the covering of the trees and around the church, moving in an anti-clockwise direction. From the other side of the church, Corović did the same. All that remained was to check the building itself.

The round-arched entrance lobby, and above it the small belfry, itself topped with a perfectly proportioned spire, formed a central bell-tower. Directly above the entrance arch, a similarly-shaped but smaller, arched opening had been provided to allow the sound of the bell to escape and plead for the presence of the faithful. The opening in the front of the belfry looked straight down over the tops of the trees towards Vitez below. A similar aperture on the opposite side invited to prayer the residents of Mosenj. In his own mind, McKay felt sure that the belfry was the place from where the sniper had taken his shots.

Stepping over the body of the dead gunman, it took them only minutes to satisfy themselves that the church was empty and that the man had been a lone wolf. Outside again, McKay sat on the seat that had been provided for the comfort of pilgrims and lit a cigarette while Josif radioed base to report that the mission had been accomplished.

"Well done Joe", he said. "We made a good team. It's going to be a little while before the boys get up here to clear up. Long enough for you to tell me all about yourself, and especially how you got that name", he said with a laugh.

3

Josif told McKay how both his grandparents had arrived in England after the second world war in 1948 and how, despite both originating from the

Balkans, they had not met each other until then.

"My grandfather Petar Corović was a regular soldier in the Yugoslavian army and saw action in 1941 when he was stationed in Skopje at the time Axis troops invaded. Later, he was moved to Belgrade where he became an officer in the Serbian National Guard. He hated the Nazis and was loyal to King Peter and to General Draza Mihailović, the leader of the royalist resistance."

"In the autumn of 1944," he went on, "when Mihailović called a general uprising because he believed Allied landings were imminent on the Adriatic coast, Petar Corović went to fight in Bosnia as chief of staff of the Serbian Shock Corps. But the landings didn't materialise, their ammunition quickly ran out, and after various skirmishes with Tito's Partisans, my grandfather's men were forced to surrender to the Germans and were taken to Austria. He eventually made his way to the Trieste area, and was there in 1945, preparing for an attack on the communists, when he met up with New Zealand troops under the command of Field Marshal Freyberg."

"It was a very lucky encounter", said Josif, "because Freyberg made sure my grandfather's men were not repatriated as so many were, only to be massacred by Tito's forces at Kočevje. He spent the next three years at camps in Italy and Germany before coming to Britain in and settling initially in Halifax."

"My grandmother", Josif continued, "was much younger than Petar. Her name was Nikola. She was one of eight daughters, born in Montenegro but her father, a post office employee, moved the family to Kosovo and it was there that she was brought up. At the age of sixteen she got married, but Yugoslavia was invaded soon afterwards and her new husband disappeared with the resistance, never to be seen again. The area was taken by the Germans who soon handed over control to Italian troops, whom my grandmother described as `a rabble'. She also became involved with the resistance in some way and this led to her and her elder sister being interned by the Italians along with several other women. Just before her seventeenth birthday she saw her family for the last time and was transported through Albania and mainland Italy to a concentration camp on a tiny island named Ustica which is to the north of Sicily. She spent two years there, basically rotting, before being moved to Naples ahead of the Allied advance. She was imprisoned in Naples, the worst experience of her life, she always said, but she told me how one night she heard a tremendous noise in the city. The following day, she and her sister learned that Mussolini had fallen and they were able to walk out of the prison. They tried to return home and somehow got as far as Zagreb before being handed over to the Germans by the Croat Ustase. After being transported around Germany, my grandmother spent the rest of the war as forced labour in a Nazi munitions factory in Austria, another place where she saw great horrors."

Josif went on to tell McKay about their life in England.

"After two years living in Halifax, Petar and Nikola moved to Chester where my father Milovan Corović was born. Milo, as he was known, joined the Cheshire regiment in 1968 and served first in Ireland and then in Berlin for a while, before in 1972 the regiment returned to the UK and was posted to Weeton barracks in Lancashire.

"It was while he was there", said Josif, "that he met and married my mother who was a local girl. I was born later that year. When my father left the army in 1980, and I was eight years old, we returned to live in Chester where, at that time, my grandparents still lived. With a family background like mine, I expect you can guess the rest. And anyway, it's your turn now I reckon", said Josif.

"That's fair enough I guess", said McKay, "but it'll have to wait for another time. Meanwhile, make the most of being a hero. I need to be out of here before the party starts."

Josif knew what he meant. They shook hands and McKay quickly made his way around the church and disappeared into the trees so as to descend unseen from the other side of the hill.

Minutes later, a military ambulance arrived, soon followed by another vehicle carrying a Military Police team. As far as army procedures were concerned, these incidents, Josif learned, were treated as `scenes of crime', even though, as far as he was concerned, no crime had been committed.

4

Vitez, Bosnia, Wednesday 23rd December 1992

In Vitez during the coming weeks, Josif soon found his family background utilised in an unexpected way. From the day the peacekeeping forces arrived, it became apparent that the need for extensive interaction, not only with the parties involved in the conflict, but with the local community as well, required a high level of language support. The solution advocated was to hire local interpreters for every office, every military observer team and every base of the many battalions which formed part of the UN force. But that was easier said than done. In a small town like Vitez, competent local interpreters, whilst indispensable, were very thin on the ground and many were unwilling to help because of the fear of reprisals. One of the Cheshires' first interpreters, despite all precautions having been taken, had been murdered after only a few weeks in the post, deliberately targeted, it was thought, by a sniper.

Recognising the importance of building good relations, soldiers concentrated on improving socio-economic relations at the level where their actions and choices had the most immediate and beneficial effect. The commander took an initiative to improve the local economy and promote social peace by hiring local mechanics and carpenters for the base's workshops. And there was certainly plenty of work to be done, starting with fitting out troop accommodation and stores and rebuilding the local mosque and school.

So it was that Josif frequently found himself required to translate the needs of Bosnian workmen at the Vitez base into something that resulted in the right materials being obtained as and when needed.

"My Son. He comes to see you I think, with his sister."

The man who had spoken was Hamid Tanović, one of the local carpenters working at the base. Seeing Josif's questioning expression, he produced a small photograph from the wallet in his back pocket. It showed Hamid with a pretty dark-haired girl who Josif took to be his wife, and, standing between them at the front, a boy of about six years old. Although probably two or three years younger in the photo, Josif instantly recognised the boy as the one who he had seen regularly in the town square and whose little sister had offered him the bag of sweets.

"Yes, I have seen him several times", said Josif. "He sometimes looks as if he wants to speak, but perhaps he is too shy?"

"His name is Nedim and he says that when he is grown, he will go to live and work in England. He thinks the British are wonderful", said Hamid with a grin.

"And what does his father think?"

"He thinks that we will have to wait and see", replied Hamid, laughing.

Over the next few months, Corović and Hamid Tanović became close friends. Josif was often invited to the house where Lejla would cook for them and Josif would teach Nedim English. At weekends, soldiers would often play games of football against the locals and Corović soon discovered that Hamid was a very useful player.

When, almost seven months later, the regiment finally left to return home, Nedim was very sad to see him go, but Josif made him promise to practice his English and to keep in touch, to write to him often.

~~~~~~~

Chapter 11

"Silent awhile he stood, as the dead calm
before the thunder rolls."
William Whitehead, `The Roman Father'

1

Orpington, Kent, Thursday 31ˢᵗ October 2019

There had been a definite fall off in the more serious
type of atrocities for some little while now. Apart
from a couple of letter bomb incidents in late
August in which two more MPs had been injured,
one of them seriously and who had resigned his seat
in fear of a repeat performance, there had been little
new traffic of interest across Burgess' desk.

He had read of there being an MP who had
gone missing, somebody called `Tiny' Symonds, but
it was nothing for him to get involved with. The
papers were full of rumours though. First, they said
he'd run off with his research assistant but then she
had turned up saying she'd simply been away on
holiday in Ibiza with her boyfriend and hadn't heard
anything about Symonds' disappearance until she got
back. Then there were those who claimed he'd `done

a John Stonehouse' and attempted to fake his own death, but the pile of scruffy clothes they had found on the beach in Cromer had turned out to belong to a local drop-out who must have been a good foot taller than little Symonds. Plus, they weren't the kind of thing the notoriously dapper MP would have dreamed of wearing, even if they had fitted him. But, in the meantime, despite extensive efforts to trace him, the man, whether dead or alive, remained stubbornly elusive.

Another member of parliament, by the name of Anthony Reynolds, had been found dead, asphyxiated in his car, in the middle of a remote woodland area, But there were not considered to be any suspicious circumstances attaching to it. Like many other MPs, Reynolds had received a number of death threats but was also known to have been suffering from severe depression at the time of his death and the coroner ruled a verdict of `suicide while the balance of the mind was disturbed'.

True, there had also been more than enough smaller scale violent transgressions to keep the police on their toes; one or two very nasty domestic and social incidents which had claimed victims, and a few workplace confrontations that had got out of hand and resulted in a couple of further deaths, but nothing that had the ring of organised terrorist activity about it. That was good he thought. Apart from anything else, it meant Burgess had been able to get home most nights for the past few weeks. He had even managed to take some much needed time off. Emily was on a camping holiday with Rebecca and her mum and dad and, he and Jenny having got Oliver settled into his student accommodation near Guildford, found themselves alone for what felt like the first time in years. Lurch had gone to stay with Everett for the week. He'd have liked that. While he and Jenny had spent a relaxing few days in France, where he had enjoyed being able to observe other people's problems from a safe distance, Everett would have spoiled Lurch rotten with long walks and far too many of his favourite *Canine Crunch* biscuits.

No, as far as real atrocities went, things had been quiet lately and now, refreshed and home again, but not due back at his desk until Monday, Burgess hoped they would stay that way, that it wouldn't turn out to have been the calm before the storm. And perhaps it wouldn't have if, yet again, the deadline had not been missed.

2

Whitehall, London, Thursday 31ˢᵗ October 2019

"Come in, Martin. Take a seat."

Armstrong had half expected to be summoned, for last night Paul Jameson had announced that the EU had granted the UK a further three-month extension and Brexit had, for the fourth time, been put on hold. He knew that Brent would not be a happy bunny today.

"It was very close this time, Martin. Three hundred and twenty-two to three hundred and eighteen. Just four votes in it. The parliamentary arithmetic is changing, mostly because of the PM's threat to deselect the rebels who won't support their own government's policy, and things are moving in our direction, but I'm worried that it's still far too close for comfort. It would only have taken that fool Symonds to turn up and we'd have lost by five. We can't even hold a bloody by-election until the treacherous bastard decides to let us know whether he's dead or alive. It beats me why he couldn't just do the decent thing like Reynolds. OK, Jameson may be able to tweak his bill sufficiently enough to be allowed to bring it back for one more try in the new year, but that will be his last chance. If it flops again, he'll have beaten Bonar Law's record. He'll be out on his ear the day after and he'll take me with him."

Armstrong did his trick with the nod and sympathetic, wry smile again.

"But anyway, Martin, these are my problems so I will deal with them. But thank you for your understanding."

It had worked again, and Brent continued.

"Now, what I actually wanted to talk to you about is another matter which I'm really hoping you can help me out with, Martin. To cut a long story short, I'd appreciate it if you could clear yourself for a meeting next Tuesday evening. Roberts is up to his old tricks again. He's set up a meeting and he knows damn well I can't be there, so I'd like you to attend. You won't be alone, there'll be others from the department present, but I need someone there I can trust. I need you be my eyes and ears."

"Sure, Steve. Anything I can do to help. Just let me have the details."

"Good man. God knows why Jameson has kept Roberts on this long. The man's a bloody Svengali. Did you know that when he was a student at university in the 1980s, he ran a pro-federal Europe group called the Oxford New Reformation Society? Word is that now he's lining himself up for a top job in Brussels and that he's feeding them with information about the current state of our No Deal contingency plans. Worse even, I'm sure that, behind the scenes, he's giving advice to those rats that call themselves the Independent Democratic Party, putting ideas into their heads about how they might be able to spike Jameson's guns. Their very name is living proof that Newspeak is a reality. Their idea of independence consists of the exact opposite - allying themselves to any ragtag outfit that will serve their ends, taking money from every disgruntled businessman or crooked donor who waves an open cheque book at them. And as for Democratic, that's got to be the biggest joke of all. Pretty much all fourteen of them represent `Leave' constituencies. No, Roberts may have fooled Heywood, and maybe even Jameson too, but he doesn't fool me and I do not intend to be his next victim."

Martin had not known about Roberts' background, or of his nefarious activities, but it explained a lot.

"If I thought we could win it, Martin, I'd be advising Jameson to go for another general election. That might be the only way to get rid of them, but Jameson and his advisors are not sure it would work. They reckon that there's little doubt we'd get the biggest single share of the vote by far but the problem is that, in their desperation to stop Brexit altogether, the opposition and several other parties have put aside their differences to create a 'Remain Alliance', in the hope of forming a coalition government. And with their propaganda machine financed by billionaire backers and mountains of overseas cash, they'd have a good chance of achieving it. But, do you know what worries me most of all, Martin?"

Armstrong didn't get a chance to answer.

"I'll tell you what it is. It's the way they've managed to pull the wool over people's eyes. It absolutely terrifies me. There's no bigger believer in democracy than me, but when I see how easily they can stand the truth on its head and get away with it, I have nightmares. They paint Jameson's deal as an `establishment coup', but Jameson is not the establishment, *they* are. The meddling, glory seeking, ex-politicians, the vile speaker, the millionaire busybodies, the prattling, pontificating showbiz luvvies, the international banks and global corporations. This self-appointed, greasily-anointed, pseudo intelligentsia, which would steal sovereignty from the people, then distort and preserve it for its own ends, is the elite. They say that Jameson is eroding democracy, when the truth is he is the only guardian the people have left.

"But, Martin, it is not what *they* have done that frightens me most of all. Politics is a vile business and, much as I despise them, I expect nothing more from such people. No, what really troubles me are some of the people themselves. The ones who just can't see through it. You can tell them black is white, day is night, and if the message comes from their Gods, the herd instinct will kick in and they'll swallow it, whole and *en masse*. It has truly shaken my faith, and I don't have an answer."

Martin thought that, perhaps, he did. But he said nothing.

3

Cheapside, London, Thursday 31st October 2019

"Good to see you again, Martin"
    "The pleasure's all mine, Jonathan."

"What can I get you, Martin?"

"I'll have one of whatever you're having."

The Whitefriars was always quiet at this time of the evening. A desperate rush as people left work kept the bar staff on their toes for a couple of hours, but by eight o'clock, only a few dedicated professional drinkers remained. Before going to the bar, Jonathan indicated the small table by the window, well away from the nearest other occupied seat and, most importantly, well out of earshot. He had been sitting there for nearly half an hour before Martin Armstrong arrived. Returning with the two pints of John Smith's, he set them down on the table next to the open Evening Standard, which he had noticed Armstrong contemplating.

"So, what is it, Martin?"

"The matter we spoke of."

Jonathan nodded.

"An opportunity has arisen and I don't think there will ever be a better one. In fact, it's almost as if it's been especially organised to suit us. Harry has put one of his best guys on to it and apparently it's going to be as easy as ABC. But before saying any more, we need to know if you're still up for it. Can I take it you haven't changed your mind? But if you have, no problem. There'd be people queuing up for this job."

Jonathan thought of Hannah.

"I'm definitely still up for it."

"Superb. I won't tell you who it is but, believe

me, it's an important one. And what Harry's man has come up with is not only virtually risk free, but not at all unpleasant for the executioner. Not like the bad old days when you had to open a trapdoor and then step forward and peer down into the depths, to see the wriggling and hear all the gurgling going on down there. All you'll have to do is make a phone call. Anyway, Jonathan, that last clue in your crossword."

Jonathan picked up his Evening Standard and looked at it. *20d. `Is the devil seed responsible for such actions?' (4, 5).*

"I'll give you a clue", said Armstrong. "It's an anagram. But, in the meantime, drink up. It's my round. Same again?"

4

Branchester, Essex, Friday 1st November 2019

No Brexiteer who knew anything about the place would ever have dreamt of entering the Brussels Tavern on Wellington Street. And to be fair, it would have been difficult not to know something about it. Outside the pub, large European Union flags hung down on either side of the entrance and the large front window displayed a variety of anti-Brexit posters; `We Demand A People's Vote', `Say NO To No Deal', `Brexiteers Are Nasty And Racist

And Should Be Ashamed Of Themselves'.

The Brussels Tavern had once been a popular local watering hole and for more than a hundred years had been called The Duke of Essex, but recently it had had been renamed by its landlord, a rabidly Europhilic District Councillor with his sights set on greater things. And since then it had become a haven for disgruntled `Remainers'. Most locals called it the `Traitors' Arms'. Many had tried to talk John Kempton out of adopting the new name. His wife Julie had told him they stood to lose a lot of business, and that, as a landlord, he should remain strictly neutral in matters of politics. The police had politely suggested he think again; had said that it could even be construed as `inflammatory'. But in the end, he'd got his own way.

Outside, fixed to the front wall by the entrance, a pair of small loudspeakers continuously played the `Anthem for Europe', borrowed from Beethoven's `Ode to Joy' and beloved by dictators the world over, from Hitler to Stalin and Mao. From opening time until the curfew on music at eleven o'clock each night, the tape loop would stealthily insinuate its supraliminal message into the sub-conscious minds of the good people of Branchester.

Julie had been right. The pub had lost a good deal of trade, but tonight was an exception and the Brussels Tavern was unusually busy; busy celebrating yet another extension to the Brexit leaving date. It being a special occasion, John Kempton had invited the local MP Alan Culshaw to address the gathering and had been delighted when his invitation was accepted. Kempton himself had taken the night off, leaving Julie and other bar staff to run the shop. Kempton sat, resplendent in the new silk waistcoat which had set him back a tidy sum. A dark powder blue and perfect in every detail, even down to the colour of its buttons. Someone having told him that a gentleman always leaves the bottom one undone, Kempton had insisted to his tailor that buttons numbers two, three and five should be the same dark blue colour as the background so as not to stand out, whereas those numbered one and four should match the gold of the other ten five-pointed stars that completed the distorted circle of European unity emblazoned on his scrawny chest.

As in a scene from a renaissance painting, the great Euro-prophet sat, surrounded by his apostles, some fervent believers and others simply hoping for a free drink. Kempton was enjoying being the centre of attention. He rose to welcome Alan Culshaw and then gave a short but triumphal speech. Raising his tankard, he valiantly attempted a paraphrase, something he knew all great politicians did from time to time. After two clumsy attempts in his already inebriated state, he eventually got as far as, "Now this is not the end. It is not even the end of the beginning. But is it is most assuredly the beginning of the end", before deciding he couldn't do any better and giving up. But it had been good enough and had brought raised glasses and rousing cheers from his motley band of acolytes.

Kempton had seen the two men enter but didn't pay much attention to them. They were strangers. He'd noted Julie serving them with a couple of pints of Guinness and had seen them sit with their backs to his party. But they had turned round to watch as he had given his faux-Churchillian toast. He had raised his glass to them and they had responded by nodding and raising theirs. They were OK. They had probably just seen the announcement of the celebration on the pub's Facebook page and decided to join in. He didn't notice when they left a few minutes later.

The first that Burgess heard of anything had been just before ten o'clock when the phone rang as he and Jenny sat watching television. It was Everett.

"Sorry to disturb you sir, I know you're not due back until Monday, but there's been another incident and I thought I'd better let you know. Looks like I'm going to be here for a while so there's no need for you to come in, unless you want to of course. It'll be on the news in a few minutes."

"OK, Howard. I'll see what they have to say and ring you back."

According to the news report, two balaclava-clad men, one carrying a shotgun and the other armed with a machine pistol, had opened fire in a busy pub. The men had run into The Brussels Tavern at around nine-twenty in the evening and had fired indiscriminately at customers in the bar. Eleven people, including the landlord and Alan Culshaw, had been killed and many others injured. Only the bar staff had not been targeted.

The newspapers would christen it the `All Saints' Day Massacre'. A distressed Julie Kempton would tell police that, although she hadn't been able to see their faces of course, she had a feeling that they might have been the same two men that had been in earlier that evening for a drink and who, going by their accents, had been Irish. Why did she think they might be the same two men? Well, they were about the same size she said, one small and skinny and the other a big, bald-headed brute of a man with a bad leg. Burgess knew the descriptions off by heart. Yes, she was sure she would recognise them again. And, when shown the photos, she had.

5

Millbank, London, Wednesday 6th November 2019

And then, on Bonfire Night, Roberts had been killed after leaving a meeting at the newly-created government office hub in Canary Wharf. The meeting, held in the HMRC offices in the South Colonnade building, had been chaired by Roberts, and its purpose had been to review, with an emphasis on trade implications, Brexit preparations, in the light of the recent three-month extension of the deadline to 31st January 2020. According to the only witness, Martin Armstrong, the meeting had ended at about eight-thirty and he and Roberts had walked together to where Roberts' car was parked. There he had left Roberts after seeing him get into the vehicle and watching him drive off. He had neither seen nor heard anything suspicious and they had passed no-one as they had walked to the car. In fact, he had said, the area had been exceptionally quiet.

Burgess was suffering from mixed feelings. On the one hand, the armistice was well and truly over, its re-emergence triggered by yet another extension of the Brexit deadline. And yet, another part of him saw each new incident as a further opportunity to move closer towards wrapping up the whole operation. If the bad men stacked and went home now, he'd be left stranded, sitting here holding a busted flush and, as a poker player, that didn't appeal to him. But the more confident they became, the more risks they'll take. They *would* make a mistake. He felt sure of it.

"This business has one important thing in common with Gray's murder. There is nothing opportunistic about either of them. Unlike all the others, they both rely totally on someone having known of their movements."

Burgess continued to address his team.

"So", he went on; Jesus, had he really said that?

God, it was catching. "Two questions for you. One. How did they know where Roberts' car would be? And two. How did they know when he would arrive to get into it?"

"Maybe he always parked there? You know, they apparently quite often held meetings at the same place."

"Possibly, Jack."

"Or maybe someone just saw him park there last night?"

"Again, possibly"

"It has to be one or the other, or both", said Everett.

"Agreed. And what about the second question?"

"They knew when the meeting would end and how long it would take him to walk there?"

"Or they could have been keeping watch on it. Waiting for him to arrive?"

"That would be my guess too, Susie."

"Right. So who does that put in the frame?"

"Anybody who was at the meeting. Or knew about it. That could be a long list."

"Have you got a list of all those attending?"

Everett nodded and handed round copies.

Burgess looked at the list of names. Apart from Roberts and his secretary there were two other members of staff from the cabinet office. Dexeu also had three staff members present, Armstrong and two others. Then there had been two from the

Department of International Trade and two from HMRC. Eleven altogether.

"Good. And we also have the list of those who might have known about Gray's movements the day he was killed." Burgess stood and pointed to the list of names on the whiteboard. "The big question is, can we kill two birds with one stone here? Are there any names that appear on both lists?"

"Well, you can rule out anyone from Gray's office. It was closed down soon after his death, so his people couldn't have known about Roberts' meeting."

"OK. What does that leave us?"

"Not many", said Daniels. "All from Dexeu."

"Names please."

"Well, there's Armstrong who is some kind of legal expert, a chap called Simon Atkins from the International trade section and a Clive Davis, a public relations officer."

"You say they often hold meetings there, Jack. Do these same three usually attend?"

"Yes it seems so."

"Right. We've already spoken to Armstrong and he seems to be in the clear. But we'd better talk to the other two as well. And while we're at it, let's also do a bit of digging around into all three of them and see if anything interesting turns up."

"There were a couple of other people who knew about the meeting but weren't present."

"Who did you have in mind, Susie?"

"Well the Minister himself for a start, Stephen Brent. And his secretary, Mrs Denise Collinson."

"Where was Brent? Why wasn't he at the meeting?"

"In Birmingham, sir, giving a talk to members of the Midlands region of the Federation of Small Businesses."

"Hmm. Well, that's it for now. Unless there's anything else."

"Just one thing, Blake. Do you still want me to keep the cameras rolling at MPM? It's been three months now and we've seen nothing suspicious."

That was true enough. From the building adjacent to MPM's complex, the surveillance cameras in the offices of Secure Software Development plc had a good view of both the entrance to Bloom's offices as well as the yard at the rear. One of Howard Everett's officers from Covert Technical Operations had been tasked with keeping a regular check on the footage. There had been plenty of comings and goings but nothing remarkable to report. The Bosnian transport firm had been in and out a few times and HMRC had provided details of the loads, mostly machine parts, but Tanović had not surfaced. According to the UK Border Force, he had not attempted to return to Bosnia. Alive or dead, he was still here somewhere.

On the face of it, Burgess knew he'd been skating on thin ice all along with the cameras. He'd had precious little to go on in the first place when

Greg Thompson had, against his better judgement, allowed him to run with his instinct, but now, with nothing to show for it, he knew time was running out.

"Run them until the end of the month, Howard. If nothing shows up by then, take them out."

6

Whitehall, London, Friday 8th November 2019

Brent looked up from his desk as his secretary entered the room.

"Mr Armstrong to see you, Minister."

"Thank you, Denise. Come in, Martin. I'll be with you in just a moment."

Armstrong sat in what was fast becoming his usual armchair by the window. Brent picked up the laptop he had been working at and set it down on the low table.

"Shocking news about Roberts, Martin."

"Absolutely tragic, Steve."

"Still, as they say, Martin, it's an ill wind that blows nobody any good."

"Very true, Steve. Who did you have in mind?"

"Well, I know it sounds callous to say it, Martin, but, if I'm honest, the truthful answer is `most people'. Jameson, for one, is looking happier already. Like he's had a great weight lifted from his back.

And it'll be good for young Ingles too."

"Ingles? I don't think I know him."

"George Ingles. Jameson's Spad, his special advisor. A good man. What they call a psephologist, an expert on voting behaviour and, unlike Roberts, Ingles doesn't take sides. I don't think he even likes politics or politicians. He just tells it like it is, which is exactly what Jameson needs right now. Anyway, I thought you might like an update on the state of play, Martin. Things are getting interesting. First the bad news though. Symonds is still holding things up and refusing to reveal his whereabouts. But, there is one bit of good news. The Liberal MP from Essex, the one who was shot and killed in the Brussels Tavern last week. We're not going to fight the by-election for his seat. The Exit party candidate is the front runner there by a country mile and we don't want to split the vote. Which brings me to the main issue. As I told you when we last spoke, Jameson's probably got only one more chance.

"Ingles has done the maths again and reckons we're almost there. He's told Jameson that in a general election, with support from the IUP and the Exit party, he could expect to get a working majority of twenty-five to thirty and Jameson himself would be happy to go for that. But, and it's a big but, Ingles has also told him it's not that straightforward. The opposition has had over three months now to call for a vote of no confidence in the government. They keep threatening to, but they haven't. What does that tell you?"

"It tells me they aren't confident of winning a general election."

"Precisely. And that puts them in a difficult position. In order to put it to the test, Jameson would need to get two-thirds of the seats in the house in favour, and if the opposition aren't confident of winning, they might vote against it if Jameson calls for one, especially if they thought he might not only win but improve his position. But then again, *not* voting for it would be an admission that they knew they couldn't win. How would that make them look?"

Another nod of the head, slower and longer this time.

"Pretty silly, I guess."

"Yes, exactly. But, they're so desperate to keep the numbers as they are, that they might be prepared to pay that price."

"So, on balance, where does that leave us?"

"Good question, Martin. Ingles is certain that the old system is dying, might even be dead already. He says that for millions of people, a basic stance on Brexit runs much deeper than any traditional loyalty they might feel they owe to a political party. He reckons that seventy-seven per cent of the electorate now identify strongly with one side or the other in the Brexit debate, as against only thirty-seven per cent who feel a similar allegiance to any particular party. And he says the figures for those who feel `very strongly' show an even bigger difference, at forty-four per cent and a miserable nine per cent. It doesn't tell us which side would win in a referendum of course, but it does tell us this is no longer a country essentially split between Labourites and Tories. We are now all either Leavers or Remainers, with large swathes of each camp in both parties and motivated by boiling passions. He says the way things have been going, we could possibly expect to win a vote on the withdrawal agreement by five or six votes in a month's time, but he cautions that it's still by no means in the bag. Quite a few Labour MPs have started to see sense, but the Liberals, IDP and Scottish Nationalists are still being obstinate. And of course, we've still got quite a few in our own awkward squad. Most of ours, and several from the opposition, would be wiped out by the Exit party if we didn't field candidates in key `Leave' areas, and Jameson has already had informal talks with Ferguson about coming to an arrangement with them, but that seems to be off the table for the time being if we're not going for an election."

Brent opened the laptop and switched it on.

"Take a look at this."

The first section of the spreadsheet Ingles had constructed showed the state of the parties when Jameson had taken office just over three months earlier. The second showed the current numbers and a third, the projections for a general election and a fourth parliamentary vote on the withdrawal agreement. The sensitivity analysis he had carried out suggested that its accuracy could only be assured within a range of plus or minus one per cent.

"That sounds good, I know", said Brent, "but it's still half a dozen votes either way."

Martin nodded solemnly. Despite a steady improvement in the numbers, it was, as Brent had said, still too close for comfort.

"So, there's your answer, Martin. We won't go for the general election yet, until we see further shifts in the numbers and get the withdrawal act through. Ingles calculates that to be safe, we'd need to gain another six or eight seats. And he says it's no good looking at the dyed in the wool Nationalists. From now on, we've got to focus all our attention on the Liberals and the IDP who, from the way things are going, will soon be Liberals anyway. I hear they're already holding meetings together and planning to stand on a No-Brexit ticket."

7

Millbank, London, Friday 8th November 2019

There was little of interest in the information Daniels had come up with. The three men had nothing much in common except that they had all been transferred into Dexeu on its formation from other government departments. They hadn't known each other before joining the department and, apart from the occasional lunch, they didn't appear to socialise. Burgess looked at Daniels' notes again in case he had missed something.

Simon Atkins. Age thirty-eight. Former HMRC officer. Degree in Business Studies from Manchester. Not a member of any political party but believed to vote Labour. Never married. A confirmed bachelor so they say. Lives with his mother. Joined Department for International Trade 2010. Transferred to Dexeu 2016 as Trade advisor to the minister for exiting the EU. Model railway enthusiast.

Clive Davies. Age forty-one. BA degree in Multimedia and Journalism Studies from Canterbury Christchurch. Joined Department for International Trade 2009. Transferred to Dexeu 2016 as Communications and Parliamentary Affairs Officer. Member of the Liberal party. Married to Lucy, two children. Plays cricket.

Martin Armstrong. Age forty-two. Law degree from Cambridge. Joined Foreign Office 2003. Transferred to Dexeu 2016 as advisor to the Minister on International Law. No known political affiliation. Member of King's College Law Society, Cambridge International Intelligence Institute and the Institute for Democratic Reform. Unmarried. No known hobbies.

All three names had been added to the expanding web of intrigue on his whiteboard but, as things stood, there was nothing to connect any of them with anyone else.

8

Millbank, London, Tuesday 26ᵗʰ November 2019

On a very wet and very windy Tuesday morning, Burgess looked down from the windows of his office, onto Victoria Embankment; to the river below where party boats and river cruisers were moored. They wouldn't be doing much business this time of year, he knew. Even the monstrous London Eye, standing on the opposite bank, dwarfing County Hall and most other nearby buildings, was motionless; it too a victim of the appalling weather.

But despite the heavy rain, Blake Burgess smiled, something he hadn't been doing much of recently. Burgess did not consider himself an unduly resentful man, but the truth was that, normally, he didn't have much time for Hanbury-Davies. They'd known each other for some years and got along well enough when their paths had occasionally crossed, but everything about the man, he thought, oozed privilege; his public school upbringing, his double M.A.s from Oxford, his arrogance, exemplified by the way he seemed to regard himself as unsackable, despite the man, in Burgess' estimation, being half-pissed most of the time. And Burgess especially resented the fact that Hanbury-Davies' family were supposedly minor nobility, something else that he had no time for. And to cap it all, there was the `Hon.' Burgess had never been sure about the `Hon.' He had heard Hanbury-Davies joke about his family's penury, had heard him refer to his father as `Baron Stoneybroke', and himself as `heir apparent to an impoverished dynasty', yet as far as Burgess knew, Hanbury-Davies' father was a mere Baronet.

But recently, the Hon. or otherwise Peregrine Hanbury-Davies, only son of Arthur Hanbury-Davies, 8th Baronet of somewhere or another, had made Burgess a very happy man and so, for the time being, all was forgiven. For, two days ago, the Hon. Peregrine had told him of the brief but illuminating conversation between Gerald Lines and Cormac O'Bierne and another connecting line had been drawn on his whiteboard. Then, after reading the two thick files that still lay on his desk, yet another had been added, this one joining the names of Gerald Lines and Martin Armstrong and leading to the bright red circle in which Burgess had written, `C^3I'. The final pieces of the jigsaw were beginning to fall nicely into place and now, to make his day complete, Hanbury-Davies was about to play to him the recording of the encounter.

Hanbury-Davies had watched O'Bierne enter the Black Pig in Poolbeg Street and make his way to where Lines sat, at a table which had been specially chosen for him by waitress for the day, Susie

Weston of MI5.

The two men had shaken hands and Lines was the first to speak.

"Good to see you, Cormac."

"Always a great pleasure, Gerald."

"I don't have long, Cormac, I'm due to give a lecture this afternoon, but I'd just like to get up to speed with the arrangements we spoke of."

"You worry too much, Gerald. You've no need to know all the details, but I will tell you this. It's going to make Bearsley look like a kiddies' sparkler party."

"You know how important this one is, Cormac, you know that they've got to be stopped?"

"Don't worry, Gerald, they will be. Everything is in place and my men will be ready", said O'Bierne. "I very much doubt we shall see any more defections after this. I'm going to be out of contact myself for a little while but you'll be able to enjoy reading about it in the papers though, I'm sure. I'm even tempted to write an article about it myself."

Burgess smiled at Peregrine Hanbury-Davies, possibly for the first time.

"Yes, we've got them. Well done."

But Hanbury-Davies' attention seemed to be elsewhere.

"I can't help noticing that something seems to be fascinating you."

"Yes. Sorry old boy, but it's your diagram", he said, pointing to the whiteboard. "Dexeu", he said.,

"Martin Armstrong, C³I. What's that all about?"

"Why do you ask?"

"Well, unless there are two of them, your suspect, Martin Armstrong, is a personal friend. An old one too. And a Wykehamist. I say, you didn't know that already did you? Only it just seems a hell of a coincidence."

"Yes, doesn't it just. But no I didn't. Anyway, do go on."

"Well, he's a very decent chap, you know, despite Cambridge and all. Sound as a pound. And, as it happens, I'm actually meeting up with him for lunch today."

"Are you really now? Well I never. Well first things first. We need to pick O'Bierne up straight away before he can do any damage. See if you can get your pals in the Gardaí on to it. You seem to have some influence there."

"And Gerald Lines as well?"

"No. Not yet. I'm sure you'd like to see your friend Armstrong taken out of the equation and you could help in that respect by doing me another little favour. But in the meantime, just ask your friends to make sure Lines is still at Trinity and keep an eye on him. I want to see if he makes a move."

"I still think you're barking up the wrong tree with this one, Blake."

"Maybe. We'll see."

Alone again now, Burgess silently asked himself the question, 'What the hell is going on here?' One fat file had led him to another equally obese tome. The story of Gerald Lines had gone back a very long way. All the way back to the arrival of Oleg Temnikov.

~~~~~~~

Chapter 12

*"Day after day they pour forth speech; night
after night they reveal knowledge"*
Psalm 19:2

1

London, Monday 23rd August 1982

On a warm, sunny Friday morning, Oleg Temnikov
and his family arrived at Heathrow after an
uneventful four and a half hour flight from Moscow.
On their arrival at the Aeroflot lounge, they were
met by embassy staff who quickly and efficiently
whisked them through the airport and onward to
what was to be their new home, a three-bedroom
apartment in a building, owned by the Soviet
embassy, on Kensington High Street.

After a pleasant weekend spent showing his
family the sights of London, Temnikov presented
his pass to the doorman at the Soviet embassy in
Kensington Palace Gardens on Monday morning at
ten o'clock and was escorted to the KGB enclave on
the top floor where he was shown to what was to be
his office. The first part of his ambition had been

fulfilled, but he was not without some considerable anxiety and was fully aware of the dilemma he would one day have to face. He knew that if his work succeeded, he would eventually be forced to defect, and might never return to Russia and never again see his mother, brother or younger sister. But if he failed and was exposed, he would be returned to Moscow to face interrogation and execution.

He reflected on his long personal journey which had begun in 1974 while he was working in the Soviet embassy in Stockholm, and where he had been recruited by MI6 and become a double-agent. Then three years later he had suddenly been recalled to Moscow. He had not known whether he was under suspicion but, regardless, prudence dictated that his activities be put on hold for the time being. Then, after nearly five years in a job he hated, an unexpected opportunity had presented itself when he learned that a new deputy head at the embassy in London was to be appointed. The London *rezidentura* was one of the most important and active in the world, and one of the most desirable postings to Russian diplomats. Temnikov had eagerly put himself forward. He held out little hope of succeeding in his application, but thought that it would, if nothing else, at least reveal what his masters really thought of him. Temnikov excelled himself, putting on a show of enthusiasm, obsequiousness and fake humility and toadying up to superiors that he secretly detested, but no-one was more surprised than he to learn eventually that he was to be appointed to the diplomatic position of Counsellor, in reality deputy head of the KGB, at the London station. Finally, he was on the move again and he would now be the man charged with handling secrets of the first importance.

Temnikov liked the English; witty, sophisticated people, full of laughter and generosity. And his wife would be overjoyed at the prospect, imagining herself taking her two well-dressed, English-speaking daughters to school, shopping at well-stocked supermarkets, visiting elegant parks and dining at classy restaurants serving international cuisine.

But if Oleg Temnikov considered himself to be a very lucky man, James Dawson thought that he was even luckier. Dawson, head of MI6's Soviet section, was ecstatic when the news reached his desk. Now, as Dawson had put it to his deputy, the `Water Lily', Temnikov's codename, had made its way to the surface of the pond.

It would be a few weeks before Temnikov's permit to enter Britain as an accredited diplomat was issued, his travel papers received and other necessary arrangements made. Temnikov made good use of this time and, as he waited to leave Moscow, he spent every spare minute studying the contents of files in Room 365, the political section of the `British department' in KGB headquarters.

Each day he would sign out a different file from

one of the room's many cabinets, and read about yet another Briton that the KGB deemed worthy of having a file all to himself. Most of the subjects Temnikov read about were not spies in the normal sense of the word, at least not yet, but all were considered worth keeping tabs on. Some, those who secretly passed information, were classed as `agents' whilst others were regarded as `confidential contacts'. Some were neither agents nor contacts, but were simply known to be sympathetic to the Soviet cause. They would have no idea that they were being cultivated by the KGB, let alone that each of them had already earned the distinction of being allocated a unique codename and being awarded their own personal file in a super-secure cupboard in Moscow.

The individuals whose names were to be found in the files were drawn from many different areas; current and former politicians, academics, writers and journalists, trades union leaders and others in positions of power that the KGB hoped to influence. In return for their efforts, some accepted hospitality, others holidays or money. But, regardless of their background and how they were classified, what most of them had in common was their usefulness. And what made them useful was their potential to influence. These were people whose opinions and pronouncements could affect and change the decisions of others.

For almost two months, Temnikov had waited

patiently for himself, his wife, and his two daughters to be cleared to travel. And every day for two months, knowing that committing his knowledge to paper would have carried unthinkable risks, he had tested himself in remembering every detail he had come across. By the time he left Moscow, he would be able to recall the name and activities of every British agent and contact in the Moscow archives, as well as that of every KGB spy based in London.

As Oleg Temnikov surveyed his new surroundings in the embassy, the austere functionality of the accommodation, which seemed to have been designed to avoid making even the tiniest of concessions to the human spirit, the stern, unsmiling, distrustful faces of its staff, he thought that, surely, the outpost must be one of the most profoundly paranoid places on God's earth. The KGB, seemingly convinced that the entire Soviet embassy was the target of a gigantic and sustained eavesdropping campaign, had ensured that every window had been bricked up and that every necessary conversation took place in a metal-lined, windowless room in the basement. Needless to say, unnecessary conversations did not take place at all. The head of the department had a particular obsession with the London Underground, believing that the advertising panels in the Tube stations contained two-way mirrors. He never entered such places and instead travelled everywhere in his personal Mercedes. The embassy was, Temnikov mused, run by an organisation imbued with a siege mentality largely based on fantasy.

A week after his arrival in London, Temnikov went to a phone box and, after checking he hadn't been followed, rang the MI6 number he'd been given. The call was answered by Grant Emmerson, his principal handler from earlier days, and a rendezvous was set at the Holiday Inn in Sloane Street, where Russian spies were considered unlikely to be lurking. At the appointed hour, Temnikov entered the hotel and a slight smile crossed the Russian's face as he spotted Emmerson at the bar. Emmerson rose and as agreed, Temnikov followed him out through the back door and up the stairs leading to the car park where a car was waiting to drive them to a block of flats in Bayswater, a one-bedroom apartment on the second floor, chosen as their 'safe house'. The apartment was screened from the street by a line of trees and the block had an underground car park with direct access via a gate from the rear gardens which led into a side street should an emergency escape ever be necessary. The flat was sufficiently distant from the Soviet embassy to make it unlikely that Temnikov would be randomly spotted by other KGB officers, but near enough for him to drive there to meet his case officers and return to Kensington Palace Gardens within the hour. Over tea, Emmerson outlined the operational plan. Temnikov would meet his MI6 case officers there once a month. Emmerson also handed him a key to a house that would be his bolthole, somewhere where he could go to ground, with or without his family, if the moment ever came when he sensed any danger. With these protocols agreed, Temnikov leaned forward and started to unload years of accumulated secrets, a great tumbling screed of all that information gathered from the files in Moscow and committed to memory: names, dates, places, plans, agents and illegals.

Among the names revealed when James Dawson and Emmerson later sat down to scrutinise the transcript of the meeting, were some that came as no surprise. Most, Dawson knew, had long been known to MI5's F Branch, which had responsibility for all counter-subversion in the UK. Earlier in his career, he himself had been assigned to F2 which had been charged with investigating areas such as trade unions, the media, education, and Members of Parliament. Others F sections had responsibility for monitoring subversion in the peace movement and Trotskyist and radical organisations.

The notes, prepared from the tape recording which had been made, named a prominent union leader, well-respected in the British trade union movement and said to be among the most influential people in Britain. The man, who regularly handed over confidential Labour Party documents as well as giving information on his colleagues and contacts and what was happening in 10 Downing Street, accepted contributions towards his 'holiday expenses'.

Another well-known name which appeared was that of Bill Edmunds, a Left-wing Labour MP and member of the Shadow Cabinet. Edmunds had leaked no state secrets, but that hadn't prevented him from being secretly awarded the *Order of the People's Friendship*, the third-highest Soviet decoration, in recognition of his undercover work. Edmunds had freely disclosed information about the Labour movement. He told them which politicians and trade union leaders were pro-Soviet, even suggesting which union bosses should be rewarded by being given Soviet-funded holidays on the Black Sea. And as a leading supporter of CND, he had also passed on what he knew about debates over nuclear weapons. The KGB gave him drafts of articles encouraging British disarmament which he would then edit and publish, unattributed to their real source, in left-wing papers and journals. He was an 'opinion-creator', more an agent of influence than an agent of espionage, but Edmunds would not have known that the KGB classified him as an agent at all.

But, in addition to the big fish, the list contained the names of a number of smaller fry, including veteran peace activist Frank Cornwell, logged as a 'confidential contact', and writer and journalist Raymond Symonds. Also on the list, one of the many names that neither Dawson or Emmerson recognised, was that of a young economist with the Foreign and Colonial Office, currently posted to the British Embassy in Moscow.

2

After coming down from Cambridge in 1975 with a joint first in Philosophy and Economics, Lines had joined the Foreign and Colonial Office in London. His work during that first year was mainly concerned with analysing papers relating to the Soviet Union and providing analytical support to policy teams in that area. The following year he joined one of those policy teams, where he impressed with his policy development skills and the apparent ease with which he had mastered Russian and other East European languages.

In 1978, Lines was offered and accepted a posting to the British Embassy in Moscow where his work required him to undertake a wide range of new roles including providing economic and trade advice to Whitehall, organising economics-related visits, managing programmes including reciprocal scholarship schemes and lobbying on market access and economic reforms. Lines was highly regarded for his efforts in providing support for the Political Team, such as basic translation and arranging meetings in Moscow and other regions of Russia and the Soviet Union. He acted as an in-house expert on aspects of Russian politics, history and culture, frequently attending public seminars and lectures on political topics.

The main purpose of his role was to contribute to the British Embassy's engagement in Russia by analysing trends and developments in Russia's internal and external current affairs. He was required to proactively assist with understanding media coverage of a wide range of major issues, including national and regional political developments, parliamentary business, electoral cycles, human rights, conflict issues and foreign policy as well as developing and facilitating meaningful links between the UK and Russia by working with UK diplomats in the Embassy's political team.

It was not until 1982, when his name appeared on the `Temnikov list', that anyone had any suspicions about him. But even then, as far as anyone could see, Lines had done no great damage. Like many others before him, he was simply considered guilty of having made an unfortunate choice of friends. It was noted by his section head that, although Lines tended not to socialise much with other younger members of the British embassy staff, he seemed to have struck up a close friendship with a young Russian embassy official by the name of Vasily Blatov whose company he seemed to prefer to that of his co-workers. He had not had sufficient clearance to give away anything of any great importance but, all the same, it would be better to have him back home.

In October 1982, Lines was brought back from Moscow, given a promotion and transferred to the Department of Transport as an economic advisor, where he stayed for four years before resigning his commission. Having left the Civil Service, Lines had returned to study for a PhD at Cambridge before going on to write and teach at university. To the British Secret Service, Gerald Lines had only ever been a small fish, a bit player, a mere spear carrier, and it would be more than thirty years before anything further was added to the file.

3

The Sunday Times, Sunday 15th February 2015

`More than seventy years after a ring of Cambridge spies infiltrated British intelligence to pass crucial information to the Soviets, it seems academics at the university are once again involved in rumours of espionage. Concern has emerged following the sudden and unexpected resignation of a number of experts from their positions at the Cambridge International Intelligence Institute, an academic forum on the Western spy world.

The men, including former government defence spokesman John Dickson, William

Harper, a former policy adviser to Number 10 and eminent Cambridge physicist, professor Clive Carter, are said to have left amid concerns that the Kremlin may be secretly funding the forum's activities.

`Suspicions were raised after claims that a publishing house which helps fund the institute's costs, may be acting as a front for Russian intelligence services. The publishing house, Informatsiya, which according to its website is based in London, is known to publish the Journal of Intelligence and Terrorism Studies.

`Mr Harper told earlier reports that his decision to step down was due to `unacceptable Russian influence' on the group and Oleg Temnikov, who had run the KGB's London bureau and been a double agent for the British intelligence service since 1974, confirmed that, `it is quite possible that they have targeted C^3I.

`It is thought that the resignations were brought about by the men having been alerted to suspicions that Russia may attempt to use the link to the institute to influence sensitive debates on national defence and security", sources told the Financial Times.

`Last night, experts confirmed that it was quite feasible for the Russians to be involved, despite no concrete evidence yet found to support the claims. A government spokesman said that he would not speculate as to the precise reasons for the departures, but admitted Russian involvement was perfectly possible given the recent torrent of Russian intelligence-related activities. He said that, `After the heady days of post-Cold War and the belief that we were gradually persuading the Russians into becoming part of a rules-based international system, we now seem to be going very rapidly in the opposite direction.

The Times understands that the new chairman of C³I is to be Dr Gerald Lines, currently emeritus professor of Political Philosophy at Trinity College, Dublin. His deputy head of affairs is to be Dr Jeremy Benson. Dr Benson is a former government policy advisor and a former attache to the British embassy in Belarus. Other appointments have yet to be announced.'

~~~~~~~

Chapter 13

*Then they said, "Ask God whether or not our
journey will be successful." "Go in peace," the priest
replied. "For the Lord is watching over your
journey."*
Judges 18:5-6

1

London, Tuesday 26th November 2019

St. James' Street was almost deserted. There was
hardly a soul to be seen. And it was quiet, although
admittedly not as quiet as it had been in the days
before the buses had been allowed in. Martin
Armstrong reflected how that had been a bad
mistake, but that nevertheless it was still a pleasant
far cry from the hubbub of nearby Piccadilly. The
walk from the office in Westminster, where he
worked as a civil servant currently attached to
Dexeu, the Department for Exiting the EU, had
taken him only fifteen minutes and would do him
good.

In a quiet corner of Boodle's, he soon spotted
his lunch partner. Excellent. Perry had remembered
to bag his favourite table. The two men, close

friends since their days at Winchester together nearly twenty years previously, were in the habit of meeting for lunch on the last Monday of each month. The `Monday Club', Perry called it. It was good to see Perry again, thought Martin, particularly because, recently, they had missed one or two of their regular lunches due to Perry being away from London. So, his friend having just arrived back from yet another trip away from the UK, they had decided to meet for once on Tuesday rather than wait another month.

Their table was at what some older members still called the `dirty end' of the dining room. Hard to believe, but there were still some who had never come to terms with the relaxation of rules which now permitted members to dine in that area without getting `properly dressed'. After a glass of sherry, both men had chosen the smoked trout and Armstrong had ordered a bottle of oak-aged, vanilla-tinged, white rioja. He had been brought up not to drink red wine with fish, but the Hon. Peregrine Hanbury-Davies seemed to think that such rules were there to be broken. And he was certainly putting it away today, thought Armstrong, as his friend ordered a second bottle of claret.

"How are things at the Fens' Polytechnic, old boy?" Peregrine Hanbury-Davies, a Magdalen man, loved to taunt Martin. "Caught any dirty spies lately?"

"Wouldn't soil our dainty little hands", Armstrong retorted. "We leave all that sordid sort of stuff to you boys down at the Vauxhall Pleasure Gardens. We're just a humble talking shop."

Martin was referring to his involvement with C^3I, where his knowledge of International law made a valuable contribution. And he was right in what he had said. Despite its name, the Cambridge International Intelligence Institute was not an instrument of the British Intelligence services. It had been set up as an academic forum, aimed at bringing a cross-disciplined approach to analysing and understanding the claims of state secrecy. The threats of nuclear proliferation, cyber-attack and terrorism; the problems generated by the demand for regional security, of governing diversity and the impact of revolutions; understanding intelligence collection and how it is used. Counter-intelligence and covert action, what intelligence can achieve, as well as understanding its limitations, were the major themes in Armstrong's `talking shop'.

Peregrine Hanbury-Davies had only this morning flown back from Ireland where he had been one of a number of MI6 officers working alongside the Irish authorities. It had been his third spell in Dublin and he was getting to know the city well. He had first been sent over following the terrorist attack on London Bridge in June 2017, when it had been discovered that one of the attackers, a thirty-year-old Moroccan-Libyan, had been living in Dublin. Gardaí suspected that Irish immigration documents owned by the man were being swapped around among a group of other North African men living in the city and officers from the Irish Special Detective Unit were investigating members of this social circle. And Hanbury-Davies had been back there again in July this year when the Gardaí had questioned Cormac O'Bierne. He knew that behind his back, his people were starting to refer to him as `our man in Dublin'.

Martin Armstrong knew only that his friend had returned today from Ireland where, as Perry had put it, he had been `helping the Irish authorities'. But there was much that Martin didn't know. For instance, he didn't know that Hanbury-Davies had listened in to the telephone call Cormac O'Bierne had made to `Henry' immediately after the visit from the Gardaí. Nor did he know that the Gardaí had been listening again when, three days ago, O'Bierne had telephoned Gerald Lines and arranged to meet him at The Black Pig, or that yesterday, Peregrine Hanbury-Davies had sat unseen behind the dark glass of the listening car, tuned in to O'Bierne and Dr. Gerald Lines' muted conversation. Nor did he know that his fellow Old Wykehamist had this very morning informed Blake Burgess of the link between the two men and made him a gift of the recording of their conversation that he had made.

"Alright are they? Decent bunch, your Cambridge cronies?", asked Peregrine Hanbury-Davies. Martin Armstrong noticed that his friend's speech was beginning to sound slurred.

"On the whole yes, Perry. Some good people there. Particularly old Lines, he's quite brilliant you know."

"Yes ... well. What I mean is, I ... er ... shouldn't get too attached to him if I were you, old boy."

For a moment, there was silence.

"I rather think we'd better get you off home, Perry", said Armstrong.

Leaving the table and collecting their coats from the cloakroom, Armstrong shepherded Hanbury-Davies safely to the front steps and out into the street. Slumped on the back seat of the taxi Armstrong had hailed for him, his outward appearance exhibited all the signs of a man who had drunk far too much. And the appearance was not in the least deceptive.

Inside however, lay a different man altogether. A sober-minded man who was pleased with, if a little ashamed of, the performance he had given. A man who had done what another man had asked of him. A man who hoped that he knew his friend better than that other man, and that all would turn out OK. But right now he was tired; all the travelling must have taken it out of him, he thought. He wouldn't report to his office this afternoon. Tomorrow morning would be quite soon enough. Now he would just go home and sleep it off.

Martin Armstrong wasn't sure what to make of his friend's remark. But it had left him feeling strangely unsettled. Should he tell Lines what his friend had said? No, he decided, that wasn't the way things were done. He would let Vasily know about it. Vasily could decide.

2

Dublin, Tuesday 26 November 2019

Lines placed his mobile phone on the coffee table. It better suited his purposes to use the public telephone in the porters' lodge from time to time, so it would not do for the duty porter to know that he possessed one. He left his rooms within the walls of Trinity's historic 16th Century campus and followed the instructions he had received. The text message, he knew, could only have been sent by Vasily, his contact at the Russian Embassy. It had been short but its meaning had been crystal clear to him; Vasily must somehow have learned that Lines' name had surfaced. Lines had always known that this day would eventually come, and now there would be no time to lose. He walked to the kiosk at the porters' lodge and, from there, began to dial the number he had been given. True to form, the young porter on duty smiled and shook his head, as if wondering when, if ever, the professor would progress to the twentieth century, let alone the twenty-first. Reading the young man's thoughts, Lines said,

"One day, John, I will get myself a mobile

phone and, when I do, I shall look to you to instruct me in its use."

"I'd be happy to, sir."

"In the meantime, John, I'm thinking of getting myself a little car."

As he spoke, the number he had dialled was answered by a voice that Lines instantly recognised as that of Vasily Blatov.

"May I ask the reason for your call please?"

"I'm calling about the advertisement for the red Skoda."

"Ah yes. Are you near your rooms?"

"Yes, yes I am."

"Good. Please listen very carefully."

A moment later, the porter heard Lines say, "Thank you. I'll come straight round", before replacing the receiver.

"Thank you, John. As you may have gathered, I'm going to have a look at a car and then I'm off to stay with my friend in Galway for a couple of days. If I buy the car, I plan to drive there myself and surprise her. In the meantime if anyone asks for me, I shall be back in good time for my lectures on Friday."

John smiled a knowing smile, as if to say `Don't worry sir, your secret's safe with me'.

"Have a nice time, sir. And good luck with the car." He watched as the tall, lean figure of Lines, dressed, as always on cold winter days, in a long, dark-grey overcoat and black scarf, his wiry, white hair covered by an old black fedora, walked back in the direction of his rooms.

It was now three-twenty-five p.m. and he was to pack a small bag and leave in time to catch the four-thirty-three p.m. commuter service to Rosslare Europort where someone would be waiting to meet him. His traveling companion would be wearing a dark grey overcoat and carrying a copy of the Financial Times. Into his ancient brown leather holdall, Lines packed the bare minimum of essentials, which in his case consisted of three spare shirts, half-a-dozen pairs of socks, some underwear, a small photo album, several SD cards and memory sticks, his lap-top, a half-bottle of *Teeling* single-grain and two notebooks. He had half zipped up the holdall when, on impulse, he decided there was just enough room left to squeeze in a small traveling chess set.

The taxi he had ordered delivered him to Amiens Street just after four p.m. and, once inside the station, Lines bought himself a return ticket and found time for a coffee in the station café while he waited for the train which would take him to Rosslare.

He looked at his watch. The train had left on time and the journey from Connolly station to Rosslare had been uneventful. It had taken a little over three hours and it was now almost a quarter to eight. Stepping off the train and looking first up and then down the platform, his gaze alighted on a small man, of about fifty Lines thought, standing a few yards away. The man, neatly dressed but wearing a coat which to Lines looked as if it had been made to fit an altogether larger customer, stood with one hand clutching the handle of a small, wheeled travel case and the other holding a crumpled, pink newspaper. Waving it and smiling, he walked quickly towards Lines.

"*Dobriy vyecher*, Professor Lines?"

"*Da, Dobriy vyecher*", said Lines, confirming his identity and returning the greeting. They shook hands.

"*Kak vas zavoot?*"

"*Meenya zavoot Levan, Levan Donauri.*"

Levan Donauri handed Lines one of the return tickets for the nine-thirty p.m. ferry crossing to Cherbourg, together with an envelope containing an Identity Card and a Driving Licence, both issued in the Republic of Poland, Lines noted. He smiled to see that he had become Aleksander Milosz.

"I will explain later", said Levan Donauri, seeing Lines' quizzical expression, and this time speaking in English. "But, for the time being, it has been decided that both you and I are to become honorary Polish citizens."

The two men walked from the train station to the foot-passenger check-in desk in the ferry terminal building. They were in good time. Foot passengers needed to be checked in at least an hour before departure and the walk in the open air from the train station had taken only ten minutes.

The two-berth outside cabin which Levan had booked for the overnight journey was tiny and noisy and had a broken shower. But so far, the crossing had been smooth and the fillet steak Lines had chosen for his evening meal had proved unexpectedly agreeable. When he woke up at around 6 o'clock the following morning, to the sound of Levan Donauri trying in vain to re-attach the shower head, Lines realised to his surprise that he had slept soundly. After breakfast, taken in a quiet corner of the ship's restaurant, Lines returned to the cabin to collect a notebook. Levan Donauri, saying that he had a phone call to make, remained seated at the table in the restaurant. Lines guessed that the phone call would be aimed at receiving further instructions regarding the journey.

Alone in the cabin, Lines briefly considered that perhaps he should try to contact O'Bierne to let him know what had happened. But then he remembered that O'Bierne had said that wouldn't be possible. Not only that, he thought, but a phone call might help police to trace his whereabouts. Returning to the restaurant, he told Levan that he planned to take a stroll on deck to smoke a cigarette. When he returned ten minutes later, Lines couldn't help noticing that his newly appointed chaperone and protector seemed altogether more relaxed. Until then, Levan had seemed serious, pre-occupied even. He had spoken very little, and then mostly in

Russian. Now, since making the phone call, he smiled more and spoke in English, showing that he had an excellent grasp of the language.

3

Millbank, London, Wednesday 27th November 2019

Burgess put down the telephone. He had stopped smiling. It hadn't been the news he had wanted to hear. It hadn't been good news at all. Hanbury-Davies had told him that Gardaí officers had called at the house in Rathmines yesterday afternoon but found it empty. They had obtained a search warrant and forced an entry but had found nothing of interest. They had contacted the offices of the Irish Times and had been told that O'Bierne had taken a week's leave, and would be away until the following Tuesday. He had said nothing about where he was going or what he planned to do. Other officers had called at Trinity College where the porter had informed them that Gerald Lines was also away and was not due to return until Friday.

"Do you know when he left?"

"It would have been yesterday afternoon or evening, but I don't know what time", the man had replied.

"Does anyone know where he has gone?"

"He told me he was going to Galway", said the young porter. "Look, I probably shouldn't say this, but I think he has a lady friend there."

"No, he didn't give me a name or an address. No, sorry, I don't know how he was going to get there. But it's possible he might be driving. He was going to look at a car, a Skoda, a red one I think I heard him say. He made a phone call about it from here."

"Does he not have a mobile phone?"

"You must be joking", the young man had said. "He wouldn't know what to do with one."

"What time was the phone call made?"

"I had only just come on duty, so it must have been just after three o'clock."

The Gardaí had asked the telephone company for details of all calls made from the public telephone at the porters' lodge and Hanbury-Davies had told Burgess that they should have it soon,

Burgess did what he always did when he needed to concentrate. Eyes closed, feet on desk, he leaned back, pressed the play button to bring Charlie Parker back to life, and silently talked to himself.

`We know they're as thick as thieves. Have the two of them gone somewhere together? No, that doesn't add up. For hadn't O'Bierne told Lines that he'd would be `out of touch for a while'? Why would he have said that, if they were planning to elope together? Why was O'Bierne going to be uncontactable? Where had he been planning to go?'

The answer to that question, although of course Burgess could not have known it, was London. In fact, at this very moment, Cormac O'Bierne was less than two miles away from Burgess' office, sitting with three other men in a small coffee shop in Berenson Street. As for Lines, was he to be found somewhere in Galway enjoying a romantic tryst? `Well, we shall know soon enough', Burgess said to himself. `He's due back the day after tomorrow.' In the meantime, it was important to make sure that his birds did not fly the nest. Burgess issued an `All Ports Alert' for the two men and, that done, he now planned to go home to find out if his wife and daughter still recognised him.

4

Cherbourg and Paris, France, Wednesday 27th November 2019

Eighteen hours after leaving Rosslare, Aleksander Milosz and Levan Donauri arrived on a wet Wednesday afternoon at the Quai de Normandie, Cherbourg, where the clocks in the terminal told them it was five-fifteen p.m. Outside at the taxi rank, Donauri spoke to a driver, in fluent French Lines noticed. The man was full of surprises. With luck, thought Lines, he might even play chess. After paying the driver of the taxi which had taken them to the Gare de Cherbourg in the town centre, Levan informed Lines that the next train to Paris would leave at seven-nine p.m., which meant they would have time for a meal before leaving.

Fully released now from his former state of anxiety, Levan Donauri continued to unwind and talk. In fact, he talked a lot. Mainly, he talked of Georgia, his love for his homeland, the ancient land of rock and stone, medieval fortresses and monasteries, majestic mountains, deep caves and rocky beaches. He told of a country of stunning landscapes, culture and history; of its importance, its beautiful scenery, food and people. He spoke of his childhood home in Sighnaghi with its breathtaking views over the Alazani valley. Levan spiritedly recited the names of many famous Georgians, among them those of the composer Alexander Borodin and the international diplomat Eduard Shevardnadze, who had played an influential role in world politics. And, like many Georgians, Levan also still revered the Soviet dictator, Joseph Stalin.

From his own visits to Georgia, Lines was well aware that many Georgians were still proud of the simple Georgian man who had risen to become one of the most influential politicians in the world. He remembered how, despite Soviet symbols being banned by law, Stalin statues had dotted the country and how his likeness had filled the shelves of souvenir shops everywhere. Less controversially, Levan talked of his own family and its noble heritage which, according to him, could lay claim to at least two ruling princes of the eastern province of Kakheti in the ninth century.

By the time the train from Cherbourg pulled into Paris St-Lazare at ten-thirty-three p.m., Lines had learned a lot about Levan Donauri. He had learned that he seemed to like the English more than the Russians, even though he was happy to take their money.

It was a short walk from the station to the hotel in the rue de l'Isly and after checking in and freshening up in their rooms, they met in the bar for a last drink before turning in for the night. Levan Donauri seemed determined to maintain his new found, lighter demeanour and, after a couple of large vodkas, he even ventured his hand at telling a joke in English.

"Have you heard the story about the cavalry officer and the courtesan?", he asked with a laugh, and proceeded to regale Lines with a tale concerning a Georgian cavalry officer who was sitting on the end of the bed, pulling on his riding boots and about to take his leave of a charming Russian demoiselle he had met the previous evening. `My darling', the woman said pointedly, `aren't you forgetting about the money?' The officer turned to her and said proudly, `Madame, a Georgian cavalry officer never takes money from a woman!' Lines felt as if he had known Levan Donauri all his life.

But now, the levity over, Donauri became

serious again. He informed Lines that the longest and most dangerous part of the journey still lay ahead of them. He went on to outline the travel plan that had been devised, Lines assumed, during one of Levan's furtive telephone calls to Vasily.

"We cannot risk taking an air-flight anywhere within the European Common Aviation Area", he said.

Lines nodded his understanding.

"Therefore", Levan went on, "we will continue, for the remainder of our journey, to travel by train and it has been arranged for us to proceed tomorrow, aboard the Paris-Moscow Express. As regards your new Polish identity, to which we are indebted to Comrade Blatov, I will explain.

The train's journey runs for more than two thousand miles in total and the locomotive will need be changed two or three times. But there will be no checks until it arrives in Terespol, on the Polish border with Belarus. This is because, until that point, we will be travelling entirely within the Schengen area, between countries which have abolished passport and all other types of border control at their mutual borders. But at Terespol, the locomotive is changed for the last time and, while the train is stationary, Polish customs and border police officers will undoubtedly make use of the time to check documents. Vasily assures me that although your Polish is good, it would be unlikely to deceive the border police. For myself, I do not know, but I trust the judgement of Vasily Blatov, who is a clever man. But, the most important consideration, and one which I cannot over-emphasise, is that it is possible that the Polish border officers will be accompanied by British Intelligence officers, who will not permit either of us to return under any circumstances. It is important that you understand clearly what I mean by that."

Lines paled visibly. He supposed that he had always been aware of the possibility, but the stark brutality of Donauri's words left no room for doubt. Shaken, he nodded his understanding.

"Good", said Donauri, "Because every moment that we remain within the European Union area, our lives will be at risk, and nowhere more so than at Terespol. It is imperative therefore that we are not on the train when it arrives there and so, to that end, Vasily has instructed that we are to leave at Warsaw and complete our journey into Belarus by an alternative route."

~~~~~~~~

Chapter 14

*"Keep me from the jaws of the trap which they
have set for me, And from the snares of those
who do iniquity."*
Psalm 141:9

1

Millbank, London, Thursday 28th November 2019

Gardaí officers had diligently kept watch on the house in Grosvenor Square, but O'Bierne had not returned. The reason for that was quickly revealed by the `All Ports Alert'. He had bought a return ticket for the fifteen-thirty flight to London, Stansted on Tuesday afternoon, and was not due to return to Dublin until Sunday. But of Lines, nothing had come to light. He had not taken a flight and no ports had any record of him. It seemed that Burgess had been right. Wherever they were, they were not together. But Burgess was not happy. The marked note Hanbury-Davis had passed to Armstrong had worked, but he worried now that it might have worked too quickly.

But at least the telephone company had come

up trumps. The call made by Gerald Lines at four minutes past three on Tuesday afternoon from the public telephone in the porters' lodge at Trinity, had been traced to the Russian Embassy in Orwell Road, Dublin. However Lines was travelling, it was definitely not in a little red Skoda car.

"Right, children. Let's have a look at what we've got. I'll kick this session off and then open it up for your ideas."

For once, Burgess was not in his chair, but was instead standing by the large whiteboard which dominated part of the wall to the side of his desk. On the board, he had written the names of everyone who had so far come up in the investigation. Where photographs existed, these too had been fixed to the board. Some arrowed lines already connected names, and Burgess was hopeful that the meeting would produce some of the further links necessary to paint a bigger picture.

"I'm going to take each incident separately and look at the names that have come up in connection with each of them. When that has been done, we will ask what, if anything, links not only the individuals, but the incidents themselves.

"First, the two incidents that we've got nowhere with; the arson attack that killed the MP Lendle and the car bomb that killed the civil servant Roberts three weeks ago. The problem with the first of these is not that we have no suspects, but rather that we have too many. Lendle was very unpopular in his constituency. He had received all sorts of abuse and threats and his local party were trying to get him deselected. But we have zero evidence. The guy they initially took in for questioning had previous form, but unfortunately he also turned out to have an alibi for the night in question."

"Is it worth looking into sir? The alibi I mean."

"Not this one, Jack. It's cast iron. Unshakeable. He was one of three men who were picked up for fighting outside a night club at around ten o'clock on the Sunday and spent the night in the cells in Hanley police station. Nevertheless, I'd still say this was carried out by a lone wolf and I'm not optimistic about ever finding whoever was responsible."

The four other heads in the office nodded in agreement.

"The second of the two", he went on, "is a little different, in that it's unlikely in my opinion to have been carried out by another lone wolf, at least in the strict sense of the phrase. It involved having inside information about Roberts' movements, it involved the construction and planting of a sophisticated device and, finally, its detonation. But, so far at least, nothing and nobody has come up. It's always possible of course that, eventually, we'll get lucky and will find things to link these first two events to other incidents, but, taken on their own, I'm not inclined to hold my breath."

"Now then, let's move on to the killing of the police officer in Sevenoaks. This is different again, and in more ways than one. First, the evidence suggests that it was not a lone wolf attack and also that the unfortunate PC Cranford wasn't the target either. He just found himself in the wrong place at the wrong time. And second, unlike the first two, we do have some leads and some links. We have the `Blue Book', the printer, McNally, William Doyle and, most importantly, the Irishman O'Bierne, who seems to be connected with them both. So let's stick with him for the moment. We know O'Bierne lied. He knows where this guy McNally is, and so does `Henry', whoever he turns out to be. And wherever McNally is, if he was involved in the Bearsley bombing, it's odds on that the other man, again probably Doyle, will be with him."

Burgess pointed to the lines he had drawn on the whiteboard and which connected the names and photographs of the three men.

"The manager of the hotel in Bearsley confirmed that these two", he said, indicating the photos of the two men taken from the CCTV footage at Northampton railway station, "are the two who were working at the hotel, and that this one", Burgess pointed to the larger of the two men, "is the `William' or `Willy', that he mentioned and who we now know is William Doyle. OK, we don't know for certain that the other one is Patrick McNally but there's a lot to suggest that it is. We know that whoever he is, he was working at the hotel and we know the BCA claimed responsibility for the bombing. We know that McNally bought the printer that produced the BCA's handbook, the `Blue Book' which was found at the scene of PC Cranford's murder at Bearsley. We also know that McNally senior was an IRA man, therefore we may reasonably surmise that McNally junior may also have links with the IRA as well as with this new outfit.

"And now moving on, the A41 murder of Charles Gray I believe is something different again. It's just not their style. I can see these IRA types as bombers", said Burgess, "but capable of the planning and precision that must have gone into this one? I just don't buy it."

His team were familiar with Burgess's conviction that somehow there was a Balkan connection and once again they were generally in agreement with him.

"And the final link", said Burgess pointing to the thick red line connecting the photos of O'Bierne and Gerald Lines. "What the hell's this all about? We know this bastard's not on our side", he said, viciously stabbing the photograph of Lines with his finger and then and running it down the arrow to the photo of Oleg Temnikov. "We had our eye on the professor long ago. And we know he's recently been heavily involved with the Cambridge outfit we're monitoring. But what else does he do? What makes him tick? Who and what connects a respected academic like Lines to thugs like McNally and Co?

What and why is he plotting with O'Bierne? How does he even come to know the man? In short, what is it about him that we've missed?"

Everett rose to point at the whiteboard.

"With respect, sir, I don't think it's just a question of understanding what links the names we already have. Even if we knew what connected all these up here", he said, pointing at the whiteboard, "there would still be a lot of unanswered questions. For a start, as you said yourself, sir, how did they know about Gray's movements that day? There just have to be more names."

"I agree", said Burgess. "But you haven't answered my question about Lines."

"Well apart from the things you've mentioned yourself, there's not much as far as I can see. He teaches, he makes the occasional appearance on radio and television, and he writes of course, scholarly articles and books, but nothing otherwise", said Everett.

"What books has he written?", asked Burgess.

Howard Everett consulted his laptop.

"Three listed here", he said. "But he's no John le Carré, by the look of it. It's all pretty dry stuff. `Man of Action', a biography of August Cieszkowski, a 19th Century Polish philosopher, `The Economic Alternative to Capitalist Dictatorship', and his most recent is, `The Rise of The New Elite - A Critical Analysis of the Threat to Western Democracy'.

"OK. Susie, I want you to dig deeper, much deeper, into the names. Howard's right. We're missing something important. Just keep digging down and down until you find it. And Jack, Lines' books. That's your homework for tonight sorted out. Take a good look at them and let us know if there's anything in there we need to worry about. In the meantime, boys and girl, where is he now? Your thoughts if you will."

"Lines has done a runner. Someone must have tipped him off."

"Agreed, and *I* know who that someone is. But to *where* has he run, young Jack? Do you suggest that the professor has abandoned the cloisters of Dublin and is, as we speak, to be found basking in the arms of a newly-bathed Mrs McGinty in their Galway love nest?"

"Ugh." Susie Weston shuddered at the distasteful thought of old people making love.

"My money's still on Moscow.", said Howard Everett.

"Well, he hasn't flown anywhere."

"Not under his own name maybe, but he could be travelling under a forged identity."

"Well, if he has somehow managed to get out on a flight, we're too late. He'll already be wherever he was going by now."

Burgess had become silent again, and when he finally made the little speech that none of them would ever forget, its purpose was to make clear to one and all his personal priorities.

"OK. Here's how I see things. We have to accept the possibility that we've lost him. I don't mean that we shouldn't move heaven and earth to find the bastard, but even if we succeed, he won't be coming back if I have my way."

The others knew exactly what Burgess meant by that.

"And if we don't find him", he went on, "it's one less for us to worry about. As far as I'm concerned, Vladimir is very welcome to him. By far the most important and urgent matter is to find the Irishman, O'Bierne. Whatever those two were planning, it sounds very unpleasant and, whatever it is, the bad professor will not be an active participant."

2

Paris to Warsaw, Thursday 28th and
Friday 29th November 2019

After a good night's sleep, and breakfast at the hotel, the two men spent a pleasant and relaxing few hours enjoying the sights of Paris before taking a taxi to the Gare de l'Est, from where the *Paris-Moscow Express* would leave at six-fifty-eight p.m.

Right on time, the train's doors opened and Provodnizas and Provodniks in spotless uniforms positioned themselves in front of each coach. Walking to coach number 240 and entering, the conductor checked the tickets and showed them to their compartment. Lines was pleased to find that the anonymous embassy functionary who, behind the scenes, had made all the necessary arrangements, had booked them a deluxe sleeper with two beds and a private bathroom with shower and WC. Better yet, the lucky occupants of the deluxe sleepers were also able to access a private bar at the end of the coach.

Through the train's windows, the two men would see nothing of the unremarkable farmland passing by as the train made its way towards Strasbourg and the first short stop. In the meantime, they would have an evening meal in the restaurant car, its tables beautifully set with crockery and cutlery, and run by friendly Poles. who it seemed communicated unproblematically with both the passengers of the train and with its Russian staff, via a mixture of German, English and Russian. The restaurant car, Lines learned, belonged to Polish long-distance operator PKP Intercity and was managed by a Polish catering firm, unlike the sleeping cars which belong to *RZD, Rossiiskie Zheleznye Dorogi*, the fully state-owned Russian Railway.

Just a few minutes after leaving Strasbourg, they were already crossing the Rhine and reaching German soil at Kehl. Back in their compartment now, the bottle of wine was empty. It was time to retire. As its passengers slept, the train sped quickly on through the night until it reached Karlsruhe, where the duty of the first of its many locomotives came to an end. The loco duly replaced, it was not long before they reached the tunnel that took them beneath the city centre to the central station, Berlin Hauptbahnhof, where once again the train stopped briefly before continuing towards the station at Lichtenberg where this time there was a longer scheduled stop and it was yet again necessary to change the locomotive.

Half an hour later, at seven-forty-six, the train left Berlin, still on schedule and now with its third loco in pride of place. Lines was awake again and, seeing Donauri put down his phone, suspected he had just finished making another call. He wondered if the man ever slept. An hour later, at a quarter-to-nine on Friday morning, the train reached the German border at Frankfurt an der Oder. Yet another river to be crossed and this one would take them into Poland. It was time to pay another visit to the restaurant car, this time for breakfast.

3

Millbank, London, the morning of Friday 29th November 2019

Burgess however had not found time for breakfast. Nor, unlike Lines, had he had a good night's sleep. Instead he'd had a bad dream which, according to Jenny who, worried, had woken him, had given rise to several bouts of somniloquy, involving, she had said, the employment of a great many unpleasant expletives.

He remembered little about the dream now, except that it seemed to involve him running very fast, chasing after a man, who despite having a pronounced limp, always got away. And another man, older and white-haired who, though he didn't run but merely walked and sometimes even stopped to look back and wave, always remained the same distance ahead. Freud might have said it was all about trying to salvage your ego, by catching someone you believe is stronger or cleverer than yourself and is leaving you trailing behind. But Burgess thought it more likely to be the aftermath of the Chinese takeaway he had taken home and eaten while Jenny slept.

The day was not, however, turning out to be altogether unproductive. Everett's colleague in Covert Operations had drawn his attention to something he had spotted on the footage from

`Camera One' at Henry Bloom's premises. Yesterday morning, at just after ten o'clock, a small black Citroen van had driven into the yard at the MPM offices and, having parked close to one of the outbuildings, a man answering the description of Cormac O'Bierne had got out. Zooming in on the image, it was possible to read the registration number and make out the words `Intervan Stansted' on the side. When Burgess saw the footage, he agreed that it looked like O'Bierne but, just to be sure, he had run it past Hanbury-Davies who had confirmed that it was indeed the man he'd watched in Dublin. At the yard manager's office O'Bierne had spoken briefly with the man inside and then returned to the parked vehicle. Soon, a man in blue overalls had emerged from the workshops and walked over to one of the outbuildings where he unlocked the heavy metal doors and helped O'Bierne load several wooden boxes into the back of the vehicle. As O'Bierne drove off, waving to the yard manager as he passed, the man who had helped him re-emerged from the workshop carrying what looked like some scrap metal objects which he dumped into a skip just outside. No, so far it was not an unproductive day at all.

"The results of your excavations, if you'd be so kind, Susie?"

Susie Weston couldn't wait to give her report.

"Well sir, the good news is I think we've found our `Henry'."

"And the not so good news?"

"I don't think you're going to like it, sir."

"We need some results, Susie, whether we like them or not. Go for it."

"Well, it turns out that Cathleen Burnette's maiden name was Phillips."

"Jesus Christ. Please don't tell me she's related to Henry Phillips."

"She's his sister."

"So, Phillips owned half of the house where Cranford was killed"

"Well he did, sir, but not for long. Cathleen Burnette bought him out after a few weeks and then sold it on a couple of months later."

"So he had no connection with the house at the time Cranford was killed?"

"Not directly, sir, but he knows a man who did."

"My God, this gets worse."

"You haven't heard the best bits yet, sir."

"Go on. Delight me further."

"The company Phillips works for, sir, White Domestic and Industrial (UK) Ltd. It's owned by Henry Bloom. And, so is the property outfit that bought the house in Sevenoaks, Blossom Properties plc. They all come under the umbrella of a company called HB Holdings. I should have seen the connection earlier. You know, the names, Bloom and Blossom. Phillips probably put his sister in touch with them when she told him she was going to sell up."

"Good work, Susie."

"Not all mine, sir. It was Jack who found out about Bloom's little empire."

"Is there more?"

"I've saved the best until last, sir. The maiden name of Agnes Merton, the mother of Henry and Cathleen Phillips."

"Don't keep me in suspense."

"No, sir. But it's complicated. It took a lot of digging around, here and in Ireland. But the long and short of it is that she was an O'Bierne. Agnes O'Bierne had a child before she married Arthur Phillips. She was a young, single Irish girl, just nineteen, and her family sent her to England to keep the birth secret. She feared going back, so the child was adopted by her older brother, Breandon O'Bierne and his wife, and brought up as their own in Limerick. That child was Cormac O'Bierne. Then two years later, Agnes married Arthur Phillips, when she was twenty-one and he was nearly twenty years older. So, Henry Phillips and Cormac O'Bierne are half brothers. Phillips died in 1979 aged fifty-nine and, three years later, she married again, this time to George Merton. Since he too passed away a few years ago, she lived at the cottage on her own. And there's one more thing too, sir."

"About Phillips?"

"Yes, sir"

"Carry on then, Susie"

"Well sir, it may not be much but it's interesting at least. We knew Phillips had been in the army, but it turns out that he served in Bosnia in the nineties. So there is a kind of Balkan connection as you call it. And also, he was in the Royal Engineers and was a trained EOD officer. He was involved in something called Operation Harvest where weapons and other devices were gathered up for disposal. So he must have picked up quite a knowledge of that sort of thing."

Burgess was silent as the implications sank in. If a faint `Jesus Christ' escaped his lips, it was for once too quiet to hear. McNally and Doyle. Sixth-generation IRA leftovers. Phillips and O'Bierne. Half-blood brothers. Phillips and Bloom. An army explosives expert and a man who imports from the Balkans. A team of all the talents if ever there was one.

Once again Susie had come up trumps. But he would let her go now because Satch was coming to talk to him. They would meet again later with Jack and Howard.

O'Bierne and Lines? What was it that Aoibheann Kennedy's deputy had told Greg Thompson yesterday about O'Bierne? That he was being funded by the Russians? Well so is Lines unless I'm very much mistaken, thought Burgess. And now, Satch was going to tell him all about it he hoped.

"Sit down, Satch. Good to see you."

Sachpal Kapoor, known to one and all as Satch, had been an officer with the Terrorist Finance Team, charged with gathering and acting on intelligence relating to the financing of terrorist operations, for three years now. And Satch was good thought Burgess, because he'd come to the same conclusion that he had. According to Satch, the Russians were pouring money into Lines' Institute for Democratic Reform. He reminded Burgess that just as the British government itself had spent a hefty chunk of public money promoting the case for remaining in the EU, many Remain campaigners had always claimed that the Kremlin was secretly backing Brexit in order to weaken the European Union. In the words of former Prime Minister Helen Fletcher, President Vladimir Putin, `would be very happy to see Britain leave the EU.' Of course, Putin denied that Russia had in any way acted to influence the outcome, or even that they had any interest in the matter. Nevertheless, in Satch's words, `there has been a distinct whiff of schadenfreude in the Moscow air since the result was announced' and many leading Russian officials had openly celebrated the referendum result. To sum up, Satch had said that could be `absolutely no doubt that Brexit would be good for Russia.'

Satch looked at Burgess who nodded for him to continue.

"No doubt you're wondering why they would go to all that trouble?", he said. But he was going to tell Burgess anyway.

"In recent years", he went on, "Putin has been pushing his own Eurasian Economic Union as an alternative to the EU. Kazakhstan, Kyrgyzstan, Belarus and Armenia have already joined the bloc. Getting Ukraine on board for the project would have been a valuable step forward but that was scuppered when the Maidan revolution toppled the Ukrainian president in 2014. Russia's business ombudsman, Sergei Petrov wrote, in the aftermath of the Brexit vote, that the UK leaving Europe could herald a major shift of power in the Eurasian landmass in the coming years. Petrov said the British exit meant that within a decade there would be a `united Eurasia', so imagine if countries like Serbia and Ukraine were offered EU membership. It would be Putin's worst nightmare. The West have called the Eurasian Union an updated version of the old Soviet Union, but of course Putin also denies that.

And Petrov is not the only one who thinks that way. The EU has imposed sanctions on Russia over their intervention in Ukraine and Moscow's Mayor, a guy called Dmitry Solzyanin, is clear that Russia wins from Brexit. He recently tweeted that `without the UK in the EU, there will no longer be anyone so zealously standing up for sanctions against us.' And the British foreign minister, David Harmsworth also agrees. He told a parliamentary committee that in his opinion, `an EU without Britain as an influential member may be less likely to take or sustain robust action against Russia.' Even the former US ambassador to Russia, Michael Regan, called the British vote to leave the EU, `a giant victory for Putin's foreign policy objectives'.

It's possible that you may not realise the contempt that the Russians have for the European Union. I recently watched a broadcast from the Russian state television's ringmaster, Andrei Kiselev, who decided that the best way to celebrate Brexit would be to mimic the EU itself, by tossing drinks from many different countries into a bucket and mixing them all together into an `unidentifiable slop' which he said `perfectly described his view of the EU.' Kiselev called it a `bastion of wayward political correctness that pushes against healthy, traditional values and dilutes national sovereignty.' Now that might sound to you and me as if it comes straight out of a Ukip campaign leaflet, but it has long been Moscow's take on the bloc. As I say, this may all sound fanciful, but in the meantime, the Kremlin is likely to continue to welcome further discord inside the EU generated by the ascent of Eurosceptic politicians, like the leaders of both our own Conservative and Labour parties as well as by several others throughout Europe."

Satch looked over at Burgess again, but this time the nod meant something different.

"Thank you, Satch. And bringing all that you have told us back to its relevance as regards our investigations, it all pretty much confirms what I've been feeling. That it was the Russians who acted as matchmakers between Lines and O'Bierne, and that it has been their money, funds provided by our friends in the Kremlin, to finance not only Brexit but Irexit as well, that has led to the two of them forging their unholy alliance."

4

Millbank, London, the afternoon of Friday 29th November 2019

Gardaí officers had called yet again at Trinity college, but Lines had still not returned and another member of the faculty had needed to be drafted in to take his lectures. His rooms at the university had been searched but nothing of interest had been found and there was nothing to indicate his whereabouts. In his bedroom, officers had found the doors to the wardrobe ajar, and inside hung several suits, jackets and pairs of trousers. In the section of the wardrobe where his shirts hung, three hangers were empty. Wherever he was, thought Burgess, he was travelling light.

"Did you manage to finish your homework, Jack?"

"Yes, sir"

"And?"

"In a nutshell, sir, he seems a complete

bastard."

"Tell me something I *don't* know, Jack."

"I was up half the night trawling through his stuff, particularly his take on the Polish guy, Cieszkowski. Not to put too fine a a point on it, Lines' idea of democratic reform seems to be for people to take the law into their own hands. I also listened to him taking part in last week's *Moral Maze* on BBC Sounds. You could tell he had Michael Buerk worried. His stance is seriously pushing the debate about where to draw the line between advocacy and incitement."

"Thank you, Jack. Good work. And pretty much the conclusion I came to. Except I reckon he's taken it a stage further. I don't think he's content any more to preach the benefits of direct action. I believe he's making sure of it. Orchestrating it from a safe distance."

And there had still been no information about Lines forthcoming from the `All Ports Alert'.

"So, either he's travelling under an assumed name, or else he hasn't gone anywhere near a UK port?", said Susie.

"Well, where else would he go?"

"He could have gone to direct from Ireland to Europe. Maybe Spain or France?"

"Either way, I'm sticking with Moscow as the destination", said Everett.

Daniels nodded his agreement.

"He could have taken the train."

"What train?"

"The train from London to Moscow", replied Daniels.

"Right." It was Everett's turn to nod.

"I don't know anything about a bloody train from London to Moscow", said Burgess. "But in any case, we'd have picked him up, either at a UK port or in London."

"As I said earlier, maybe he hasn't gone to a UK port", said Susie. "What if he made it to France for example? He could have caught the train there, in Paris."

"So basically, you're telling me that he could be anywhere?"

"Well, not exactly anywhere. Regardless of whether he's travelling by ferry, bus, car or train, he may well still be en route."

"OK, Howard. Let's run with that possibility", Burgess began. "Can we get hold of the timetable for the train?"

Howard Everett's laptop produced the information within a minute.

"It only runs once a week from Paris to Moscow. It leaves every Thursday at eighteen fifty-eight and arrives in Moscow at ten forty-five on Saturday morning."

"So, if he's on it, we have a little under twenty-four hours?"

"I'm afraid it's nowhere near that", said Everett. "If we're going to pick him up, we'll have to do it before he gets to Belarus and leaves the Schengen area."

"And how long does that give us?"

Everett consulted his tablet again.

"Looks as if the train will arrive at Terespol on the Poland-Belarus border around seventeen-thirty tonight. That gives us just six hours."

Burgess, realising now that it was near on impossible for any of his team to get to Terespol in time, immediately alerted MI6 at the British embassy in Warsaw and made it clear to them that this was a matter of `extreme prejudice'. Two officers would join the border police at Terespol but, even if they found him, Lines would not be returning.

5

Warsaw, Poland and Grodno, Belarus,
Friday 29th November 2019

Wide open plains and forbidding forests passed by outside the carriage window as, for the next few hours, the train sped eastwards across Poland. Just after noon, Lines and Donauri paid what would be their last visit to the Polish dining car for, when the train reached Warsaw Centralna, the central station where they were to leave the train, the Polish carriage would be removed. It would be replaced eventually by a Russian restaurant car, but not until the train stopped next at Terespol, and by that time the fugitives would be long gone. Returning to their sleeper carriage, Donauri packed his case and Lines his holdall in readiness to disembark, but as the train neared the suburbs of the Polish capital, it was early, too far ahead of schedule to be permitted to enter the tunnel beneath the city leading to Centralna. Instead, the pretty, dark-haired Provodniza informed Levan Donauri apologetically, the train would have to be held back for a while at Zachodnia, the Warsaw West station, until it could be accommodated at Centralna.

"This is an unexpected but very welcome occurrence", said Donauri, "and for two reasons. Firstly, because although it is unlikely that that anyone would have been waiting for us at Centralna, we can be sure that our departure will go unnoticed at an unscheduled stop. But it is also good because, with a little luck, we may be in time to board an earlier train and gain a little valuable extra time."

Having once more stressed the importance of getting as far away from Terespol as possible, and as quickly as they could, Donauri then went on to outline the next stage of the plan he had discussed with Vasily Blatov. When the train pulled in to Zachodnia station at fourteen-forty, Donauri would go immediately to the ticket office where he would purchase two tickets to Bialystok, the largest city in north-eastern Poland, some one hundred and seventy kilometres north of Terespol, on the banks of the Biała River. And fortune smiled on the two men for the second time that afternoon. Donauri's guess proved right and they would have only a few minutes to wait. The next train to Bialystok was due to depart from Zachodnia at fourteen fifty-four and arrive in Bialystok at seventeen thirty-eight, by coincidence, Donauri noted, at exactly the same time as the Paris-Moscow express would arrive in Terespol.

At Bialystok Central, they left the train and crossed to the adjacent bus station, from where regular buses made the journey to Grodno, just inside the Belarusian border. Donauri bought tickets for the next bus which was due to leave at eighteen-ten and arrive four and a half hours later at the bus station in Grodno.

In Terespol, the Paris-Moscow express had stopped, and armed Polish border guards kept watch from the platform as customs and immigration officials in their military style uniforms boarded the train to check documents. As the Polish officers carried out their checks, they were accompanied by two other dark-suited men who had boarded the train with them, one of whom had spoken briefly with a senior Polish officer. They asked no questions as, in turn, each compartment was entered and each of its almost two hundred occupants required to produce the necessary documents, an exercise which took a little over half an hour to complete.

Only two people had anything of interest to tell

either of the two MI6 officers when shown the photograph of Gerald Lines which Burgess had emailed to them. One was an elderly French businessman travelling to Minsk, who thought he might have seen the man pictured in the restaurant car on one occasion. The other was a pretty Provodniza who seemed to remember seeing someone who looked a bit like him shortly before the train had arrived in Warsaw. As the Polish officers left the train, their work done and their place taken by Belarus officials intent on carrying out visa checks, John Simpson made a phone call to the British embassy in Warsaw, to report that neither of the two men had been on the train when it had arrived at Terespol.

The bus had left Bialystok on time and, a little over fifty minutes later, arrived in Kuźnica, the picturesque little village on the Polish border which had suddenly become an important external border entry point when Poland had become part of the Schengen area a few years earlier.

While Lines and Donauri waited tensely for the border guard, who had boarded the bus, to clear it to leave the checkpoint at Kuźnica, police and armed guards at Terespol combed the town and the wooded areas around the border, while other officers diligently scoured CCTV images from Warsaw and elsewhere for any sign of the fugitives.

Finally released from captivity, the bus began slowly to traverse the one hundred and fifty metres of no-man's land between the Polish and Belarusian checkpoints and, as it did so, the next in the long line of vehicles edged towards the barrier to take its place. In his office, the checkpoint commander looked at the photograph he had just received. The image, taken from CCTV footage at Zachodnia station, showed two men standing on the platform earlier that afternoon. Running out of the kiosk, the commander spoke to one of the two officers on duty and handed him the photograph.

Levan Donauri rose from his seat at the rear of the bus and walked down the central aisle between the rows of seats. Once in the toilet, he took from his coat pocket the two ID cards and the driving licence and carefully pushed them into the small gap behind the hand dryer mounted on the wall above the washbasin.

At the checkpoint, the younger of the two Polish border guards gave an excited shout. Waving his arms to attract the attention of his colleague, he pointed at the bus, the rear of which by then had just rolled across the line marking the border between Polish and Belarusian territory. Raising his gun, he took aim at the black fedora, visible through the rear window of the bus.

"*Szybki, człowiek w autobusie.*"

"*Nie, Nie.*", came the urgent and immediate response from his senior colleague, shaking his head from side to side. It had been he who had carried out the checks on the bus and had allowed it to depart.

"*Za późno. On odszedł*", he said. It was too late. They had gone, and were now in Belarusian territory.

Making his way back down the aisle to his seat, Levan Donauri froze as, through the rear window, he saw the two guards. Then, as the older of the two gently guided the barrel of his young colleague's weapon towards the ground with his hand, he breathed again and sat down. Lines who, having seen the look of fear on the face of his travelling companion, had turned around to see what he was staring at. Seeing what was going on, he had dropped down, terrified, and cowered low in his seat but now, slowly, he sat upright again. For a moment, neither man spoke. Then, opening his case, Donauri took out two passports and handed one of them to Lines.

"Now, my friend, you are to become a Russian citizen", said Donauri, laughing. Opening the passport, Lines saw the photograph of himself and looked at the name, Feodore Kuznetsov. It was his turn to smile. In Russian, Kuznets was `blacksmith'. Was it possible that somebody knew that his maternal grandfather had been a blacksmith?

Now at the Bruzhi checkpoint on the Belarus side of the border, Belarusian border police and customs officers, all in spotless uniforms with impressively large peaked caps, boarded the bus. Customs officers asked passengers if they had any alcohol or anything else to declare but, Lines noted with relief, they seemed to understand the word `No' in almost any language. When passengers replied, `*Nie*', `*Niama*' or `*Net*', as most did, or like some others, simply shook their heads in response to the question, the officers would continue on to the next seat and so, very soon, the bus was permitted to leave.

A little under two hours later, the bus crossed the road bridge over the Neman river into the city centre of Grodno. As it did so, Lines, for some reason unknown to him, thought of the river and its historical importance. Once, long ago, before Europe had taken on its modern form, it had marked the eastern border of Germany. It was even commemorated in the *Deutschlandlied*, the anthem of the Wiemar Republic, although under its German name, the Memel. `*Von der Maas bis an die Memel, Von der Etsch bis an den Belt* ', went the words. Now, the river formed part of the border with Lithuania, where people referred to it as `the father of rivers'. It seemed appropriate that the hotel where they were to stay overnight was named after the Neman.

Shortly after ten o'clock, the bus arrived at the central bus station in Grodno, where Donauri and Lines took a taxi to the hotel. Tired but relieved beyond description, they found the `Beer Restaurant' still open for business.

"But before we eat, I think you owe me a very

large vodka, my friend", said Donauri, his humour clearly restored.

They would not be early to bed tonight, but they would rise early tomorrow.

6

Grodno to Minsk, Belarus, Saturday 30th November 2019

The dawning of the cold but bright Saturday morning had seen a great change in Lines, as if a very heavy weight had been lifted from him. And for once, a very pleasant change he thought, they would be travelling by day. For the first time since they had left Ireland, he felt more like a tourist than a fugitive.

The train from Grodno to Minsk departed on time at six thirty-nine on Saturday morning. The journey to their destination would zig-zag, travelling first south-east, stopping briefly at the small town of Mosty forty-five minutes later, and then turn sharply north-east towards Lida and another short stop.

Most of the four-hour journey took them through farmland and orchards, wide open spaces with views of distant forests, all typically Belarusian Lines reflected, everywhere very neat and very green. One more stop, this time at Molodechno and then abruptly south-east again, passing close to the impressive Zaslavsky reservoir and on into Minsk

Passazhirskiy station where the train arrived just before a quarter to eleven. Donauri had told Lines they were to report to the Russian embassy at midday.

Lines was very fond of Minsk. Outside the train station, he looked up at the two spectacular Soviet-style towers that he remembered, the one on the left proudly boasting the biggest clock in all of Belarus, while its mate on the right still displayed the coat of arms of the Soviet Union. Every street, corner and square in Minsk is truly grand, thought Lines. He knew that most of the city had been destroyed in World War II and had been rebuilt in the 1950s with the towering Soviet-style buildings that Stalin loved so much. He also knew that this had led many to hail Minsk, with its massive concrete edifices, wide avenues and huge open squares, as the most perfect example anywhere of a Soviet city.

But in reality Lines noted, it was a city of three distinct architectural styles and periods. The beautiful brutalism of the Soviet influence contrasted as sharply with the old Belarusian buildings in downtown Minsk that had somehow managed to escape destruction, as it did with the many new modern buildings that had sprung up around the city since his last visit. No, Minsk, he thought, was nowadays definitely a lot more than a ghost of its brief Soviet past.

The taxi delivered them to the Russian embassy where Ms. Olga Sokolov, the senior foreign policy counsellor, was waiting to greet them. Ms. Sokolov guided them to the lift which took them up to the top floor of the impressive new building and the office of the Ambassador, or to give him his full title, The Ambassador Extraordinary and Plenipotentiary, Mr. Vladimir Piminov. The ambassador welcomed them on behalf of the Russian Federation and informed them that arrangements had been made for them to fly to Moscow on Monday. For the next two nights they would stay at the Manastyrski Hotel, a short distance from the Svislach river which flowed through the city centre and in the meantime, he hoped they would have a pleasant weekend in Minsk.

Lines was quite sure that they would, for that evening, he had willingly agreed to let Levan Donauri take charge of the arrangements and Donauri had discovered that, by chance, Georgian opera diva, soprano Madina Varazi, was in Minsk. Better yet, she would tonight be performing the title role in his favourite opera, Richard Strauss's *Salome*. The performance at the National Opera House, Lines would later say, was undoubtedly the finest production of the work he had ever seen.

But before that, Donauri was to take him to his pick of the several Georgian restaurants in Minsk. And on Sunday he would rest.

7

Minsk, Belarus to Moscow, Russia,
Monday 2ⁿᵈ December 2019

At mid-day on Monday, an embassy car delivered the two men to the international airport where Belarusian border guards led them through the airport complex, bypassing the usual checks and controls and instead making their way along corridors and walkways that the travelling public would not be aware existed, until finally they emerged from the building onto an area of tarmac set apart from those used by commercial and domestic traffic. The plane stood waiting, an unmarked, shiny black Antonov An-148, in the service of the Russian Ministry of Defence. Reaching the top of the plane's steps, they were greeted by a smiling Colonel from the FSB, wearing a plain, dark suit.

"Welcome, Comrades", said Col. Stanislav Zykova. "I should like to extend my congratulations to you both on completing what, I am sure, cannot have been an easy journey."

The Colonel laughed at his own little joke while motioning them to enter the cabin and take their seats. Minutes later, at twelve-thirty, the plane began to taxi towards the runway. Col. Zykova turned to address Lines.

"Our flight will be a short one, Professor. We

are due to arrive in Moscow shortly before two o'clock, but during the flight we shall need to talk through the events that brought you here. I hope you understand?"

"Yes, of course", Lines replied.

"And, I imagine that you would perhaps wish to begin by acknowledging the part played in all this by the man to whom ultimately you owe your life, the man without whose presence of mind and swift reaction you would not be here today."

"Indeed", said Lines. "Levan has been my saviour and my constant guide every step of the way, ever since we left Ireland almost a week ago."

And then, remembering Vasily's part in it all, he hastily added, "and of course, I shall also be forever in debt to Vasily Blatov for his invaluable assistance."

"Of those things I am sure, Comrade. However, it is neither to Comrade Donauri nor to Comrade Blatov that I refer in this instance, but to one of your own countrymen, Mr Martin Armstrong, who was I believe your colleague at Cambridge. It was he who alerted Comrade Blatov to the imminent danger facing you."

"My God", said Lines, genuinely taken aback. "I had no idea."

During the short flight, Col. Zykova explained to Lines that he had been instructed to familiarise him with certain aspects of what would be his new life. He would be given a `grace and favour' apartment in a pleasant residential suburb of Moscow and a pension, very generous by Russian standards, of an inflation-protected 60,000 roubles per month. He would never have to worry about money, especially as he had already managed to send a considerable amount from the PRAXIS account at Warden House bank to his personal account with Credit Suisse in Moscow before UK banks had started to look more closely at such movements. Lines was particularly pleased to hear that he would also be given a full travel visa, which would enable him to travel freely to any country within the Eurasian Union. In return, he would be expected to undertake work as directed in the new Institute for Western Economic Studies in Moscow. This he knew, was the price he would be expected to pay for the very considerable trouble the Russian state had gone to on his behalf. He was not a free man, but neither was he greatly troubled. He had always looked forward to the day when he would leave his old life behind and start anew.

At thirteen fifty-four, when the Antonov touched down at Sheremetyevo airport, Moscow, Lines and Donauri followed the Colonel to the waiting car sent by the embassy to collect them.

~~~~~~~

Chapter 15

*"Evil shall slay the wicked: and they that
hate the righteous shall be desolate."
Psalm 34:21*

1

London, Monday 2nd December 2019

The headquarters of the new, euphemistically named
Independent Democratic Party were located in a
once grand building which, in its heyday, had
boasted mansion status. Now, only the glossy black-
painted entrance door with its ornate stonework,
topped by a carved coat of arms, remained as a
testament to its former glory. Affixed to the
stonework in the doorway, a modest brass plaque
reading, `IDP offices, 1st floor', confirmed that this
was the entrance to the suite of rooms belonging to
the new party. The accommodation, comprising two
small former bedrooms, now used as offices, a
kitchen, two toilets and a larger meeting room, took
up the whole of the first floor.

At street level though, internal partitioning now
divided the ground floor of the building into a

number of small, separate `units' which were rented out to small businesses. The unit to the left of the entrance was a small coffee shop and the larger unit next to it a Turkish restaurant, with an entrance on the corner where Berenson Street and Morden Street met. To the right of the doorway, directly underneath the first floor meeting room, a Jewish tailor had conducted his business for many years but the old man had recently died and the unit, now unoccupied, was being refitted.

The shopfitting work was in progress but although the place had been gutted, there was so far not much to show for the efforts of the workmen who had been there for several days now. An electrician had finished re-wiring the premises and a new suspended ceiling had been put in place but, otherwise, work appeared to have come to a halt. To the casual observer, the new ceiling would have appeared no different from those commonly found in many shops and offices but, as they say, appearances can be deceptive. For, in reality, this ceiling was very different indeed, insomuch as the space above it contained a number of custom features, perhaps the most puzzling of which, had they been visible, would have been the ten copper-coloured metal cones that had been positioned in between the joists above the ceiling, so as to form a wide ellipse around the perimeter of the room.

When the explosion occurred, it ripped through the first floor of the building, creating a huge hole in its front and causing a chimney stack to collapse and crash through the centre of the building. Virtually the entire midsection of the building collapsed into the ground floor, leaving a gaping hole in the mansion's facade. The BBC reported:

`A bomb explosion ripped through the offices of the newly-formed Independent Democratic Party in London at around nine o'clock on Monday evening. All fourteen of the party's MPs are believed to have been killed in the blast which also injured several people including two passers-by, and caused extensive damage to the building. Police and fire and rescue officers rushed to the scene but a police spokesman has since issued a statement saying that, given the problematic working conditions, it may be several days before they would be able to return the street to normality.'

At first, it seemed possible that it could have been a tragic accident and there were rumours about a gas leak. But as investigators pieced the evidence together, a more disturbing picture emerged. Examination of the remains of the building found evidence that several explosive devices had been deliberately planted above the ceiling in the ground floor shop unit, timed to go off simultaneously during the evening meeting, and police had circulated CCTV images of three men who had been working there. Once again it seemed that those targeted had been chosen because of their stance regarding Brexit. The Independent Democratic Party had been formed just a few months earlier when disaffected MPs, drawn from both of the two major parties and united only by their determination to prevent any form of Brexit, had joined forces with the single aim of preventing the result of the referendum being implemented.

In a Churchillian moment, Paul Jameson made a speech in parliament in which he described the bombing as having been, "An attempt to cripple Her Majesty's democratically elected Government." "But," he said, "the fact that we are gathered here now, shocked, but composed and determined, is a sign, not only that this attack has failed, but that all attempts to destroy democracy by terrorism will fail. Over the past few months, we have suffered a series of tragedies which not one of us would have thought could ever happen in our country. And yet, after each, we have picked ourselves up and stood firm as all good British people do. We must unite and stand together, for we are British. These evil individuals are trying to destroy the principles that underpin the freedom, justice and democracy that are the birth-right of every British citizen."

The Prime Minister's view of democracy and justice however, contrasted sharply with the interpretation of some other observers, like Donald

Partridge who in his book, *Brexit - The Great British Betrayal*, published shortly afterwards, commented that, `The greatest regret of the London bombing must surely be that there were no cabinet ministers present.' In an article in the *Northern Observer*, Alan Potter wrote that, `a working men's club in Lincolnshire is seriously considering taking up a collection among its members to pay for the bombers to have another go, this time at the Houses of Parliament.'

By the time the forensics team arrived, the front of the building had been boarded up and the pavement and part of the road cordoned off. Inside the building, the full extent of the damage was clear. Above the shop unit, the floor and ceiling separating the ground and first floors had been completely destroyed. Some of the substantial Victorian timber joists and almost all of the first floor floorboards had been completely splintered and dislodged and fallen into the space below where they now lay, along with other timbers, dangling electrical cabling, the lath and plaster of the old ceiling and brick rubble from the chimney stack that had been destroyed. As a testament to the quality of the nineteenth-century materials and workmanship, however, a few of the old joists had somehow remained intact although some, now being tied to the brickwork at only one end, hung down into the space below.

The back room behind the shop, which had

once stored cloths, threads and other sewing materials, had been partitioned to provide a small kitchen and toilet. Among the debris, officers from the investigating team discovered evidence of the room having been recently occupied, including the remains of what had been three camp beds, takeaway food containers, beer cans and an empty, but miraculously still intact, *Green Spot* whiskey bottle.

After the police photographers had done their work, the larger pieces of brick, stone and timber had been removed, but not until officers had taken numerous samples and sent them for analysis. After dozens of such samples had been sent off, much of what remained, mostly dust, rubble, other debris and numerous body parts, was shovelled up, collected in buckets and also despatched to FEL to be further searched, sorted and analysed.

2

Millbank, London, Tuesday 3rd December 2019

Burgess had taken great pleasure in having Martin Armstrong pulled from his bed at three in the morning. Armstrong had very sensibly put up little resistance as the two officers hauled him down the stairs and into the waiting car where Howard Everett sat behind the wheel. Still half asleep, he had demanded to know, `what the hell is going on?', but had received little in the way of a satisfactory answer from Burgess who, from the front passenger seat, had turned to face him and had simply said in an apologetic tone that he was, `sorry for the inconvenience', had respectfully called him `sir' and had promised that a fuller explanation would be forthcoming `very shortly'. Now in the living room of the house near Camden Lock, he would be as good as his word. Burgess indicated to Armstrong to take one of the three chairs around the small dining table and, taking another for himself, sat facing the man, still pyjama-clad under a dark overcoat and, sockless, sporting a pair of brown corduroy slippers. The words came slowly, each phrase separate, punctuated by pauses to allow each to make its mark. The others sat drinking tea in the adjoining kitchen, listening through the door

"Charles Gray, our esteemed former PM. Mr Brendan Roberts, until not very long ago, your boss. And now a number of other politicians, some of whom we shall no doubt be able to establish you were in contact with in the course of executing your civil duties. It is beginning to look to me as though you, Mr Armstrong, are a very dangerous person to know."

"You can't surely think I had anything to do with any of that? You must be mad."

"It's always possible I suppose, but in the meantime I propose to give myself the benefit of the doubt."

"Which is more than you appear to be extending to me."

"That is undoubtedly true, sir, however, whereas in my case there is no evidence to support the hypothesis that my highly-prized marbles have, all but one or two, rolled under the sideboard, never to be seen again, the same unfortunately cannot be said for the cause of the predicament in which you now find yourself. To wit, sir, I know damned well that you are up to your nasty little neck in this business."

Howard Everett entered and set a tape recorder down on the table. He inserted a cassette tape and plugged it in. Burgess had not yet found himself able to put his trust in digital devices.

"This is blatant persecution. I don't even know who you people are. I want my solicitor."

"All will become clear in due course, sir. In the meantime I'd like us to have a nice informal chat."

Armstrong was beginning to perspire.

"You were with Mr Brendan Roberts on the night he was killed."

"Of course I was. And so were a lot of other people."

"But when the meeting was over and Roberts walked to his car, you were the only one who walked with him. May I ask you, sir, why that was?"

"No. I can't. I mean I can't tell you why no-one else did. I assume they just wanted to get straight home, but I can tell you why *I* walked with him. It was because I was going in that direction anyway."

"And in which direction would that be, sir."

"In the direction of the Bengal restaurant. I'd scarcely eaten all day. I was hungry. Famished in fact."

Armstrong told Burgess that after leaving the restaurant, he had walked to Canary Wharf station and taken the tube to Southwark from where he then walked the short distance to his flat just off the Borough Road. That was it, he said. He knew no more than he had told them and would not answer any more questions.

The flat that he had mentioned would have been the same flat of course that Burgess' men had been methodically searching; looking for evidence, any clue, however small, that could link him to any of the incidents. But they had found nothing of interest. Armstrong had been careful. Following the call to Vasily Blatov, his mobile phone had been deep cleansed of its call history and his laptop disposed of. Burgess decided to let Armstrong stew for a while.

Unfortunately for Armstrong though, someone else had not been as thorough, and other officers, who had simultaneously been engaged in removing equipment and papers from the C^3I offices, would soon find something interesting. Interesting at least to anyone who might very reasonably wonder why, among a number of seemingly innocuous emails sent by Armstrong to Gerald Lines' inbox at the Institute for Democratic Reform, was one short message, sent on the evening of Tuesday, thirtieth July, which read, `Gray will be meeting the new boy 15.00 hours, Whitehall 6 August'. Even more interesting was the fact that the email had been forwarded by Lines, without additional comment, to a Mr Henry Bloom.

At eight o'clock in the morning a very tired Armstrong once again found himself facing Burgess, this time accompanied by Susie Weston as well as Everett.

"What do you know about a Mr Henry Bloom?"

"I've never heard of the man. Who is he? What's he got to do with me?"

Burgess ignored both questions.

"Would you mind telling me about your relationship with Professor Gerald Lines."

"Purely professional. I knew him from my time at Cambridge and met him again when I was invited to join the Intelligence Institute there."

"Professor Lines has described politicians trying to derail Brexit as", Burgess reached for his notes, `traitors to their country. Men devoid of all principle. Men who would sell their grandmothers for thirty pieces of silver. Totalitarian bullies, self-interested cheats and liars who despise democracy' and who are `on a par with the worst the world has seen.' I could go on if you wish. Do you share his views, Armstrong?"

"As a matter of fact I do. But so what? It's not a crime, is it?"

"Perhaps not, Armstrong. We shall decide on that in due course. In the meantime, why don't you just tell us everything you know? It will go well for you. We know you're neither the brains nor the brawn behind things. We know Lines is the brains and he's gone. I expect you're pleased to learn that."

"You really think I didn't already know?" Armstrong laughed.

"On the contrary", said Susie Weston. "we know that it was you who tipped him off."

The penny dropped. Armstrong realised what had happened. That he had been set up by his old school friend and that he had sleepwalked into the trap laid for him.

"Why did you send Professor Lines an email telling him of Gray's planned visit to Whitehall?"

Armstrong paled, but with some difficulty managed to retain his composure.

"Because he asked me to let him know if I heard anything about Gray visiting Dexeu. I don't know why he wanted to know and I didn't ask."

"How did you come by the information?"

"I saw it in the minister's diary"

"Stephen Brent's diary? Do you have access to the diary or did you just enter his office while he was out and take a peek at it?"

"Neither, he showed it to me."

"Just a stroke of luck then?"

"I suppose so", said Armstrong. But now he wasn't entirely sure.

"Professor Lines is also known to have advocated that the people rise up and take direct action against `the system'."

"I'm not answering any more of your questions without my solicitor being present."

Burgess was not in a hurry. He was quite happy to keep Armstrong on tenterhooks for as long as it took. He would drop in at the house without warning and fire more questions at him whenever it suited his convenience. And so it was that at the convenient hour of midnight, Armstrong was once more hauled from his bed to face his adversary.

"So", Burgess began. Jesus, it's even getting to me, he thought. "Tell me more about Roberts. Was that in Brent's diary too?"

"No, the minister asked me to attend the meeting."

"I don't imagine there was much love lost between them. Brent and Roberts I mean?"

"Of course not. The man's batting for the other side."

"So, it's all working out rather well both for you and for Brent then? First Gray and then Roberts. Did you tell Lines about Roberts too? You do realise that assisting in a murder is a very serious crime?"

"Murder. What murder?"

"Well, we're fast getting to a point where you

can take your pick. Gray, Roberts, the Berenson Street brigadiers. Which of the many crimes do you want to put your name to?"

Armstrong's demeanour changed. Until now, despite suffering from sleep deprivation and, as a consequence, not being at his best, he had largely managed to deflect Burgess' questions and, although clearly rattled, had maintained an outward calm. But now Burgess had just crossed an invisible line, had trespassed into Armstrong's Weltanschauung and now, his anger boiled over. His face contorted with rage, eyes narrowed, cold and hard, he pointed a finger at Burgess as if holding a stiletto to his face. It would have scared some people. But it would take a lot more than that to scare Burgess. Everett rose and stood ready to step in if necessary.

"Crime. Don't talk to me about crime. You don't know the meaning of the word. The only crime I'm guilty of is thinking for myself. You, you're just a lackey, a miserable, unthinking, servile fool, the willing tool of a corrupt system. You and your sort are in hock to those who have designed a system to keep a small class of people permanently in power. First convince the people that they matter, that they are listened to, but at the same time make sure you own and control the means, not only needed to disprove the foul lie, but to take any meaningful action. That is the true crime, which useful idiots like you are aiding and abetting. But Lines sees through the great deception. The man is a genius. You're not fit to shine his shoes."

"Jesus Christ. You've swallowed Lines' poison hook, line and sinker, haven't you?"

"Just as you have swallowed theirs", retorted Armstrong in a contemptuous tone.

That's more like it. He's cracked. The man's a bloody lunatic. How come no-one had spotted the signs? This called for a celebration.

"Just get him out of my sight, Howard."

Burgess waited until he was alone before pressing the play button. Perhaps something from Errol Garner's, `Concert by the Sea'. Whenever he played the album, he fancied he could smell the Pacific ocean, hear the Californian waves rolling onto the beach at Carmel. Burgess chose `Misty'. He wondered if Clint Eastwood still lived in Carmel and, if so, whether he ever played it too.

3

Stansted, Essex, Tuesday 3rd December 2019

The NCA had issued the European Arrest Warrant and O'Bierne was booked on the eleven fifty-five flight to Dublin. The plain-clothes officers who had kept watch on the car park adjacent to the office of Intervan where the vehicle O'Bierne had hired a week ago was due to be returned, had so far seen nothing. Then, just after ten o'clock, other officers monitoring the drop off points watched as a green Peugeot 308 estate stopped and dropped off a heavily-built man in his early sixties outside the entrance to the departure lounge. After a minute or so, the Peugeot drove off, followed by an unmarked police vehicle which would tail the Peugeot as far as Cambridge, where it would turn off to be replaced by another, different vehicle. A third would follow the car from Stamford and watch from a lay-by as the Peugeot turned off down a track leading to a small farmhouse near Oakham, where Henry Phillips would arrive at twelve-fifteen and where also a small black Citroen van would be seen standing outside a barn.

Inside the terminal, plain-clothes officers watched as O'Bierne went first to buy a newspaper and then, carrying only hand luggage, stopped to check the gate number of his flight. They were watching him still as he then walked straight through, not stopping at the Ryanair baggage check-in, to the Cabin Bar where he ordered a large *Tullamore Dew* and a small caffè latté and sat at a table near the window reading the newspaper. By the time he sensed their presence and looked up to see Peregrine Hanbury-Davies of MI6 and the two officers clad in ballistic vests it was too late.

O'Bierne put up little resistance and was found to be unarmed. In Dublin, Gardaí officers were immediately notified of his arrest and searched his office in Tara Street, where, in a locked metal cabinet, they discovered the Mitsumo laser printer and several copies of the `Blue Book'.

4

Fort Halstead, Kent, Wednesday 4th December 2019

"Twice in one year, Guy. We really must stop meeting like this." John Walton sat with his chief technical officer Alan Simpson as Burgess entered the room. On the table in front of them was a small wooden box containing objects that Burgess would need to be shown. Simpson, he knew, was an acknowledged expert in the field of criminal investigation and the forensic analysis of evidence associated with arson and explosions, a specialised area of forensics where, because of the inherent destructiveness of the events, much of the material left behind is very difficult to process and analyze. The grandson of the distinguished pathologist Professor Keith Simpson, whose photo looked down from behind Walton's desk, rose and smiled.

"Hello, Blake. Long time no see."

"Hello, Alan. He's got you involved this time has he? Must be something interesting."

"You'll have to be the judge of that, Blake, but, yes, I think so."

"You may as well carry straight on, Alan", said Walton.

"OK, John. Well, much of it's pretty standard and won't surprise you. Our old friend Frangex again, only more of it this time, but the deployment is very different from the last one. What do you know about shaped charges?"

"Not much, but somehow I feel sure you're about to educate me."

"OK. Well, to put it simply. If you were to just put a few kilos of Frangex into a metal bucket and then detonate it, where do you suppose the blast would go?"

"Everywhere I guess", said Burgess. "All around in every direction, more or less equally."

"And you'd be about right", said Simpson. "But suppose that you didn't want that. Suppose you wanted to control where the force of the explosion would go. Say upwards and outwards for instance. What then?"

"Put it into a much stronger bucket and leave an opening at the top?"

"OK, so you've got the general idea. But the most effective devices are a bit more sophisticated than that. Imagine if you will a conical metal container that tapers inwards near the top where it is open. The sides of the container made of, for example, copper. Strong but not strong enough to contain the explosion. But the base made from something much tougher and heavier, say steel, the container holding the explosive material and maybe some shrapnel, above it a space filled with compressed air and below it the detonator."

"Are you telling me that you found one of these things?"

"That's pretty much what the stuff we found is telling us, yes. But not just one. I estimate there were at least ten of them, each containing a kilo or so of Frangex and arranged in an elliptical pattern under the floor of the meeting room."

"Did you find evidence of shrapnel too?"

"Plenty", replied Simpson. "Ball bearings. Everywhere."

"How do you reckon these things were set off?"

"The detonators of the devices appear to have been linked via a recently installed smoke and heat alarm circuit and detonated by a plug-in timer."

"Jesus Christ", said Burgess.

"Quite."

"Take a look at these".

Walton reached into the box and lifted out a circular piece of steel plate about a quarter of an inch thick and ten inches in diameter. It had been deformed by the blast but was still in one piece. He handed it to Burgess.

"It's OK to handle. We found ten of these. If you look carefully around the edge, you can see that something had been welded to it and that something is copper."

Reaching into the box again Walton pulled out a polythene sample bag containing several small, jagged and discoloured pieces of copper sheet, none of them much more than an inch or so across.

"You might be interested in this", said Simpson reaching for a sheet of paper. What he handed to Burgess was a drawing he had made of what he thought the finished objects would have looked like.

"It's probably a bit rough and ready, but it'll give you an idea of what you're looking for. Whoever was behind this knew what they were doing, Blake", said Simpson. "You can't buy this sort of stuff off the shelf. The charges were custom-made for this particular job. They were designed to exactly fit the height of the ceiling joists and they were supported underneath by scaffold boards fixed to the joists to help ensure most of the blast went upwards. It might not look it to you, but nothing about it is straightforward, particularly not the welding. You're looking for someone who had the knowledge necessary to design these things as well as the facilities to build them. Probably someone with an EOD background."

Burgess said nothing but thought of what Susie had told him about Henry Phillips.

"But even then, Blake", said Simpson, "it's not easy."

No, I don't suppose for one moment that it is. You'd probably mess a few up to start with, thought Burgess, remembering the deformed scrap metal bits and pieces he'd seen going into the skip at MPM.

"I hope you'll bear with me, Alan, while I ring one of my guys. I've got some footage I'd like you to see."

"Sure", said Simpson. "In the meantime, is there anything else you'd like to know?"

"Fingerprints?", said Burgess, and then, not wishing to be reminded of the answer Walton had given the last time he had asked the same question, adding, "other than those of the victims."

"Not many. Your best bet is the whiskey bottle. It's plastered in them. Find someone who drinks *Green Spot.*"

And I know just the man, thought Burgess.

~~~~~~~~

Chapter 16

*"For the Lord of hosts will have a day of
reckoning against everyone who is proud and
lofty, and against everyone who is lifted up, that he
may be abased."*
Isaiah 2:12

1

Thowton Allop, Northamptonshire, Thursday 5th December 2019

"Mr Henry Bloom?"

"At your service. What can I do for you?"

Howard Everett looked at the man who had answered his ring of the bell at the front door of the small Tudor Manor house that was Thowton Place, and stood there now, wearing a monogrammed, dark-maroon coloured dressing gown and matching corduroy house shoes.

"Dreadfully sorry if it took me a moment", said Bloom. "Wife's away and I was in the dressing room."

"My name is Lewis", said the SO15 Inspector holding up his warrant card. "We'd like to have a word with you, Mr Bloom."

"Yes, of course." Bloom shivered in the night air. "But please, do come in out of the cold." He pushed the door open wider and stepped inside to allow the two men to enter the hallway.

"Through here", he said smiling and opening the door leading into a comfortably appointed reception room where a blazing log fire provided a welcome warmth.

Bloom sat down in what Lewis supposed must be his favourite armchair and, indicating a nearby sofa, motioned the officers to do the same.

"Now then, Inspector, what's it all about? How may I help?"

"We'd like you to accompany us to answer some questions about recent events."

"Good heavens. That all sounds very mysterious. May I ask what's going on?"

"I'm afraid I can't tell you that, sir. But I should tell you that other officers are, as we speak, involved in carrying out a through search of your company offices and other areas. I also have to tell you that evidence has come to light which is not to your advantage. You will learn more about the exact nature of our findings and enquiries when you are formally interviewed."

"Yes, well I can't imagine for a moment what you chaps are looking for or what you have found, but just give me a moment or two to pop upstairs and put some togs on and I'll be with you."

"I'm afraid I shall have to accompany you, sir",

said Lewis.

"No problem at all, Inspector. This way."

Bloom rose and opened the door into hallway. Lewis followed him up the stairs, onto the landing and into the master bedroom where he sat and watched as Bloom opened a drawer and rummaged through the socks it contained. Perhaps he took his eyes off the man for an instant, or perhaps the movement was so quick and unexpected that nothing could have stopped him, but too late he saw Bloom raise the gun to his head. Downstairs, Everett heard the shot and was in the room within seconds. Lewis looked at Everett and shook his head. Bloom lay slumped dead on the bedroom floor, a Makarov 9mm semi-automatic pistol still in his hand and a tiny rivulet of blood running from his right temple and staining the pale carpet.

Just a mile down the road at the offices of Midlands Plastics (Machinery) Ltd, other officers had sealed off the premises and now guarded the entrance while the search was under way.

2

Oakham, Rutland, Thursday 5th December 2019

If it had been possible, from twenty-five miles away, to have heard the gunshot that had killed Bloom, Burgess would not have needed to look at his watch to satisfy himself that the two operations were well synchronised. Exactly nine o'clock. Time to go.

He nodded to the officer holding the ram and with one stroke of the `big red key', the front door of the farmhouse gave way and flew open. Burgess and two officers from the armed response unit entered the front lobby.

The two men who sat in the living room at the rear of the property watching television were alerted by the sudden explosion of noise. As the cause of the commotion coming from the front of the house registered, they heard the shouts of `Police, police. Nobody move.'

McNally leapt from his seat and flicked the switch to turn off the light. Cautiously, he peered out of the window into the moonlit yard at the rear of the farmhouse but saw nothing. Simultaneously, he saw William Doyle grab the Franchi shotgun from behind the armchair he had been sitting in.

"No, Willy. Put it down", shouted McNally frantically. "Not this time. They've got us. We've got to get out of here quick. Follow me."

McNally ran out of the living room, into the hallway and up the back stairs, hoping perhaps to escape via a bedroom window. But Doyle had not followed. He had stayed put. That had always been his mistake. Not listening to anybody.

Clutching the weapon, Doyle ran out of the living room and into the entrance lobby only to come face to face with Burgess and the two officers.

Burgess momentarily found himself giving serious consideration to the the idea of planting a fist right on the jaw of that ugly bald head. Mourning the loss of spontaneity that had steadily accompanied the loss of his youth and his several promotions, he was still considering it even as Doyle raised the shotgun a little, until it pointed somewhere between Burgess' ankle and shin. Doyle heard Burgess' words.

"Put the weapon down, Doyle. You nearly did for me once before, a long time ago. It's not going to happen again."

Doyle had no idea what Burgess was talking about. He still wasn't listening. He raised the Franchi further until it now pointed at Burgess's navel. Burgess aimed to disable the Irishman and the well-aimed single round from the Glock that Doyle seemed not to have noticed him holding hit him in the shoulder, shattering his scapula and causing collateral damage to his collarbone en route. Unfortunately for Doyle however, the bullet from the gun of the officer standing behind Burgess had got there milliseconds earlier and Doyle fell to the ground, dead. Looking at the body lying face up on the parquet floor of the lobby, Burgess recalled how Satch Kapoor had once explained to him that, traditionally, the area between the eyebrows, where a bright red Bindi now decorated Doyle's forehead, was said to be the the seat of concealed wisdom. The irony was not lost on him.

From the kitchen, Phillips had heard the

shouting and now the gunshots. Turning the light off and looking out of the window he saw, by the light of the thin, pale moon, shadowy movement and noted the police car which, lights switched off, had rolled silently into position and now blocked the track leading to the road. His only hope was to get out unseen, then, maybe, he could escape on foot across the fields. There seemed no other option. Quietly, he opened the back door and started to run towards the fence. Suddenly a black-clad figure stood in front of him and a young woman's voice shouted at him to stop where he was. Arms flailing desperately, he threw himself at the dark outline. When Burgess got there a few seconds later, he found Phillips lying on the ground clutching his groin and groaning in pain, while Susie Weston stood over him, brandishing a Heckler & Koch 5.56mm semi-automatic carbine and grinning like a Cheshire cat that had just lapped up the last of the cream. Leaving Susie to stand guard over her prize with all the self-satisfaction of a proud vixen that has just downed an enemy rabbit and brought him home for dinner, Burgess went to investigate a new commotion coming from the rear of the property. McNally had shinned down a drainpipe outside a back bedroom window, straight into the welcoming embrace of the two policemen. But at least he'd had more sense than Doyle. He was unarmed and had left the Scorpion machine pistol in the living room.

3

Thowton Allop, Northamptonshire, Thursday 5th and Friday 6th December 2019

Nearly there now. Lines had been lost and Henry Bloom and Doyle were dead. That was a pity. Burgess always liked to tidy things up properly. But it wasn't a disaster. Officers had entered Bloom's premises at nine o'clock and by the time Burgess' driver delivered him there after leaving police to tidy up at Phillips' farmhouse, things were progressing nicely. Everett had been there for almost an hour.

"How's it all going? Anything interesting?"

"All under control. And yes, come and take a look at these."

Going by the drawing Simpson had supplied, four of the scrap metal items retrieved from the skip seemed to be prototypes of the shaped charges in various stages of completeness. Everett had laid them out on a bench in the workshop, and next to them had put other pieces of scrap found in the skip together with samples of similar materials taken from the stores.

"Not much doubt about those, Howard, but we'd better get them off to FEL to make sure. I'll hang on to this one for the time being though."

Burgess selected one piece which appeared to be almost complete and most nearly resembled the object depicted in Simpson's sketch.

"Did you bring Bloom's keys?"

"Yes, but we haven't used them yet. I knew you'd want us to wait until you got here."

"Well here's another set for your collection which, if I'm not mistaken, will turn out to be an exact match."

Burgess handed Everett the keys Susie had taken from Phillips and followed Everett across the floodlit yard towards the `Customer Projects' building.

After trying several of the keys, the door finally opened and they found themselves in a workshop area. The outbuilding itself was divided internally into the workshop, a storeroom and a small washroom and toilet. An internal door led from the workshop into the storage area which was also directly accessible from the yard. Bolted to the top of one of the heavy wooden workbenches were two hydraulically operated bullet presses and, in drawers below, a manual, described as a `reloading handbook', together with a variety of components of weapons; firing pins, bolts, recoil springs and other parts. Another drawer contained what looked like two broken receivers, the serial numbers of which, when the parts were sent off to FEL, would enable them to be identified as being from a Scorpion machine pistol of Czech manufacture, subsequently exported to Bosnia. A cupboard below the other, smaller, workbench contained hand tools and electrical bits and pieces including several soldering irons, reels of various cables, switches and digital meters as well as what looked to Everett like rotors from a drone.

In the far corner of the workshop stood a large metal safe which eventually yielded to another of Bloom's keys. Inside on the top two shelves, two dozen one-kilo blocks of Frangex sat, wrapped in wax paper and, on the shelves below, several plastic trays, each containing twenty-five rounds of bullets in 9mm and 5.56mm calibres. On the shelf directly underneath were several boxes of blank cartridges and bullet heads, as well as two eight-pound containers of powder. At the bottom of the safe sat a small wooden crate containing eleven M75 type hand grenades, each still in its plastic transportation can. There was one missing.

The label on the box read, `*Hercegovacea Blatina - Dvanaest boca*`, but underneath it was another, `*BRB Bugojno - 12 x Kašikara'*. FEL would later confirm that the grenades which had lain at the bottom of the case, each originally hidden by one of the twelve bottles of Bosnian dry red, had indeed been manufactured in the factory of BRB in the Bosnian city.

Howard shook his head in astonishment.

"Bingo. Some haul"

"Bosnian bingo", said Burgess, with a smile of satisfaction.

Back in the main building, Satch Kapoor and an assistant had spent the night interrogating the computers in the accounts office and, trawling through the various ledgers, one item in particular had already caused him to raise his eyebrows; a donation of fifty thousand pounds to the Institute for Democratic Reform. But his search was set to continue for many hours yet.

4

It was now seven forty-five and from information in the staff records, Burgess noted that fourteen employees from the yard, workshops and stores were due to start work at eight o'clock. The portakabin in the yard had been earmarked for the preliminary interviews. That worked out well because it meant that, using both rooms and allowing ten minutes for each interview, he could hope to clear most of the early arrivals within an hour. The other six employees were office workers who didn't start until nine and they could be interviewed in the offices. He and Daniels would occupy one of the rooms and Everett and Susie Weston the other, each accompanied by one of the SO15 officers to read them the necessary cautions. What, he wondered, would be their reaction when told that they were being detained under Schedule 7 of the Prevention of Terrorism Act (2000).

At seven fifty-four, Charlie Jacobs, the yard foreman, was the first to arrive. He had intended to drive his beloved old Volvo round to the back of the premises to unlock the yard gates and park in the yard as usual, but had found them already open and himself being taken to one of the rooms in the portakabin. There he explained who he was and that it was his responsibility to arrive a few minutes early each day to open the yard. Officers asked him about the bunch of keys that hung from his belt. Did he have access to every part of the complex? `No', he had said, `apart from the gate, only for my office, and the rear entrances to the workshops and the stores.'

Next to arrive, a few minutes after Jacobs was a man called John Stevens, one of the sales engineers, who was taken to the second interview room. He didn't normally arrive until nine o'clock, he said, but today he had to collect some machine parts and pieces and deliver them to a customer where they were to be fitted. He was told that that would not be happening today. As for keys, he had none.

While the first two interviews were taking place, Joe Corović and Branko Kovač arrived together in Corović's car. Corović explained that although his official job title was `Transport Manager', in reality it involved a lot more than that. In addition to organising transport, he was responsible for the entire process of tracking orders from their place of origin to their destinations, and everything in between. Corović had worked for MPM since leaving the army in 2012 but Kovač had only joined the company as a driver a few months previously, after being put forward for the job by Corović. Neither had keys to any part of the premises. While Corović was being questioned, several other employees arrived, first the workshop manager closely followed by one of the machinists. Both had worked for Bloom for several years.

Burgess began by addressing the workshop manager, a man called James Edginton.

"I want to ask you a few questions, Mr Edginton. Questions concerning certain items we have reason to believe were manufactured here recently."

"Sure, no problem. What were they?"

"I was rather hoping you could tell us that."

Daniels produced the distorted metal object that Burgess had kept back and placed it on the desk.

"We all wondered about them ourselves", said Edginton. "I remember Mr Bloom giving me the drawing. It had no name or title on it and I asked him what on earth it was."

"And what was Mr Bloom's reply?"

"He said they were for an old friend, a retired railway engineer who builds steam powered engines, locomotives, pumps, that sort of thing. Not full size you understand, but small scale working models. The boss didn't actually seem to know himself exactly what they were for. My guess was they were some kind of boiler.

"Does Mr Bloom often do that sort of thing,

bring in special jobs, for himself or friends?"

"It has happened before, yes. It's annoying because it puts other jobs back but, well, he's the boss so there's not much we can do about it."

"Which of your men were involved in making the `boilers'?

"Gordon did the shaping and forming and then passed them over to Jason Langford to weld the bottom plates on. It was a bloody difficult job though. Took my lads days. But you'd be better off asking them about that."

"Thank you. I will. And just one more question. What keys do you hold to the various parts of the premises?"

The workshop manager had keys to the roller shutter door of the workshop, the portakabin and two of the outbuildings in the yard, one of which he called the `Oxy store' which contained oxygen cylinders, and the other, which held acetylene and other fuel gas containers. `That's all I have', he told Burgess, `apart from when Charlie Jacobs is on holiday. Then I have to temporarily take over the duty of opening the yard.'

"What about the other building?", Burgess had asked. "The one marked, `Customer Projects and Orders Only'?"

"No", Edginton had said. "Only Mr Bloom and Mr Phillips can get in there."

"But the building contains a workshop. Surely somebody must work there."

"Not very often", said Edginton. "As far as I know it's unused most of the time. I've seen Mr Bloom take customers over there a few times and there are a couple of guys who come in with Henry Phillips occasionally."

"What do you know about them? Do you know who they are or what they do?"

"No, I'm afraid not. I'm pretty sure they don't work for us. The one I've seen most often, I think might be a friend from his army days. I've heard Henry call him `Mac', a scruffy looking Scotsman but I've no idea what he does. I know Henry has to sub-contract out some of the work he carries out for customers, where we haven't got the in-house expertise, stuff like electrical and electronics modifications, so maybe that's what he does."

"And you're certain you've never seen any other member of staff enter the building? Think carefully before you answer."

Edginton was silent. He closed his eyes and pursed his lips, deep in thought.

"Well. There was one time when I think I saw Joe coming out of the the place. I remember being surprised because I thought he was still away. It was a few months ago. In the summer. He'd been away with Mr Bloom and I didn't know they were back."

"What do you mean when you say you only *think* you saw him?"

"No, you misunderstand me. It was definitely Joe that I saw. What I meant was that the door was open and he was talking to Henry Phillips who was standing in the doorway. Joe was holding a wooden box and I remember thinking that maybe he had just brought it out but, thinking about it now, he could have been taking the box to Henry. I mean I never actually saw him either go in or come out."

"And this was just after he and Mr Bloom had returned from Bosnia?"

"Must have been the very same day. Otherwise Mr Phillips wouldn't have still been here."

In the other interview room, the employee being questioned by Howard Everett was telling him that he had no keys to anywhere.

"Jim took photocopies of the drawing and gave one to me and the other to Jason."

The man who had spoken was Gordon Frith and his work, he told Burgess, mainly involved operating the cutting and shaping machines.

"So, tell me, how did the job go? I mean, was it straightforward?"

"It might have been if the dimensions had been more accurate but the answer is no. I had to tidy them up a lot before I could even start."

"Tell me if you will, why that was necessary and how you went about it."

"Well, the geometry was all out for a start. If I made a base plate the diameter specified and kept to the angle of taper shown on the drawing, the overall height of the thing increased by nearly an inch and Mr Bloom said that wouldn't do."

"Did he say why?"

"No, but when Jim showed it to him, he said the height was the most critical dimension. So, to get the height right, we ended up with the base having to be a bit smaller than how it was shown on the drawing."

It seemed Frith had `got it about right' on his third attempt and had been relieved to be able to hand the construction over to the welder to complete by attaching the stainless steel base. But even before that another modification to what was shown on the drawing had been necessary.

"I'd seen the drawing before Gordon even started on the job", said Jason Langford. "And I knew straight away it would be tricky, so I got him to make another modification."

"Tricky in what way?", asked Everett.

"Well, more than tricky actually. It's a nightmare. Trying to weld copper and steel. Ask anyone who's ever tried. And the weld design didn't exactly help."

"Do you think you could explain that to me in a way that I might understand?"

"I'll try. You see the problem is mostly with the copper. It's highly reflective to laser beam light and the way the thing was designed, we'd have had to weld through the copper first, and that's where the trouble starts. Because it reflects most of the light, copper takes a lot of welding energy before it melts, and that causes two problems. First, the extra heat causes distortions. Second, copper's a very effective conductor of heat so as the energy comes through the copper into the steel, it basically disintegrates the steel and can cause holes and blow outs. A much better design would have been to have the weld energy come through the steel first and then into the copper. Then the right amount of heat can be applied to fuse them, and any extra energy is quickly dissipated into the copper. You get a better weld, and use much less energy. It's a lot easier with an electron beam welder, but we don't have one here, just an old CO_2 laser. I don't know why he didn't get the entire job done by his Bosnian mates. They've got a lot of experience in this area. But, according to Jim, he apparently said it had to be done quickly and in house. So I got Gordon to form a flange in the copper shell so I could weld through the steel base onto it."

Everett wished he hadn't asked. But when the tape was played to Simpson, Simpson would confirm that the man knew what he was talking about. And now for the big one, thought Everett.

"Just one final question."

Looking relieved, Langford nodded his understanding.

"You told me earlier that you don't hold any keys?"

He watched the man's face.

"Yes, that's right."

"So, how do you explain that last Friday, the

twenty-ninth of November, you accessed the building where completed customer orders are kept, awaiting delivery or collection, and and removed a number of items?"

Langford hesitated, but only briefly.

"Yes, I remember that. Mr Bloom told me that his friend would be calling in the afternoon to collect his order. He gave me the key and and asked me to make sure he got everything."

"Why was that do you think? Had that ever happened before?"

"No, never. He just said he would be away on business and that he'd already asked Jim, Mr Edginton, but Jim couldn't be there because had a hospital appointment that afternoon."

"And what happened to the key?"

"I kept hold of it over the weekend and gave it back to his secretary on the Monday."

During the next two or three minutes, a further four employees arrived and waited their turn, but by eight fifty-five all had been released to return home. Three others whose names were on the list had not arrived at all, one of whom was Bloom himself. Burgess thought he would let him off. After all, he had a good excuse. But he needed to know about the other two.

At eight fifty-two, Bloom's secretary arrived and was allowed to enter her office. Soon, one little point that had long puzzled Burgess had been resolved. When he had asked her about `Henry', she had confirmed what Everett had told him. That nobody ever called him that. It was Harry to his friends and Mr Bloom to everyone else. So how did she explain the phone call that the receptionist had put through to `Henry' when O'Bierne had phoned? She didn't think to ask how he knew about the phone call, but simply suggested that `perhaps it was Mr Phillips who had taken the call', saying that `sometimes when Mr Bloom is away on business, Mr Phillips stands in for him'. `Had that been the case on Tuesday, the ninth of July?' She couldn't remember. But when she checked Bloom's diary, it all came flooding back to her. Bloom had been away, visiting customers in Bosnia. `Yes, I remember now. Mr Bloom was away all week and Mr Corović went with him too.' And, `Yes, Mr Phillips had occupied Mr Bloom's office for three or four days'. Wasn't that a bit odd? After all, Mr Phillips didn't work for MPM but for another of Bloom's companies. It had `never occurred to her that way', she'd said.

Still unable to rid himself of his gut feeling about a Balkan connection, Burgess asked her about Corović and Kovač. `Yes, Mr Bloom does a lot of business with people from that region, particularly Bosnia.' and, `yes' again, `Mr Corović helps him with that'. What about Mr Kovač? Mr Kovač had `only joined the firm in the summer.' He was `a friend of Mr Corović', she said. Her words confirmed what Corović himself had told him earlier, that he had known Kovač for many years, `ever since my stint in

Bosnia in the early nineties', and that it had been he who had recommended him to Bloom because `he wanted to recruit a Bosnian speaking driver'. `And the two who had not arrived for work?' One, she had said was a sales engineer who today would be working at a customer's premises. The other, another machine shop worker, was away on holiday. She also confirmed that Langford had returned the key to her.

Josif Corović was recalled for a second interview. He did not deny having carried the wooden box over from the boot of Bloom's vehicle and having given it to Henry Phillips. What did he think the box had contained? Bloom had told him it was wine. `You'd better take Henry's plonk over to him, Joe', Bloom had said. He knew Henry had a liking for Bosnian red. Did he take it into the Customer Projects building? `No, Henry must have seen me coming because he met me in the doorway. I've never seen the inside of the place'.

5

Downing Street, London, Friday 6th December 2019

"Ah, do come in, Stephen. Be with you in just a moment."

As Brent entered the PM's inner sanctum,

George Ingles was just leaving. Brent couldn't help noticing that Ingles was smiling.

"Bad news about your man, Stephen."

"Yes indeed, Paul, I can't help feeling sorry for him."

"Yes, I know what you mean, Stephen. But, all the same, he did rather get himself into it. I mean, taking advantage of his position, mixing with the wrong people. You know, all that sort of thing."

"Quite."

"He'll lose his job of course, and probably his pension. And they'll probably charge him under the Official Secrets Act and put him away for a while you know."

"Do you have any idea at all as to how he came to be suspected, Paul?"

"Well, off the record, and strictly between you and I, Stephen, I've heard that he may have been caught out by a friend of his, a chap in one of the secret services. Quite dreadful. Just goes to show that you can't trust anyone these days. Anyway, putting all that to one side, we have some good news at last."

So that's why Ingles had been smiling.

"Ingles is ecstatic. He says that with the demise of the IDP, which he describes as `manna from heaven', we're pretty much unassailable. For the first time ever, the arithmetic is firmly on our side. So, on that basis, I'm making a few more minor tweaks to placate the Speaker and planning to bring back the deal for another vote in the new year. It's scheduled for the seventh of January, the first day of business when parliament reassembles after the Christmas recess."

"Excellent, Paul."

"And if, by some unforeseen mischance, Stephen, the Goddess Tyche should decide to defecate on me from a great height yet again, now that Ingles is confident of getting a working majority, I shall not hesitate to call an election for late February. I doubt I'd get the two-thirds of the house behind me that I'd need, but that doesn't matter so much now. But if I do, and if we win, I'll get another five years and you'll be Chancellor. How does that sound?"

"It sounds very good to me, Paul."

~~~~~~~

Chapter 17

"These all died in faith, not having received the
things promised, but having seen them and
greeted them from afar, and having acknowledged
that they were strangers and exiles on the earth."
Hebrews 11:13

1

Moscow, Monday 16th December 2019

From the large window of the living room in his
Vrubelya Street apartment, Lines looked out across
Panfilova Street and noted with satisfaction that,
from the ninth floor, the trees surrounding the block
did not obstruct his view of Vsekhsvyatskaya Grove.
But he pitied those who lived on the other side of
the block, who would instead be greeted by the ugly
sight of the intersection of the Leningradskoye and
Volokalamskoye highways. No uglier of course than
those in any other major city, but ugly just the same.

The sun hung low and pale in the clear, cold
blue of the early morning Moscow sky. It seemed to
him that there were far more trees surrounding the
whole area around his enclave than he remembered
from his last visit only a few years previously. And

although only a few conifers here and there now provided any hint of colour, when spring arrived, he thought, the tree-lined avenues of his new surroundings would resemble nothing so much as the leafy cityscapes of Sheffield which, long ago as a young lecturer, he had admired during a brief tenure at the university there. It reminded him too of the trees that lined Griffith Avenue in Drumcondra, where he had lived for a time after accepting the post at Trinity and arriving in Dublin.

Lines had been in Moscow now for almost two weeks. The apartment he had been given in Vrubelya 8 was small; apart from the living room, it had just a single bedroom, a kitchen and a private shower. But compared with the accommodation he had been allocated during his time in Moscow many years earlier, it was very comfortably appointed. He remembered still the uncomfortableness of the ancient sofa, the hard mattress on the bed, the single, unwholesome-looking, gravy-stained table with its small, hard chairs and the single radiator which hardly ever worked. Here, by contrast, the soft furnishings, the bed, the comfortable armchair and couch, did not give the lie to the adjective. Here also there was a small flat-screen colour television with satellite channels, WiFi, even a telephone, although it still waited to be connected, a desk and a large bookcase, almost empty now, but which he would soon fill. Best of all, the lift, as well as the central heating, actually worked.

From his apartment, it took less than ten minutes to walk to either of Oktyabrskoye Pole or Voykovskaya Metro Stations, from where he could be in the city centre in less than twenty minutes. Lines picked up the portable chess set from the coffee table. Tomorrow, he would start work at the Institute for Western Economic Studies but, this morning, he would get on at Voykovskaya and spend a pleasant couple of hours at the Moscow Art Theatre. After that, he would walk the short distance to the 18th-century-styled Café Pushkin on Tverskoy Boulevard for tea and cake, and to play a game of chess with Vasily, which this time he would win. He had been developing a new opening, based on a modified *Grob's Attack*. The fool Grob had made an error which had led to his opening being considered inferior by many, but Lines felt sure he had found and corrected it, and now he couldn't wait to try it out on Vasily.

And then, later, before returning home, he would visit the little food shop run by the Karavaevs brothers where he hoped to be able to buy some eggplant rolls, the Georgian delicacies, aubergines stuffed with cottage cheese, mint and fresh cucumber, that Levan Donauri had introduced him to in Minsk and had told him were assuredly the food of the Gods.

He had been greatly saddened to read of Bloom's death. Saddened, but in a way. not surprised. Henry had always been old school. It had been typical of him to take the gentleman's option. It was not likely that any of Bloom's employees, other than Phillips, could be charged with anything, but he wondered how Armstrong would be coping. He was not strong like Cormac or Henry Phillips. He might break down eventually and talk. But he was not stupid. He might admit to having warned me, but he would say that it was because he was my friend. So long as they could not link him to Vasily he would be safe and might eventually even be able to carry on the good work. He doubted whether they would ever be able to pin anything on Brent or Jameson, but Jonathan's position was less certain.

As for himself, all things said and done, it had worked out well. He was happy in his new life and glad to have seen the last of the liberalism that, for decades now, had been eating away at European culture and was now close to destroying it forever. He had done what he could and he was proud of that, but only time would tell. His new masters were confident that Jameson would finally succeed in pushing through his withdrawal agreement early in the new year. And in his experience, they were rarely wrong about such things.

He certainly hoped they were right, for it would deliver an end to the violence and allow parliament to reflect on what had been learned. The division itself would take time to heal fully, but at least there would be an opportunity to address the issues which had given rise to the troubles; to begin the process of asking and answering the questions which had been allowed to lie dormant for far too long.

But if they were wrong, and parliament continued to thwart true democracy by claiming sole ownership of sovereignty, the division would deepen further and it would be down to his successors to ensure that the fight back continued. Benson would assume leadership. He was a capable man, and there were many others waiting in the wings to carry on the struggle if necessary. The few that had been uncovered had only been the tip of a very large iceberg. Ultimately though, it would, as ever, be down to the people themselves for, in the end, only they could bring down the fools that considered adherence to their crazed ideology more important than either the wishes of their own citizens or the preservation of traditional values.

But that life was all behind him now, and he didn't miss it one bit. He had more than enough to occupy himself; his work at the institute kept him busy for a few hours each day and his new book was progressing well, but now, he found time for the things that gave him the most pleasure. Tonight, he was looking forward to treating Vasily to an event that promised to be the highlight of his year, for tonight, they would be attending a performance given by the great Latvian cellist Mischa Maisky at the Tchaikovsky Concert Hall, where Maisky was due to play selections from concertos by Prokofiev, Shostakovich and Richard Strauss. And Maisky had been trained by the master himself, Mstislav Rostropovich. Life, he thought, doesn't get much better than this.

And then, soon, it would be Christmas. The streets and squares were already starting to receive their festive decoration and, although most Muscovites don't celebrate Christmas until the seventh of January, the foreign communities would organise Christmas bazaars and concerts to create the spirit of festivity and to link the period between the two Christmases. No, he would not be waiting until the seventh of January. Instead, he looked forward to attending the festivities at the annual international Christmas festival musical event, which takes place every year in the Cathedral of the Immaculate Conception of the Holy Virgin Mary in Malaya Gruzinskaya Street and which somehow succeeds in joining together into a single celebration the Christmas traditions of many countries. There, musicians from Austria, France, Germany, Spain, Latvia, Estonia, some even from as far away as Mexico and Ecuador, would play traditional Christmas melodies from different cultures and times. Mexican rhythms and Baroque music would join forces with folk songs, eternal classics and even, occasionally, some jazz.

And while, in Moscow, the winters are long and cold, he could look forward to the spring, when he would be visiting Levan Donauri and his family in Georgia.

Chapter 18

"Each man is forever thrown back on himself
alone, and there is danger that he may be
shut up in the solitude of his own heart."
Alexis de Tocqueville

1

South Kensington, London, Wednesday
25ᵗʰ December 2019

The Queen's speech, and the Christmas message from the Archbishop of Canterbury which had plagiarised it so shamelessly, had consisted largely of the usual stream of well-intentioned platitudes. Pleas for tolerance, for an impossible reconciliation and for greater understanding. Did they not realise that understanding was the one thing that existed in abundance? That it was precisely because each side understood the other so well that the division existed?

Jonathan was as a man who had lost his religion. He felt now that, his whole life, he had been deceived, that almost everything had been a pretence. Was there anything or anyone that could be trusted? Lines hadn't cared about democracy. But he had known that Jonathan did. And he hadn't cared about Ireland. He had used O'Bierne too. And he only cared about Brexit as a means to an end. To weaken both the EU and the UK. He had used them all. And Brent. Brent had used Martin Armstrong. Perhaps even Brent himself had been used.

But it was his lifelong trust in democracy that had taken the most painful hit, and he could not pin the blame for that on the deceptions of others, for the truth was that he had deceived himself; that the vacuum that had taken the place of his former faith was of his own making. The theory held good, but in practice it failed the test. Most people were too easily manipulated for their own good. Though he hated to admit it, Monnet had been right on that point. Most politicians were unashamedly and unalterably self-interested, as well as being unprincipled and barely half as clever as they imagined. All of which left everything at the mercies of the unelected idealogues, global corporations and, he shuddered at the use of the word, `experts'.

He had always understood and accepted that no country could be run by direct democracy alone. Quite apart from the chaos that would inevitably result from a system that required a never ending stream of referendums, not to mention the likelihood that the differing opinions resulting from such a system would make it quite impossible for society to act as a single body, the people simply do not possess the skills necessary to deal with the complexity, breadth and inter-relatedness of the issues involved. And nor should they be expected to possess such skills. Just as we do not expect every man to be competent in medicine, nuclear physics or aeroplane design, so we cannot expect that the people would be capable of acting together in a unified way to design and run a National Health system, implement a taxation policy, run the Exchequer or manage a national house-building programme. Having elected our representatives, and they having formed a government, it is only right and proper that such things are left in the hands of those elected to get on with the job, supported by those best qualified to deal with the implementation. It is sufficient that democracy ensures that a government which fails to do so can be removed without the need for revolution.

But there is another category of matters. A different category altogether. A category into which fall those issues which require neither that expert knowledge nor those special skills, indeed, where the application of either is entirely inappropriate.

The views of the man who believes in God or supports the monarchy, or believes it wrong to kill animals for their meat or to destroy the earth's forests, must not be overridden by those of an `expert'. Society employs experts to find solutions, perhaps to give us information, even advice. But we do not employ them to challenge our beliefs.

Such people, whether they be businessmen,

economists, politicians or philosophers, act rightly when they make their views known before a referendum takes place. It is right that people should be given any relevant information that is available, and right that they should be exposed to all the arguments and points of view relevant to their decision, and from both sides in the debate. But it is not right that, when the people have given their answer, that when that decision has been made, they should be told that they were wrong.

One does not have to be an expert in order to have a valid view on matters based on conviction or principle. Do we want a National Health Service, free at the point of delivery? Should Scotland seek independence from the UK? Is it desirable for certain industries and services to be given special status, to be owned by the state and protected from both private and foreign ownership? These are questions on which your member of parliament cannot and should not speak for you. It is not his opinion that counts. It is yours.

And it seemed to Jonathan that these were matters in which expertise was not only entirely irrelevant, but dangerously sinister, for such `experts' seek to replace ethical values with cold computations, to denigrate faith while promoting doubtful facts as certainties, to sneer at such things as altruism, custom, common sense and, particularly, patriotism. As Orwell had once noted, the self-appointed intelligentsia took for granted, as though it were a law of nature, the divorce between national pride and intelligence. For them there is no place for emotion, judgement or experience.

And, when the propaganda and sophistry fails them, there is always technicality to fall back upon. Like crooked lawyers, they scour the law books of parliamentary and judicial precedent in search of a technical loophole to get a guilty man off. As a bent accountant, they will trawl through Butterworth's tax handbook hoping to find a useful ambiguity in the rules of the revenue men. Thus, the New Elite keeps busy, busy trying to destroy democracy, to replace majority rule with rule by themselves, because they think they're smarter than everyone else. Not just smarter than the people either, but smarter too than the politicians they secretly despise. Yes, even the politicians were being used. And so, for once, Jonathan thought, politics itself was not to blame. In fact politics had become the victim.

All the major political parties had welcomed the Trojan offerings of the New Elite with open arms. If it helped them to win elections, it was all good. But some of the people were a lot smarter than they were believed to be. Granted that, as Brent had said, there would always be some who could be convinced that black was white so long as the message came from their own Messiahs, but there were others not so easily fooled. So while some were deceived into thinking they were marching for democracy when, in reality, they were being used to help destroy it, others had sensed what was going on and, as a result, elections were now being fought less along party lines than between those who believe in majority rule and those who believe in rule by experts. To Jonathan the flaw was obvious. There can be no such thing as an expert in matters of belief, conviction or principle. It is a complete fallacy. And because expertise is not required in order for such questions to be answered, the lack of it can never be a satisfactory reason for not asking the questions or respecting the answers. This is properly the realm of direct democracy.

Jonathan remembered what John Locke had written long ago; that, 'There is no practical alternative to taking the consent of the majority as the act of the whole and binding every individual; that it would be, 'next to impossible to obtain the consent of every individual before acting collectively' and that therefore, 'no rational people could desire and constitute a society that had to dissolve straightaway because the majority was unable to make the final decision and the society was incapable of acting as one body.' And yet, that was precisely what had been allowed to happen.

In Jonathan's lifetime, it had never before been put to the test. In fact, this most valuable of democratic tools had been shamefully under-used throughout history. And now that it had seen the light of day, it had failed miserably. It had exposed the extent to which our appointed representatives had come to believe that sovereignty was theirs alone. What on earth, they thought, but did not say, had sovereignty to do with the people? It had made him angry, but even so, he felt remorse now for his own actions.

2

What if you wanted to make a clean breast of it? Where would you start? Google would know, he thought. And Google did know. In fact Google took him straight to a web page headed `Contact us', the website of the Security Service MI5. He hadn't been expecting it to be so straightforward. Surely, he thought, there had been a time when such organisations lived their lives completely in the shadows, and now contacting them had become as easy as ordering from a local take-away restaurant.

The message displayed on the screen of his PC had read, `If you know something about a threat to national security such as terrorism or espionage, we want to hear from you. We will treat your information and any personal details in confidence unless you tell us otherwise, or exceptionally if there is a need to share it with appropriate parties such as the police.' Three options were offered.

`You can send us information through our online contact form. Your message will be sent securely. You will see an acknowledgment when you have sent your message. All messages will be read, however, we cannot promise to respond to all of them.' It even promised that, `You can remain anonymous if you wish', although Jonathan thought that promise unlikely to be honoured.

A PO Box number was given, which allowed you to post a letter to them. It seemed like a hangover from an era which had all but vanished, especially as it warned it could take up to a week for them to receive your letter. `Alternatively, you can contact us by telephone.' Three alternative telephone numbers were given, followed by a plea not to use them for `making enquiries about general matters or recruitment issues.'

Jonathan imagined dialling the Freephone number. The robot voice would ask for his name, his address, his date of birth and eventually lead him to a range of options, in much the same way as when he had contacted HMRC about his tax coding. And, just as then, the voice would ask him to choose one of several options, one of which would probably be `espionage' or something like it. And if he pressed that option, there would be no turning back. He poured himself a whisky, a small one this time but still his third of the morning. Perhaps Hannah had been right.

What would happen if he pressed the number for `espionage', and was put through to speak to someone face-to-face as it were? He imagined the frenzy of activity that would be taking place. In

Millbank, an assessment team would look at his name to check whether it came up in connection with an existing investigation. His phone and email records would be accessed and read, his contacts noted and cross-referenced to other names. They would definitely want to talk to him. He imagined how the contact would be made. The phone would ring.

"Mr Jonathan Shawcross?"

"Yes."

"My name is Smith, Mr Shawcross. You were kind enough to contact us and we've decided we'd rather like to talk to you. As soon as possible in fact."

"OK, that's fine", he would say.

"Well, Mr Shawcross, we don't think it's a good idea to discuss the matter over the telephone. Are you at home this morning?"

"Yes, I've taken the day off."

"Good, you'll need to come to my office, but don't worry, I'll send a car for you. A black Mercedes. It'll be with you very shortly."

If he looked out of the window, the black Mercedes would probably be there already. Jonathan lit a Marlboro, poured himself another whisky and sat down to think. What would he say? Something along the lines of, `I don't know where to start. I'm afraid I've been rather a fool?'

And what if he did nothing? Lines had gone, Bloom was dead and O'Bierne knew nothing of his involvement. Armstrong couldn't say anything without incriminating himself. The Telegraph article had been vague and short on detail. The security services, it said, had uncovered a group which appeared to be behind the recent spate of atrocities. Two men, named as Henry Bloom and William Doyle, had been killed in shootings and several others had been arrested. There appeared to be some connection with the Russians and with the IRA. There was no mention of Lines, but his disappearance had not gone unnoticed, and the cloisters in both Cambridge and Dublin were buzzing with rumours.

3

Beir Al-Shaghala archaeological site, Dakhla Oasis, Egypt, Wednesday 15th January 2020

In the end, we are alone. Allegiance was something that, properly distributed, spread outward from the heart of each individual in concentric circles, like the ripples in a pond that emerge and grow, each more distant, from the point where the child's stone has landed. But, like the energy that created the waves, it was not inexhaustible. It must gradually dissipate until it runs out and there is no more to give. It could not sensibly be otherwise.

One did not properly start with allegiance to the

whole world; not to a continent, nor even to one's nation. Allegiance must not be allowed to become diluted, spread ever more thinly until it becomes as meaningless as it is impotent. As Plato's Phaedrus had come to realise, one must first learn to know oneself. Allegiance was then owed first to one's family and friends. Only when they had been protected could further allegiances sometimes be justified, and even then great care must be taken to ensure no conflict between them. Just as only a traitor would have any good reason to keep his true loyalties hidden, so only a fool would give allegiance to a cause on the periphery which could put at risk one at the core.

And this, Jonathan thought, was where it had gone wrong. Whereas allegiance to the greater family caused no harm at all, those in charge had failed to see that blind, dogmatic allegiance to an imperial ideology was bound to cause conflict now, just as it had repeatedly done throughout all time. They had not only created and obstinately maintained an unnecessary allegiance, but they had placed it at the very epicentre, from where it could do most damage.

For, whilst human beings have shown themselves capable of remarkable acts of courage and devotion, towards friends and family, and even to the larger community, they have also, in the name of allegiances to larger causes, be they God's glory, communism, fascism, democracy or patriotism, often demonstrated that they are capable of acts of cowardice, treachery and indescribable cruelty. That surely, was what Joseph Conrad had meant when he had said, `I know only that he who forms a tie is lost. The germ of corruption has entered into his soul.'

Above all perhaps, Jonathan had learned that love is clever. And that it is deceitful, but for the highest of motives; because it needs to be. Love will convince two lovers that what they have between them is irreplaceable; that it does not exist, and therefore cannot be found, elsewhere. Love lies. But it does so with the best of intentions. It does so in order to make us happy and to keep us its faithful, voluntary prisoners. Only if and when it becomes absolutely necessary, does it ever reveal the truth. And the truth was that Mandy had become absolutely necessary to Jonathan. There was no betrayal involved. The fact that both of them would always love Hannah did not mean they could not love each other. It had been her gift to them.

Jonathan knew now that he had made the right choice when he had decided that, for the time being at least, the phone would remain on the hook.

ABOUT THE AUTHOR

Mick Morris is a writer and musician. Educated at Dover Grammar School for Boys, Mid-Kent College and the University of Kent at Canterbury. He is the author of several other published works including the guitar tutor book *Play Straight Away* and *Six-String Stories,* a compendium of quotes and anecdotes about the guitar and those who play it. Other books include *The Life of the Limerick*, and *Tall Stories. Division* is his first novel. He has also written numerous short stories and has contributed articles to music magazines as well as composing many poems and songs. He is currently writing a biographical memoir entitled, *Don't Give up the Day Job.*